G000097674

"*Caposcripti* is just effortlessly mes[...]
that is impossible to pigeonhole - a[...]
like thriller, a coming of age story[...]
anthropological study and literary[...]
continents and times. Zelda Rhian[...]
the chilling obsession and practica[...]
is at recreating the intensely alive [...]
the Amazon. Totally compelling stuff - I can't recommend it
enough!"
Emma Pickard, Freelance Publishing Marketer

"I loved it. It is tense, thrilling and terrifically ambitious. And
it has shrunken heads in it."
Scott Pack, Publisher, The Friday Project

"It's quite shocking to realise that one of your regular
customers is secretly a serious literary talent. I read her book
and my hands shook when I poured her a pint."
Kit Fraser, Publican and Author of *The Joy of Talk*

"A wonderful, well-paced story about those individuals who
seek to illuminate the shadowy corners of human existence
- forgotten over time or never fully understood. The plot
moves easily between the tumult of the modern city and
the suffocating lushness of the South American jungle.
Meanwhile we are given a sense of those faint wisps of half-
known wisdom that obscure the heart of darkness pulsing
beneath the thin veneer of our civilization."
Jim Gleeson, Writer

"Beautifully constructed... immaculate prose... John Grisham
meets Carlos Castaneda"
Patrick Kelly, Bookmongers Bookshop, London

"I loved the way the dialogue builds and builds, but is very
subtle...a different way of looking."
Anna Druka, Illustrator and Curator

"It was such a good read. I enjoyed its clear lucid prose and vivid compelling narratives. Nina was a fabulous character and I felt so moved by the tribal people and their way of life. I am left with a nostalgia and sense of loss for the time when we as people trod softly upon this earth. Above all I loved the ending."
Melanie Swan, Book Rep

"Just finished *Caposcripti* and what a cracking good read it is too. Genuine sense of menace throughout."
Ron Meerbeck, Artist and Writer

"Mesmerising, exquisite, and beautifully crafted!"
Alex M. Dunne, Microsoft

"*Caposcripti* is a densely constructed, deeply disturbing book. It touches on the fears at the heart of all of us, and exposes how the desire for knowledge can be as corrupting as the lust for power."
Ben Scott Robinson, Director, We Love Mobile

"I saw one of your stickers in the toilet and wanted to scrawl 'beware the photographer!' - but I'd lost my pen."
Julia Roberts, Teacher

"I was hungry for more, each of my busy days, to indulge myself in this book. Each time I opened the pages I was there, with the characters, my six senses working the pages, sitting on the edge of my seat throughout my *Caposcripti* experience. This is an incredible book! Zelda Rhiando's first novel reads as if she is already a seasoned writer... a natural talent like hers is undeniable and hats off for a superior first novel. Highly recommended reading!"
Lisa Billson, Singer in *The Loose Salute*

"It's a great read!"
Rod McLaren, Director, Mobbu

*Suzie – thanks so much
for your beautiful
presence
xZelda*

caposcripti

Zelda Rhiando

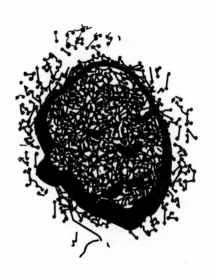

&
Ampersand Press

A CIP catalogue record for this book is available from the British Library

ISBN: 9780957220300

Published by Ampersand Press
Registered offices: 44 Helix Road, London SW2 2JS

More info at: http://www.caposcripti.com

Contents

Now the whole earth had one language and few words. And as men migrated from the east, they found a plain in the land of Shinar and settled there. And they said to one another, 'Come, let us make bricks, and burn them thoroughly.' And they had brick for stone, and bitumen for mortar. Then they said, 'Come, let us build ourselves a city, and a tower with its top in the heavens, and let us make a name for ourselves, lest we be scattered abroad upon the face of the whole earth.' And the LORD came down to see the city and the tower, which the sons of men had built.

And the LORD said, 'Behold, they are one people, and they have all one language; and this is only the beginning of what they will do; and nothing that they propose to do will now be impossible for them. Come, let us go down, and there confuse their language, that they may not understand one another's speech.'

So the LORD scattered them abroad from there over the face of all the earth, and they left off building the city. Therefore its name was called Babel, because there the LORD confused the language of all the earth; and from there the LORD scattered them abroad over the face of all the earth. (Genesis 11:1-9)

1. Personae

The Photographer
A heavy and unruly creature, he habitually dresses in black or grey: for many reasons, but not least because he is living celluloid. He's probably fooling himself – at root he is a pragmatist, a state symbolised by his footwear: his boots are solid with good thick soles.

His apartment is a rat's maze of frenzied overblown house-plants, and concealed cameras. From the monstrous cine-camera in his hall cupboard (activated by the doorbell, it has contained the same reel of film for a long time – company is rare) to a cunningly devised cigarette lighter, which snaps wide shots Bond-style. He is a man of few words, and two obsessions, one of which is to make pictures speak for him.

The other? Don't be impatient please; all will be revealed in good time.

Despite his retiring nature he has achieved some notoriety in the world of photography. Infrequent exhibitions and a total lack of interviews contribute to this. And no it is not clockwork that makes him tick, as one critic suggested.

Love Interest? Cold comfort.

The Tribe

The year is 1851 – the year of the Great Exhibition, optimism and palaces of glass.

The Amazon is full of magic. Travel is difficult. Jungles are impassable. Rivers form the main arteries for trade, but most are so sclerotic that traffic is limited to canoes and the occasional raft, all that can survive the rapids and endless deltas of the Amazon basin. Alcoholism, the clap and the common cold have not yet decimated the indigenous population and the ancient arts and languages are not yet ancient – for the people that live there the legends are real and spirits, rather than morals, censor their actions. They are not yet children – it will take them a few years longer to become that.

The Tribe are a semi-nomadic people, their wanderings determined by the floods that submerge large tracts of the jungle for several months of the year, when the rivers break their banks. They live in small, temporary settlements, each loose scattering of families taking up a few hundred feet square of jungle. When the rains come they will frequently abandon a whole pueblo, returning to it the following year when the Amazon has deposited a rich layer of mud on the dry shores. They range over a fairly large area – always choosing land avoided by more settled people.

Keenness of hand and a rich oral tradition have bequeathed to them the gentle art of head shrinking, and the ability to brew the equally lethal concoctions curare and alcohol.

There are substances in the jungle which give them visions, and on attaining adulthood they take these daily, so as not to become confused by the lie of this reality.

Their language is infinitely complex: they tattoo it on their bodies so they don't forget it, starting on their feet for common phrases in youth and scripting sacred truths and personal histories on their faces, on the lids of their eyes, and on the lobes of their ears.

As the intellect begins to develop the head is shaved, and various areas of the skull are marked with the traits and characteristics that arrive through maturity. Typically an elder of the tribe will be completely bald, hair replaced by an intricate tangle of points and lines. There is a paste made from tree bark that prevents follicle regrowth.

They exist on a diet of fish and whatever they can hunt in the jungle – almost anything big enough to eat and not actively poisonous is fair game to their blowpipes and poisoned darts, their almost invisible traps. Although sometimes the crops falter, and the staple *manioc* fails to yield its large and nourishing roots, hunger is not a problem in the jungle. There are more than enough fruits and nuts to sustain the few people that inhabit the region. And yet there is much to fear, good reason to ask the protection of the spirits against accidents, floods, storms, against poisons, fevers and the attacks of animals.

Those lost this way are the ones that are forgotten – their heads missing from the massed ranks that bear witness to the history of the Tribe, providing the only constant record of their existence in the unsettled and ever-changing jungle, ringing with the echoes of wandering spirits looking for another shell to animate. For all those who have ever been are not gone, but merely imperceptible to the living.

Suicide is less an escape from this existence than a passport to the next, and in fact an honourable way to remove the burden of one's existence from one's family. To avoid the fate of not existing, of never having been, those who are too old or tired or sick to continue take poison, mixed for them by the

Speaker, who sends them on their journey to the next world. Their heads are preserved in the ritual manner, life reduced to an ideogram tattooed on the shrunken scalp.

After death, the body is mummified in a seated position, and suspended from the branches of trees high up, to be disposed of by the elements – the cleansing depredations of birds and tree-dwelling carnivores, the sudden, fierce squalls of the late afternoon.

The heads are prepared by quite a different, and secret method, which preserves the sacred scrawl in perpetuity. They are hidden underground in concealed caves reminiscent of the Photographer's cupboards and drawers – all the paraphernalia of a chronicle rests with them, the wisdom of the future and the potential of the past.

The Explorer

Once he was a big man: his shoulders were as wide as
two axe handles, and young ladies sighed over their dance
cards. Now the years of travelling, bad food, and loneliness
have given him a wizened, jaundiced look. Dirt ground
into deep creases, clothes badly stained, candid, fanatical
eyes piercing from beneath untrimmed brows. He has two
passions: travelling and chronicling – nothing hidden here,
all is transcribed into small dog-eared notebooks which set
forth, detail, narrate and enumerate moment by moment the
minutiae of life.

In his youth he had been a literary man; possessed of a large
vocabulary, and the full complement of the fashionable
philosophies. The years have conflated these into an all-
embracing pseudo-humanism – ennobling the savage and
placing learning on a pedestal for all to admire. Reduced
though he is in possessions, he has nevertheless held onto
several books: the essays of Montaigne; the Confessions of
Rousseau; a volume of Keats; a pocket bible. The rest of his
belongings fill a number of solid trunks in the family home –
sent back to London from all corners of the globe, and held
in storage against his eventual return.

He is still uncertain of what has brought him to these remote
and savage lands to chronicle their inhabitants. There is
disillusionment with optimism – the childlike wonder in
the machine, in technology, in industry, that has gripped his
fellows with fever. Some disgrace, a lapse in his fortunes;
anger at the profusion of inaccurate descriptions already
in existence and daily multiplying. And there is wonder in
the thought of describing what has never been seen; of
challenging the certainty of those who believe that because
they hold the secrets of machines, they are infallible. For
whichever of these motives you prefer, he has for the

latter part of his life taken to chronicling lands distant and mysterious – arcane tongues and barbarous practices – in a self-imposed exile from civilised society.

His should have been the guardianship of many secrets. Instead all are bequeathed to vellum and paper; mixing his piss with berries when ink runs dry, making a canvas of his skin, his body.

This last is probably what saved him from extinction.

2. Scouting

The Photographer is out looking to score with his callipers
and cameras. All around, he feels the pulse of the city; the
grumble of traffic, the constant near contact with other
pedestrians on the pavement. He is edgy, taut. Controlled
precision and a certain detachment are evident in his posture.
He has chosen that uncertain hour between daylight and dusk
when the puddles in the gutter start to reflect darkness and
the stark outlines of cornices, aerials, and fire escapes. Today,
however, the Photographer is not particularly interested
in puddles – although once upon a time he took pictures
of them, as well as street scenes, barrow markets, smiling
children, obscure buildings.

Back then the urban landscape had inspired him with its
complexity – awed him with the continual juxtaposition of
the unexpected. He would go to Liverpool Street station to
attune himself to the city's rhythms, wheels within wheels,
natives interacting with one another like cogs turning,
clockwork and unvarying measures; contrapuntal movement.
Nine-to-fivers in from the suburbs every day; the swarms of
black suits fleeing the city at five-fifteen; soaring buildings,
park-sized atriums, giant tropical plants belying their sterility
and dwarfing the scurrying workers below; skyscrapers
suspended from great steel arches, glistening pyramids
of glass – all invited the Photographer's lens, demanded
interpretation.

But now in the gathering dusk he ignores these and other
possibilities. He is conducting a dialogue of one: with himself

and his camera, the method and the goal, the Cartesian dichotomy. He believes in dualism.

"In the beginning was the word: and the word was with God. Who can we believe? The priests and the philosophers, these lovers of wisdom? Should have been a camera there. Black and white. Never lies."

"Seven planets, God and the Devil, and man travelling a known path one way or the other. Someone is up there with their CCTV, filming inside the mind, no lies. Camera never lies."

The Photographer doesn't own a television: he had a black-and-white one once, but the dull eye watching him from across the room unnerved him. God and his eye piercing his very soul, pinning him insect-like under the solar microscope, caught in the panopticon. No escape. Sometimes he thinks he is Lucifer – he too carries his hell inside him.

And so he is outside as the dusk falls, while the sun is too engaged in its struggle with the moon to keep an eye on him. Eyes scan the faces of passers-by for the one whose head fits his specifications: he has it down to a fine art now. The callipers are just a prop, part of the mythos. These days the only genre that interests him is portraiture, and he has no time for clouds, solar eclipses, or the bottom of the ocean. Motion photography he flirted with briefly, in his youth, but lately he's been after the freeze frame, the moment of truth.

Camera and callipers; callipers and camera. The others on the pavement give him a wide berth: his gaze is discomfiting – measuring them from head to foot as they near him. He has chosen a busy time and the roads are at capacity. The city's dwellers are displaying a refinement of evolution: the ability to condense population past the point where another species would choose to selectively cull their own kind. Evolution has a part to play in this narrative. The Photographer has more respect for it than for the scurrying pedestrians in his path.

Still they serve their purpose.

3. Amazonas, 1851

*Nanay River, March 21*st

Morning. I awake on what feels like the seven millionth day of my journey. The Jungle is beginning to swallow me whole. I feel my spirit evaporating day by day. My voice feels rusty from misuse. I have taken to muttering to myself as I walk, to combat the loneliness & to convince myself that I am still here & not wandering, a figment, in some self-imagined country.

I know not whether I am in Ecuador or Peru. Borders have little meaning in terms of the Jungle. I have heard rumours of a secret Tribe somewhere in the vicinity, followed them up in the settlements upriver, garnered what information I can from rum-sodden natives gone to seed in tiny river outposts. But for some reason the Tribe has never been classified – mere rumours of their existence culled from the records of successive waves of colonizers. Exploration in the area has been minimal. Attracted by the gold & rare minerals; the guano & oil & ancient treasure troves to be found in the more accessible areas of mountain & coast, the Spanish & the British & all of the other greedy or well-meaning colonisers have so far ignored it.

Perhaps in years to come the ethnographers, those missionaries of civilization, will arrive, taming the natives with ideas of property & sin, cheap gifts & alcohol – replacing traditional medicine with iodine & quinine, the meeting huts with neat schools. For now the Amazon is guarding its secrets well.

'Yet shall I build a fane In some untrodden region of my mind, / Where branched thoughts, new grown with pleasant Pain, / Instead

of pines shall murmur in the wind'. I have few books here with me, everything rots; yet my mind is a library still unsullied.

⁓

I cheat the Jungle of my blood by making words of it, the dark fluid clotting on the pages of my notebooks, a self-created epitaph. Still I am becoming dispirited. The earth is all water, the flora all slime, the air half steam. The vegetable life around me is oppressive – the Jungle alive with sounds all muted by the foliage, an ambiance that changes with each step, throwing back now the sounds of running water, now the high & melodious whistles of birds, now the harsh calls of parrots, the whirring & clicking of grasshoppers, the rustling of breezes & of my passage. Each step is a struggle & every step feels wrong. The lack of direct sunlight makes direction almost impossible to determine & time a meaningless abstraction.

For the first time in many months I feel lost. For the first time in many years I feel fear, for somewhere on the edges of my vision I can sense eyes, a suspicion that has been plaguing me for some time. Maybe my mind is finally betraying me.

My clothes, boots, food, books are rotting in the humidity: the pages gradually turning a virulent green – the ink correspondingly purple. They are rotting, but they addict me – I have learnt to appreciate the smell of musty paper; & still I am writing, recording, reproving this existence.

Because the Jungle never changes (although it continues to astonish me) I have begun to delve deeper beneath reality. The life around me seems to me too sentient to be merely the sum of several different types of monkey, innumerable birds, fish, plants, insects, strange iridescent lizards.

I am gradually developing an equation, out here on the perimeter:

a series of truths hard-gained & dear paid for. These I have proven on my body, scribbling arcane figures in the crooks of my arms & on the palms of my hands. Finally, distilled into these pages.

For now, I suppose, I must continue.

4. Betty

Night-time in London – or rather the electric dusk that passes for night in the city, where the sky develops a perpetual orange glow that conceals all but the brightest stars, and a thin haze softens everything into indistinctness.

Patches of light from the street lamps intensify the areas of shadow under the long landbridge supporting the railway line, and cast doorways and corners into obscurity. Beneath the overhang arches curve along the pavement. The shops and offices are shuttered against the night, rendered uniform by the dark outlines of graffiti etched into them. The street is littered with the debris of daytime and has that peculiar sense of isolation of the shuttered outdoor market.

Save for the dim glimmer of reflection thrown from his lens, the Photographer is near invisible in his hiding place, black coat melting into the dark stone, dark eyes dim hollows in his pale face, camouflaged in stillness, checking for cameras.

His quarry, an old drunk entering the final stages of dipsomania, is about half-way down the street bedded down for the night in the entrance to the station. Like the market and the shops it's closed now, quiet and deserted, and she is only just visible through the metal cage that forms the stairwell. A near shapeless bundle in the darkness, even the filth and the stink of piss and stale cider have not been enough to dissuade her from the shelter that the stairwell affords in coldest hour before dawn. Shelter, the Photographer reflects, that will provide his activities with some cover too.

Everywhere these days there are cameras watching; cameras,

hidden by them, tricks and feints. Even the concealed ones might be dummies, double bluffs, no escape. Watching me? He marks her and bides his time; there's no need to rush. Does anybody really see such people? Maybe not, but the camera catches everything.

The Photographer pictures a grand controller, seated in front of a giant switchboard, wired into a chamber studded with monitors in obscene symbiosis: a monstrous eye. Images flash on the screens, zoom shots, wide pans – from the grainy black and white of CCTV to the lurid polychrome of cheap porn.

Suddenly everything vanishes, every screen switches to a single shot, a magnified view of the very street, the very doorway where he is hiding, camera lens glinting in the streetlight, sight and senses straining. But what would they see? Nothing. For how can they see what they're not looking for? Blind. Blind leading the blind. Eyes closed to the patterns in the noise, fragments of the lost language. He's been watching this one for some time now, saving her up like a banquet, waiting for the moment of significance, the confluence of signs.

Even in the dark he can form a perfect mental picture of every contour of her person – from the filthy and crusted layers of petticoats, and blouses, and skirts, and coats, and cardigans, to the bloated feet wrapped in layers of plastic; conjunctival eyes squinting from the lined and bloodshot face. He is impervious to the decay, for this face still holds a promise of beauty for him, hints given in the high cheekbones, weathered cheeks, sockets spaced wide and eyes of an extraordinary colour.

He's observed her in all weathers: panhandling for change or drinking Tennent's Super on a bench by the library with the other regulars; shouting and spitting at the pigeons, at the government, at the rain, and at the great confusing conspiracy of it all; sleeping it off on the pavement, as oblivious to the passers-by as they are to her.

How many times has he asked himself: does anybody see such people? Really see them or just register their presence as they pass in the morning as an annoyance or obstacle or object of sudden pity, quickly forgotten? How many hundreds of pairs of eyes glance at this woman on a daily basis without ever seeing her at all? And if challenged to describe even one small aspect of her appearance, what would they recall? Naturally this last is an important consideration.

It's different for him, for them; he's intimate with her, close as no other. Who else could describe, as the Photographer can describe, the colour of her eyes, the moles on her face, the deep lines carved down to the mouth? Who knows the precise number of her teeth, and which are crowns? Who traces the lines on her hands, the varicose veins marbling the back of her calves, measures the tone and tenor of her voice, when she wakes, when she sleeps, where she goes?

Who had last touched her emaciated body – as he would – filled with a kind of awe before the microcosm of humanity; the machinery of natural language latent in her cells, like some complex DNA strand waiting to unfold? She will be more than the sum of her parts, society's discard, nameless and invisible. She exists for this, fragment of an equation that embodies that primary relationship between the identity of the individual, and the millions of dim reflections of the original form that people the universe, the fragments of Babel that she carries within her.

And all this contingent on the cameras, the CCTV, his present concealment and his long observation of her habits: Will anybody miss her? Will anyone register her absence, and having registered it, ask questions, instigate a trace, compile footage of her haunts to establish just when and where and how she disappeared? Will they delve into the black economy of the nameless and unrecorded to discover her true identity, that long-forgotten National Insurance number, the place on the Electoral roll surely lapsed?

So much easier to suppose that she has moved on, succumbed quietly to the maw of the streets, been rescued to rot her days away in institutionalised peace....

All potential truths, all possibilities, all made concrete to confuse the pursuer – a paper trail laid for those who might be looking.

"Black and white. Clear-cut. No, there is nothing preventing this: she is nothing. Camera never lies. People do. I must remember as life is art, she is symbolism. Nearly time now: woo her with the camera; always works, black and white: Camera never lies. Fool the eye. Time. Now."

When he was younger he relished these opportunities. Anticipation and the quick strike, snap, run. But this is only the first step in the process. Each element is deliberate, each a part of the ritual.

Above all there must be no haste in his actions.

As with each of his victims there's an element of the lover's nervousness in this first contact. Despite all his observation, even having seen inside them with the eye of his lens, clear as the cross-section of a cell on a microscope, even then first contact is a shock, recognising in each of them a fragment of the true language. Whilst others dismiss their drunken ravings, he rejoices in their deafness to the language of Babel, the speakers of tongues – Have they no ears to hear? Here, in this dark and filthy street, shuttered for the night and watched by the blind lens of a score of CCTV cameras, here, would he hear the voice of God? Her cries could be the only remedy for the lost symmetry of his soul.

Not all of his subjects have been women: although there have certainly been a few. Outwardly they differ from each other, but linked by a common theme; the shibboleth latent in their musculature, in the juxtaposition of cheekbone and eye socket, the grammar of the sacred language encoded in each like a cipher. Each of these individuals could be prepared and reduced to their essence, the barest equation. Each would become an elegant notation in the vast and complex calculation, the answer to which is the original word, the knowledge the first humans stole from the Garden of Eden, which was lost in the destruction of the Tower of Babel.

It was time now, painfully, to reconstruct that language to unpick the myths and conspiracy theories of society's remnants, living on the borders of its conscience, and rework them into his own private mythology.

Time. Strike. Thrill of fear or is it anticipation? He feels himself becoming hard, the street silent enough to hear her gently snoring in the stairwell, his measured tread as he approaches.

Softly he speaks her name, all reassurance – Betty come now dear, come with me, calming her with his mild voice and gentle hands, talking to her all the time as he gathers her up from her den. Somehow it's easier than expected to convince her that he poses no threat. She comes quietly, holding his hand in hers, grasping his fingers like a child, despite the illusion of bulk created by her many layers. She is so light and frail she seems barely anchored to the ground.

Her hand: cracked and slightly crusted – is it exposure, or

some skin complaint worsened by dirt and lack of washing? The contact is uncomfortable but necessary to reassure her; the last thing he needs is a scene in front of the cameras. He glances at her profile in the darkness, walking head-down, one foot in front of the other, and the next gets you where you're going; how many years of the same round? Deliverer.

The rented car is around the corner, but it feels like miles, like they're crawling, open targets on the battlefield. Finally they reach it. He opens the passenger door.

"It's all right Betty, I'm going to help you, can't have you sleeping on the cold street at night. Got a nice warm bed and a few ciders for you at home, come along now, in you get."

Slow, slow talking in a gentle monotone, reassuring smile, no sudden movements; in his pocket, the solution – just in case.

Once she's in he closes the passenger door gently and walks slowly around to the other side of the car, settling his large frame into the seat. Turns the ignition and starts the car; turns to look at Betty, already dozing, head on her chest in the comfortable seat. Good. They can drive for a while.

After half an hour or so, sure that she is deep in slumber, he slowly brings the car to a halt in a residential street beneath a large tree. What infinite patience it requires to wait for a couple more minutes. The street is quiet and dark, and she has not stirred at all. Time. Now.

5. Wanderings

March 24th

82 degrees on the Thermometer. Another hard march today. I am traversing dense Jungle; huge tree trunks litter the landscape & where once they shaded a sparse Jungle floor, now are grown up every type of vegetation & the whole wrapped around by Lianas & mosses grown over the rotting boles so that it makes for very treacherous footing & much machete work. Birds of a brilliant plumage, in shades of gold, green & ochre occasionally flit across my path & the air is strongly aromatic.

In this region grow many of the douradinha; it has a yellow flower & looks something like our dandelion. The Indians use it as a powerful emetic, the which I have no need for just now.

It is only the thought of all the invisible Jungle, the lure of the empty spaces on my map that keeps me going. It is solely the promise of an Eden, a place of purity & simplicity utterly foreign to the Babel of London, the insensate progress of the Western world that drives me on. It is not my first such journey. Other journals now stored safely in London (where one day this volume too, shall rest, God willing) contain passages describing mandalas built up painstakingly from sand by Tibetan lamas, only to be brushed away on the instant they are finished with yak's hair brooms. I have illustrated first-hand locust plagues in Africa & passed on recipes for aphrodisiacs, philtres & near untraceable poisons, learnt from the medicine men of Haiti & the Congo, to my descendants – in the journals that lie safely back in London.

*Sometimes I have used guides to take me to those distant &
unrecorded tribes, to traverse areas so remote & strange that none
of my race has ever ventured there to map their valleys & hills &
secret places. Each sentence clawed out of painful ascents into the
mountains, to the rocky heights where nothing grows, surviving on
a few dried-out grains of corn, goat's milk, edible lichens, melting
snow water in my mouth, staggering through blizzards over high
mountain passes, eyes slitted behind wooden goggles.*

*But none of it has prepared me for the Amazon, for the rich &
hungry Jungle, for the river, its life-blood & for the unseen &
unrecorded interiors, where life superabounds.*

*Night falls suddenly, the Jungle becoming a negative of itself,
deepening shadows where the palms & saplings & vines & trees
grow into & around each other. The dark is almost complete – apart
from the spark of fireflies & the occasional star pricked out against
the ink of the sky where the Jungle breaks.*

March 25th

*This morning I stumbled across a clearing that looked as though it
may have once been cultivated – perhaps with maize or manioc – but
the Jungle grows back so fast that it's impossible to be sure, or to tell
how recently the ground was used. It could be a clue or a chimera. I
have come to the conclusion that I will almost certainly be the last to
know when I encounter the people of this Jungle.*

*Despite the rumours of bloodshed & war between tribes, an almost
pathological distrust of outsiders, dark hints of cannibalism & the
practice of head shrinking, I have made no attempt at concealment
as I hack my way through this Jungle. For one, the sheer density of
vegetation seems to insulate against all sound, even the crunch of
branches beneath my feet are strangely muted, so that I feel the urge
to scream bubbling up within me, if only to reassure myself that I*

am not forgetting language, losing my voice & the habit of shaping words. Then, too, concealment would be pointless. These people know the Jungle so much better than I.

There have been reports of whole expeditions killed & tortured by Indians, angry & terrified at the strangers invading their territory; people who have learned the hard way to associate the white man with death, with slavery, with the loss of land & children. The Chaman that I hired back at Iquitos has long deserted me. I awoke one morning to find that the rogue had left & taken the canoe & himself & returned to more familiar lands. I had no hint of what had frightened him so & little warning of his intended defection except for mutterings about bad magic & death.

These people are too superstitious; As a humanist I am tainted neither by religion nor fear of unknown spirits. I have no intention of being a missionary; nor am I a tourist. I have looked death in the face; we are old friends now. It is knowledge I am after – a thirst that will never be quenched until I am in my grave.

March 26th

Another hard day's walking through impenetrable terrain. Only my compass assures me that I am travelling in my intended direction through this matted felted Jungle, knitted together by cabled creepers. The plant life is excessively abundant, characterised by prodigious variety and creates a terrible & wonderful landscape, yet I find myself almost blind to its strangeness & occupy my mind chiefly with imagining the tribes who have had, as yet, no contact with Western man. In this Jungle dwell people who have never heard of steam, glass, Faraday or gunpowder. Their customs could be the strangest I have ever encountered; their religion incomprehensible, pantheistic, sublime. How do they imagine the heavenly bodies, who can only catch glimpses of the firmament between the lowering trees?

According to the rumours that I was able to glean in Iquitos, there is one Tribe in this area that writes & what is more they have reportedly been doing so since 'the beginning time'. The rumours suggest that they are unlike the other tribes in these lands, the Jivaro & Shuar & Machichuenga, who are one & all bloodthirsty & savage in the extreme. This Tribe is rumoured to be peaceful; a nomadic people who nevertheless have magic powerful enough to protect them from their more warlike neighbours.

It is my dream, put simply, to make First Contact with this people, isolated from the world outside their Jungle home. That world feels as distant as the moon here, with the great walls of green rising on all sides, the tangled vegetation, warring for space & light.

Here the possibility of creating multiple worlds exists, the real far away & half-forgotten.

All my life I have been in flight from society, in search of a greater truth, the answer to a single question. What knowledge did Man lose when God destroyed the tower of Babel? What had so terrified Him that he cast Man back into the chaos before speech? It has been the chief labour of my existence to find an enlightened people who have the answers to these questions that plague me so. I can never rest until I do. When I find them they will take me in, teach me their customs & their language & through me will discover & come to know their fellow man. I will be their sole interpreter; their unique point of contact. Alone in the world I will understand their ways & a grateful humanity will thank me for revealing the secrets that they have discovered. Secrets of medicine, levitation, magic & divination. Who knows what boundaries of the Mind they have conquered, untainted by blundering Science? All of this will be mine to interpret; to add to my chronicles, to augment the pattern I am creating of the world.

But now the light fades & it is time to sleep. I write to drive away the demons of loneliness, but neither pen nor paper is limitless. To sleep, perchance to dream...

March 27th

Over the years I have become less & less convinced of the efficacy of language in recording, correlating & explaining the customs & tongues that I have uncovered & chronicled. Thus have I have developed a system of Mathematical Notation combining that of the Ancient Greeks, Egyptians & Sumerians, as well as those of Mesmer – & including symbols & constructions previously undreamed of in any Western or Eastern lexicon. This system functions as a kind of shorthand, allowing me to cross-reference these elements from so many different cultures. It has the additional advantage of requiring far less space than longhand.

My hands, wrists, forearms are covered in notes that I have made whilst travelling through the Jungle. They overlay themselves & with my fading vision & the guttering of the tallow, it is a struggle to transcribe them all before darkness or sleep claims me. I dare not expose the notebooks to the continual dripping of moisture from the high canopy, so I try to memorise & reproduce – in detail as faithful as is possible – poor sketches of the marvels that surround me.

Decades of squinting at tiny characters have all but destroyed my vision. My greatest fear is not death, so much as the loss of my spectacles! I preserve these against the damp & dirt of the Jungle by keeping them in an inside pocket wrapped in silk. Sadly it is now slowly rotting away like the rest of my equipment. The humidity here is well nigh total.

Night is falling now; at last it is getting a little cooler. The tallow is holding out, so I shall permit myself the leisure of writing a little more than usual in here; sometimes it is the only way to combat the solitude.

In the background always I hear the sounds of the Jungle. No longer do the chorus of calls, whistles, barks & shrieks that start up at dusk terrify me. At first sleeplessness hollowed my cheeks & lent a grey pallor to my skin. I experienced delusions & imagined horrors – waking with a jaguar or a puma snarling on my chest, vampire bats sucking my blood at night, giant snakes crushing me & swallowing me whole.

So far, none of these terrors have come to pass. I have seen monkeys, lizards, tree sloths, giant rodents, capybaras & porcupines, but evidently the fanged predators of the Jungle have sought easier meat for their tea. Still, when the firewood situation permits, I build a fire before I camp & trust that the hammock will protect me from the depredations of ground-dwelling creatures. The merest inch of flesh uncovered is a virtual invitation to the bites of bloodsucking bats & insects alike.

I must remember not to leave anything on the Jungle floor, for it does not stay there for long; a good piece of biscuit was carried away this morning, and my food stocks are very low. There seem to be a limitless number of ants & all determined to purloin every scrap of anything left unsecured, as if the Jungle is intent on gradually assimilating me.

March 29th

The sun is rarely visible & direction further confused by the variety & monotony of the landscape, the murmur & lap & drip of water, millions of leaves brushing against each other, parrots calling to each other, monkeys screaming in protest, packs leaping through the trees, cicadas whirring. At dusk the daytime sounds segue into *those of the night; the Jungle is at its loudest for the brief period of semi-darkness when then sky is a riot of flame & the stars have not yet begun to emerge. At this time the frogs begin to sing & join their voices to the spider monkeys calling for rain.*

Thus far have I seen little sign of the people for whom I am searching – only the barest traces of settlements, tools or fires. According to the fragments of information that I have been able to gather, they should be somewhere around this area – always assuming that I have not lost my way or become confused by recurring bouts of Fever. The unwholesomeness of this place may well be the death of me, but I refuse to entertain the possibility.

The journey through this inimical yet beautiful landscape can only create in me the most perfect rapport with the invisible people. Hard fought-for, my experiences become the tools with which to decipher their language. I will find them & when I do I will be the first & only of my race to discover their unique world, to create a bridge between their reality & our own.

From my earliest youth I conceived a fascination for language. Just as we cannot exist save for our thought, so language defines people & ideas. Language is grown from environment as the flower grows on the vine. Thus, one can make no serious study of a language in isolation of both the people & the place that has shaped its lexicon; & it follows that it is only through a minute & careful study of the life around me that I can have any hope of understanding the detail of their existence.

If I am fortunate enough to be able to talk with the Tribe & so stumble through mutual discovery to a sense of language, it will be solely because I have learned in the very lineaments of my body the shape of their experiences. The World is in its essence made of words; for how can we have any concept of that which we cannot describe? Descartes understood this.

I have interpreted & catalogued innumerable languages the world over & although sounds repeat, the meaning is never the same; the words are never repeated. It is as if the shattering of language created a million million tiny echoes of the first word; each corresponding to a facet of the consciousness of the earth, in potentially infinite variety.

6. Nina

Where is it going a good question and one that she was only just after asking herself as she walked down the road. Just where indeed is it all going, Nina – and are you up there at the front, or only just after catching the tail end of it. Life's running away and one of these days you'll not be holding the reins girl: that's for sure. Coming down off a trip and she's feeling blue, blue and mottled, thoughts scattered and useless.

She is tall and pale from a decade under London's gunmetal sky, with red hair and faded freckles. A slightly too sharp nose points upward and (at this moment in time) her mouth points downwards. Her eyes are shadowed; one keeping an eye on the pavement while the other looks inside. She might be enchanting but she tends to the tawdry. Her clothes are garish.

Her one firmly held belief is in chaos. In the beginning was the word? Bullshit. So what was before the beginning? What was outside the universe? What was inside the apple? Chaos. There is no truth. There is no law. There is no reason. We are not even a humorous error: geometry and nature are only by some strange synchronicity connected. What is left, then, when the creed of irrationality rules? Language only hides the fact that there is no truth.

What makes her distrust truth, all truth, to such a degree? Who held her back with custom, with prejudice and with guilt? Who still daily smothers her with silent grief?

People are far more complex than they appear. These are not characters. The only names that have been changed are to protect the guilty.

There are no innocents.

Her room is small, untidy, littered with books, with bright things, things she's found and things she'll find a use for sometime. Mistress of disguise, her collection of wigs, false eyelashes, hats and glasses allows her to express her protean personality and exercise her obsessions; self is after all, only a construct. Books are visible scattered amongst underwear, feather boas, glossy magazines and shoes. Energy without expression, painful vision of a world in shades of grey, lost to the simple dichotomy of black and white, opposite and equal, and one in the middle makes Trinity, Church, Our Father, Hail Mary – and Christ I still know all the words after all these years; cold knees and the chill hand of the devil down the back of her neck.

She drags her past behind her like a trawl net.

Her age? Indeterminately twenties. Stance? Defensive. Voice? Mellifluous. Object of desire? Freedom. For desire.

What do we mean by freedom? All of these threads will at some point conjoin. She will discover, and they will realise, and he will decipher, and yet another will record freedom, under three, under seven, or infinite criteria. At which point there will be a denouement and it won't matter any more. Sure someone will care, but you and I won't know about it, and sure what's the point when I'm only young and I've no desire for a church wedding or knitting lessons. Because after all St Peter's retired, and the hinges rusted off the pearly gates, and God gave up, and man got stubborn: and now here we are faced with this crap. They always say you can spot a convent girl a mile away. Especially the ones with the veils and black habits.

She has no piercing in her body: her earlobes are unblemished, her tongue in one piece, her nipples and navel framed only with fine hairs. She has no scars, no tattoos; none of life's signifiers. She doesn't dye her hair. In this respect she is entirely as nature intended her and thus eminently suited for this narrative. For someone as precise and devoted to rules as the Photographer she is ideal. Her skin is variegated: he could read volumes from her wrists, the flesh on her cheekbones. She is an obsession waiting to happen.

She doesn't have a job in any recognised sense. She gets by on the dole, and on a series of get-rich-quick-earn-££££££s-at-home schemes that haven't yet made her fortune but consume enough hours to stop her feeling guilty for doing nothing constructive with her time – and keep the DSS off her back. When she's not scratching a living from London's unwelcoming streets she spends her time in libraries, watching the other readers; ostensibly there to borrow books, but perhaps like herself lost in contemplation of the library's patrons, constructing imaginary lives and fantasies around them. The British Library is best. She loves the smell of books long untouched, the dark corridors of shelves and the dim recesses where gems of intellect rest. She has her regulars there, each tenuous connection: students, writers, harmless crackpots engaged in researching their genealogy and serious academics with their air of abstracted genius, gestating theories. Glances across the wide tables, eyes not quite meeting, relationships formed but not consummated.

The reader's card she has had since her college days gives her access to the stacks. Down here direction is confused by the fact that the shelves are on casters and can move in any direction, creating a maze of shifting passages where bearings are soon lost in the dim light. You see a few people, but they are often the most interesting; each struggling with their own private obsessions. Practice has helped her to develop techniques of observation so subtle that her victims have no idea that they are under surveillance, and she is able to reconstruct their research with astonishing accuracy – checking the notes that they make for themselves, and then carelessly leave on tables, the queries made of the vast catalogues, monitors detailing the location of volumes buried deep in the library's bowels; vicarious intellectual. Is she looking for truth amongst those millions of words, a copy of every book mapped out like a blueprint of humanity's imagination? If so, she hasn't found it. Yet.

But she senses that they have: and one in particular. The Photographer. He was the first that she had wanted to follow outside the Library; to discover what other secrets he had found.

⁓

She lives near Elephant and Castle in a council block that's been condemned. In this sense she's technically homeless, but the block has been squatted for long enough that its inhabitants feel reasonably secure. The corridors have been trashed beyond all recognition, graffiti scrawled in an unreadable palimpsest on the filthy walls. The floors are a mess of rubbish, broken furniture, syringes, old newspapers and other, unrecognisable, detritus. She tries not to examine it too closely, and watches where she puts her feet.

Some of the flats have electricity and water – the utilities companies don't care if the tenants are legal or not so long as someone is happy to feed coins to the meter. Five or six people share the flat she lives in. She doesn't trust any of them and padlocks her door when she is at home, and even more securely when she is not.

She has no friends, but innumerable acquaintances. She's known on the scene, always at the edge of parties, always caning it. She has her contacts with the e-dealers, speed freaks, acid punters. Base, coke, 2CB, pure MDMA when she can get her hands on it – which isn't hard, at the right parties. The wasted addicts lying in the corners in the hallways – eyes glazed and cunning, sizing her up for her cash, looking through her at the next fix, are enough to dissuade her from indulging in anything harder. They make her think of a certain genre of film, the 'gritty hardness' of the 90s, smug revelations of society's decay, drug addiction, violence, crime; – but the comparison is meaningless in the face of their reality. The books she had read, films she had seen always glamorised the addict to some extent. But there was nothing seductive about these wrecks. So she watched her step, was careful and kept her eyes shuttered.

She comes from everywhere and nowhere: one of London's dispossessed, her accent has mellowed and been adulterated in the city of Babel until she speaks in a flat London drawl, with just a tinge on the Rs to suggest her origin. The honey pot of the city has drawn her in, as with other characters in this story – and now holds her fast in a web of seeming coincidence, where all time's strands conjoin and conspire inexorably to draw her into the centre.

If you asked her where she comes from she would probably name some anonymous small town in middle England – but it's not home to her any more. Going back there she's a stranger. She remembers a couple of bars, but they're different. She's unlikely to meet anyone she once knew on the street – and if she does, it only confirms her lack of contact. They will have nothing in common, and will soon drift on, having established their separateness. Her life is a list of outdated contact numbers.

7. Taypi's Discovery

Taypi crouched lower in the cover of the giant palm, praying that he'd not been observed. He took long shallow breaths, and closing his eyes concentrated on relaxing every part of his body. Gradually he became aware that the perspiration was cooling and that insects were exploring his motionless skin. He opened his eyes and began to tune his senses to the jungle around him, the myriad of sounds, colours, smells and textures that made up his environment.

The stranger was still in the vicinity, about twenty paces away from where he lay hidden. He couldn't see him, but he could hear him and smell the acrid odour of his body – a mixture of stale sweat, urine and a damp musty stench. Beneath the odours of sap and sweat and piss he smelled quite unlike any human that the boy had ever encountered. This in itself was frightening – especially when combined with the sounds that the man was making. Low mutterings, their rhythm strangely broken, clicks, dissonant humming; altogether a meaningless jumble of sounds that sounded like the raving of someone in a dream spell. Maybe he was preparing to cast a spell, and was some kind of magician? Maybe this was a test, a vision, and part of his initiation.

Taypi was in the middle of the period of his isolation, part of the ceremony that would make him a man. Only if he could survive in the jungle on his own for a full month, until the moon turned again and showed his jutting cheekbone and cold smile to the world, would he be allowed to return to his people, no more a boy. Until that time he lived in solitude, spending his days foraging for food and chewing the various roots and herbs which the Speaker (who held the knowledge of the Tribe and communicated with spirits) had given him so that he could discover his spirit animal. The Speaker had warned him that demons might try to trick him during this period – so Taypi was not sure if the apparition before him was human, or a spirit who had taken on this disguise to confuse him.

After some time Taypi relaxed his immobility and dared to stretch one of his legs, which had begun to cramp a little. Emboldened by the fact that the man did not seem to have noticed his presence he decided to risk sneaking a look at him. The palm he was hiding in was one of a stand, on the edge of a small clearing formed when one of the giant trees had toppled, crushing the vegetation beneath it. The Stranger was sitting on one end of the massive trunk, examining something that he held in one hand, and writing with the other, and the boy was able to crawl to a place where he could see him through the leaves. This took some time – he didn't dare risk disturbing the leaves in case it startled the birds roosting on the upper branches, so his movements were infinitesimal; he almost grew from one spot to the next.

The clearing was bright with sunlight, slanting down into the ragged hole left in the cover by the fallen palm. The Stranger was outlined clearly against the foliage by his light clothes, his head covered by a decrepit hat that had once been a creamy magnolia, but was now somewhat greenish in hue. Every so often he would remove it, and wipe his face and brow before replacing it on his head. Taypi noticed several things at once: he was covered from head to foot, except for his hands and face, with garments of a kind that he had never seen before. The skin that was visible was yellowed and leathery, and marked with deep grooves. On his beaky nose some kind of adornment was perched which covered his eyes and hooked over his ears. He was hunched over, making it hard to judge his height – but gave the impression of having been a tall man. He was holding something in his hand which he squinted through, and which kept flashing in the sunlight. As the boy watched he put it down and began to write on a tablet with many leaves, sometimes pausing and scribbling on the back of his left hand.

Taypi forgot his crouched position, the branches that were digging into him, and the ants that had begun to make a regimented exploration of one of his feet. He was frozen in place; the sensation of movement a memory. The world narrowed to the bright clearing, and the Stranger, oblivious to his presence, busy cataloguing a new species of orchid in a sunbeam.

The spell was broken when the Stranger began gathering his things, obviously preparing to continue his onslaught on the jungle. The boy suddenly woke up to his predicament, realising that there was no way he dared make a move until the man was gone. He only allowed himself to breathe again when the Stranger, having gathered up his travelling equipment, departed from the other end of the clearing. Within seconds he was out of sight, machete poised for chopping at any roots or vines, and leaving a swathe of mangled vegetation in his wake.

Taypi was left alone in the clearing to try to make sense of any of the things that he had seen. It still lacked a handful of days to his appointed return to the camp – the moon was not nearly full yet. To come back before that time was unheard of, nothing before this had ever made it necessary as far as he was aware. They came back, or they didn't; but not before the allotted time. And this? The presence of this man was something that Taypi thought the Speaker and the Chief of the Tribe would want to know about. What would happen if he delayed, and the Stranger stumbled across the pueblo?

Still, they were a few days walk from his home, and Taypi didn't have any proof that the Stranger was even aware of his people's existence. He could watch him for the next few days, and return to the pueblo after his time was up with the news. That way he would not risk the disgrace or banishment (or worse) that he imagined waited for one who broke his pact with the moon.

8. Flora; My Attempts at Hunting

April 3rd

The deepening shadows remind me that the day is almost over. My little lantern throws friendly light from a bough above my head; my hammock is snugly rigged & now tis time to write up observations of the day.

The going being a little less irksome, I have been able to be somewhat more leisurely with my pace & even to collect some samples & perform a rough dissection on a tree frog which I had first sketched as you see on the facing page. Its markings were quite extraordinary & I fancy would occasion much comment at the Zoological Society.

It is somewhat dispiriting that travelling on my own this way & thus acting as my own porter somewhat inhibits my ability to catalogue as I go, but still I can aim for some level of accuracy & veracity, as far as is possible given the tools to hand. As well as the frog, I followed the trail of some leafcutter ants, to their cunningly constructed nest & searched out the funnel spider's trap-doored lair (though you can be sure I was well apprised of the danger to myself in so doing). Less perilous, but wondrous, the colonies of clay globes built by termites. These minute architects suggest the hand of some creator, yet my humanism makes me distrust such conclusions; nature is passing strange in its manifestations. "There are more things in heaven & earth…"

April 6th

I have spent the day half maddened & dazed, feverish & dreamlike as I hack & cut my way towards my goal, brushing flies from my lips & eyes as they feast on the stinging sweat, the suppurating bites. Bits of leaves & branches, beetles & unidentified seeds add themselves to the tangle of my hair & the folds of my clothes. My route is determined equally by compass & intuition, for it is rarely possible to travel in a straight line for long. Some of the land that I am crossing has evidently been cleared at some point in the past – the Jungle has reclaimed its own with extra ferocity, throwing up tangled areas of plants.

This afternoon I encountered a marshy area, and as I could see no clear route around it I had perforce to go through it, precariously balancing on fallen logs, on stones, on anything solid enough to hold my weight in the valleys of mud between the river's tributaries. After this I came to an area where the Jungle floor was clear, huge trees soaring over the ground carpeted with their dead leaves & strange species of fungi; mosses, creepers & roots hanging down from the secondary growth, high above the ground. Looking up I could see ferns & orchids & parlour palms, parasites on the trunks of giant sequoias. I wish I were a spider monkey; I envy their graceful passage through the highest reaches of the Jungle.

I have fallen into a pattern of travel now. I walk from daybreak to dusk with infrequent stops for rest & refreshment, supping on fruits that I recognize & pools of water collected in Jungle hollows or tapped from the trunks of trees. Today I was most fortunate & caught a small bird, but there's precious little meat on them, barely worth the trouble of searching out dry firewood. The river has its own dangers; swift moving & silent water snakes, many-teethed amphibians & the animals & birds usually avoid my somewhat clumsy traps.

This afternoon I tried to shoot a peccary, using the heavy musket I carry with me, the report deadened against the deep gloom of the Jungle. But it is difficult to aim & fire the clumsy weapon *fast enough to hit anything & I was certainly no match for such fleet-footed game. I do not know enough of the habits of the Jungle creatures to follow the trails of capybaras, or catch possums in their lairs. Now I dare not waste what little powder & ammunition I have left in case I should need it to defend myself.*

9. Watching the Stranger

Taypi had spent the last few days watching the Stranger, and struggling to fit the things that he observed into any frame of reference that made sense. For a start the Stranger seemed to be ridiculously ignorant of the jungle, like a child who has never left his mother's hip. Even whilst walking he kept examining and touching everything, even at one point standing on a nest of poison ants to sample the bark of a tree, scraping away at it with his machete. This tool of wonderful sharpness was as different from the palm machetes of the Tribe as everything else about the Stranger. Who knew, he might have some purpose for the bark that the Tribe were completely unaware of? It wasn't much good for anything, as far as Taypi knew. It was too crumbly to use for binding, inedible, no good in tea and with no known medicinal properties. The Stranger seemed to become very excited about it and packed the sample carefully away in one of his many pockets, after wrapping it in some banana frond, along with a leaf from the tree.

Every so often he would stop, take out something bright from his pocket, cast around for some light between the leaves, and measure it up against the sun. He would scribble symbols on his arms and on the tablet around his neck. This reassured the boy somewhat, as he understood the sun and the practice of recording knowledge on the body. For the Tribe it was a sacred process, the indelible symbols pricked on the flesh with sharp thorns, whereas for this strange creature it seemed as instinctive as breathing. There was no ceremony to the Stranger's writing – he made notes as he went, and the letters were not indelibly pricked on the skin, but scribbled in all on top of each other, new symbols etched over the faded tracery of the old. The implement he used for the markings could have been made of bone, yet it was the wrong colour; the handle intricately worked. There were rumours of tribes that had the secret of metal: it could be that he was one of those... But he seemed entirely foreign to this place, and Taypi was not even sure if those tribes still existed. There seemed to be far fewer drums rumbling through the jungle each year.

Taypi has not been able to get close enough to see what the Stranger is writing in his book with many leaves, but the writing on his hands and arms stands out clearly. The script seems regular, repeating the same few symbols in a bewildering variety of combinations. Perhaps the man is making prayers on his skin, endlessly repeating the name of his guardian spirits. The idea that the written language could combine the same few symbols to reproduce any word in the language was foreign to Taypi – for the Tribe had thousands of symbols, each reflecting the essential properties of the object, idea or event they described. You could not lie, or describe something incorrectly in their language; each event, each story has its own notation and style, variation but never repetition.

The Stranger eats and drinks as he travels but is clumsy in his foraging – ripping fruits from the trees and bushes and leaving scars on the jungle as he passes. Taypi has no need to cut his way through the thick vegetation, instead using almost invisible paths that weave through the clearings, sometimes travelling along the beds of streams, sometimes taking entirely to the river. This is always a last resort as the Tribe are afraid of the open sky. The spirits of those who have left look down at them at night, glinting like so many fireflies between the clouds, and they are jealous of the living, stealing their spirits when they can.

10. The Photographer's Apartment

The Photographer's apartment is in an old-style mansion block with a central well in the buildings, and barred windows, netted to prevent pigeons nesting. Only a single, small and heavily obscured window lights the rooms giving onto this space. The Photographer has blacked out even this small aperture with soundproofing material, and installed a complicated ventilation system to replace the window, so that once inside the room you could be anywhere or nowhere.

The room itself is not large – a box room, or bathroom perhaps. It would make a perfect darkroom, but the Photographer has long since adapted another room in the apartment for this purpose.

Inside the room there is no furniture. The walls, floor and ceiling are padded with soft black rubber. Concealed in black rubber studs are tiny microphones which pick up and amplify the slightest whisper, connected to a recording system in the Photographer's study that holds two three-hour tapes. When the room is occupied they are changed every six hours.

The only entrance is through a heavily soundproofed door, with a specially reinforced lock that secures the door to the frame on both the hinged and opening sides. From inside it's hard to find the door, as the back and the surrounding walls are padded in the same material. The Photographer keeps the key on a chain around his neck at all times, and the lock well-oiled, so that it turns smoothly and silently. A hatch is built into the door, allowing food or water to be placed inside the doorway for the occupant of the room, but even this works through an ingenious airlock system, so that no light or sound is allowed to enter. The room could be a womb or a sensory deprivation tank. The Photographer has himself spent some hours enclosed between its padded walls, but the total solitude, the silence, and the whispering of internal voices frightened him; he felt as though his soul was being eaten. Now he uses it solely for observation, sending others on the journeys that he is too terrified to make himself, recording the pleas and entreaties absorbed by the padded walls, the gradual loss of identity and the dissolution of language. Each time he attempts to piece together a deeper meaning from the babble on his tapes. But there is never quite enough to grasp a pattern, and frustration sends him out looking for fresh victims.

11. Fever

April 9th

Today I saw a striking bird & had a strange sensation of deja vue. Although it seemed new & strange, being of a genus I have not encountered before & at same time it was strangely familiar, as though I had already seen it somewhere. & thus I am combing my Journal for a reference to it & yes – just days ago I had sketched it & have already forgotten both that & what else?

My senses are much disordered; & I am much plagued by stomach cramps, vomiting, diarrhoea, sweats & all the other consequences of my experiments in the edible. Each episode is a painful lesson in the vocabulary of sustenance, a language I must learn soon if I am not to perish from want of food. Twould be an irony to starve in the midst of such natural plenty.

April 11th

A nasty shock today – I think my reactions are slowing. Nearly stepped on a fer-de-lance – a snake of a highly poisonous variety (although I hear that the Indians make an antidote of the plant of the same name, which mashed and applied as a poultice, produces a speedy cure). This threw me off balance, the hand I threw out to catch myself landing almost dead square in a column of biting ants. My diet is still very poor, though I have found breadfruits to eat. The mosquitoes are very plaguesome. I must keep myself covered from head-to-toe to avoid their bites. That & the bloodsucking of leeches & ticks have left me prey to recurrent fevers, which take me out of myself for days, wavering between unconsciousness & vivid hallucinations, so that I no longer know where or who I am. Either of those small mistakes could be fatal to me out here & who knows if anyone will ever discover my rotted bones, the rusted remains of a beltbuckle, the gold of my pocket watch perhaps all that remains after all else has decayed?

April 14ᵗʰ

I could not swear that is the correct date. I see visions, and hear unexplained sounds. Flashes of coppery faces, strangely ornamented and tattooed, alternated with a speech seemingly composed of clicks and vowels, singing and whistling, the smell of smoke and headgear made of feathers. I feel another fever coming on.

Hard to tell what is dream and what reality; hallucinating caused by fever or hunger? Someone (or something?) is watching me. I feel eyes always upon my back. I hope to God they are friendly eyes, as I have become weak as a kitten.

12. Return To The Pueblo

The days passed quickly. Taypi was so absorbed in the
stranger's actions that he almost forgot to note the phase of
the moon, or to carry out the meditation exercises that the
Speaker had taught him to help him contact his spirit animal.
One morning, however, the stranger did not stir from the
hammock he had slung between two trees. Instead he lay
moaning and thrashing in the net in the grip of some fever.
His glazed eyes opened occasionally – staring at nothing or
at something only he could see, mumbling and shouting
meaningless words. Taypi could sense that his spirit was
travelling far from his body, engaged in a mortal battle on the
spirit plane, and wondered if he should sing one of the chants
that the Speaker used to guide the spirit back to the body
after it has been wandering.

Although Taypi had to a large extent lost his fear of the
Stranger over the preceding days, nevertheless it took him
the better part of the morning to gather up the courage
to approach him. Gradually he moved closer and closer,
scrambling silently up the trunk and branches of one of the
trees to which the hammock ropes were fastened. Securing a
vantage point directly above, but still screened by a couple of
layers of foliage, he could see through the nearly transparent
netting that covered the Stranger, and directly into the man's
face.

From this close he could see that the Stranger was translucent
and white-hot with fever, literally burning up, with the
bones in his already gaunt face seeming to pierce his tightly
stretched skin. It hardly seemed possible that a man so

emaciated could still be alive. At a distance, and concealed by bulky clothing, he had not been able to guess at the wrists reduced to bones, the legs all femur, jutting sharply through the cloth. The Stranger's hands were like those of a skeleton, sheathed with parchment and inscribed all over with interlocking scribbles. His flesh looked desiccated, the flesh that of a corpse; but his eyes, startling the boy when they opened for a moment, were a bright and intense blue.

From the way they wandered, glazed and unseeing, Taypi knew that he was already half-way between this world and the next, and that he did not want the responsibility of admitting that he had done nothing if the man died in their lands. It was time to let the Speaker know everything that he had seen, and to let the Tribe decide what should be done.

The moon that night was bright, but it was not yet full. Taypi was stiff from crouching over the stranger, and light-headed with hunger as he had not dared leave him to forage for food. He had balanced the damage that the man's unsung death would have against the possible disgrace to himself for returning before the appointed day, but faced with the figure before him, emaciated and barely clinging to this world, he knew that he had no choice. If the man was to have any chance of survival then he must return to his people with all possible speed and report everything to the Speaker, who would be anxious to learn the man's reasons for being in their land. Giving the man a little water, and singing a quick prayer over him to keep him safe, Taypi began to run back to the settlement. When the jungle became completely black, and he could not even rely on the light of the moon and stars for direction, he walked, picking his way by landmarks that he recognised, and trusting to his instinct.

It was already full morning when he arrived back at the camp. He was hot, breathless and thirsty; filled with a sick urgency for the Stranger and dread of the consequences of his return. A few children were playing in the dust, older children watching the younger ones whilst the adults were out hunting or planting. Some of the women were pulping yucca to make Masato, and scraping the flesh from gourds, but apart from their low voices and the laughter and scolding of the children, the camp was quiet. The boy made his way to the Speaker's hut, hoping he would be there. Sometimes he went into the jungle for days to meditate and carry out various rituals and initiations, now and then returning in the middle of the night, and always unpredictably.

It was with a profound sense of relief that he saw the Speaker seated on one of the platforms inside his house. The elder took one look at Taypi, whose breath was still coming in quick gasps and whose eyes were slightly wild, and motioned him to sit, calling to one of the women to bring them some bowls of Masato. He squatted and watched the boy with a quizzical expression in his eyes whilst Taypi took long slugs from the bowl, and then replaced it on the ground beside him. Wordlessly the woman took the bowls and refilled them from the giant clay pot where the Masato was left to ferment. When he judged the boy was ready the Speaker addressed him gently:

"Taypi, you have returned early. And you look frightened. You have obviously come back here as fast as possible to tell me something – what can be so important that it would send you running through the jungle like an animal in flight to find me, and the moon not full until tomorrow? Hmm?"

"I found a stranger in a clearing, a couple of days ago, not one of us. I didn't come back here and tell you about it then because the moon was not yet full, but followed him, and watched what he did. But yesterday he didn't stir from his hammock. I went up close to him, and he was feverish. He saw nothing with his eyes, as though his spirit had gone away from his body. And they were blue. I think he is dying. I came back here, to tell you before it was too late."

The words tumbled out in a rush, and the Speaker spent a few moments taking it all in. Taypi waited silently, blinking the stinging sweat from his eyes, but otherwise making no movement.

"Go on, I am listening."

"He's about half a day's run from here – much longer than that, carrying him, as the land is rough. I first saw him a couple of day's walk away from here. I've been following him ever since. He's definitely not one of us, or of any of the tribes that I have heard of. He was like no one I have ever seen. Everything about him was different, even the way he spoke and walked – except for one thing. Whilst I was watching him he spent some time inscribing symbols on his skin, that I could not read."

The Speaker had his eyes closed and was listening intently. He motioned for the boy to continue with his story.

"I do not even know if he was a man – or even human, although I think he was flesh and blood, and not a spirit – I am only calling him 'he' because he seemed to be a male, rather than a female. I couldn't see his body, since he was all covered up from head to foot with only his hands and his face and neck showing.

"He made a lot of noise, and didn't seem to be familiar with the jungle at all – he was examining some flowers as if he'd never seen such blooms before, and seemed to be making pictures of them on a tablet with many thin whitish leaves."

"I think he is an old man, as his skin was very wrinkled and he stood a little hunched. He spoke to himself from time to time, but not in any language that I could recognise. And his smell is unfamiliar – but very strong, for he used water only for drinking, after he had boiled it and mixed it with various substances."

"Another thing. He is looking for us, or at least for something. And he is coming closer. For the last couple of days I have been following him towards the pueblo, although at the rate he is going it would take him much longer than that to reach here, for he is travelling in circles and seems to have little or no sense of direction. This anyway is what I observed."

The traditional formula indicated that Taypi had finished his description, at least for the moment, and was the cue for the Speaker to reply. The boy knew that there was no point rushing him – at the moment the Speaker would be sifting through the history of the Tribe to see if there was any precedent for this situation, which would give him an indication of how to act in this matter.

The Speaker began to go into a spirit trance, to consult the massed knowledge of the Tribe that he held in trust along with the preserved heads of those who had gone before. This would take the greater part of his awareness, but a part of his spirit would be free to talk to the spirits of the jungle – the frogs, who are everywhere and see everything, the crocodiles who speak with the spirits of the water and the spirits of the land, and the most sacred and powerful of all, the jaguar. He would watch through their eyes.

The Speaker began to strip himself methodically, removing his loincloth, his bags of herbs and roots, the beads and necklaces and bones of his office. Finally, when he was completely naked, save for the tattoos which covered his body, he seated himself cross-legged on a piece of wood and lighted a cheroot, filling his lungs hungrily with the pungent smoke, spitting it out with a whoosh of air, clearing the space around him of distractions and malignant spirits.

After a few minutes he began to hum and sway, keening in a low tone, with his eyes fixed on the air in front of him: air that shimmered lightly, perhaps with thermals in the tropical heat. Sweat poured from his forehead, making the tattooed script shine, and on the cords of his neck it rippled like living snakes. The Speaker was oblivious to this – his attention was all for the images that were beginning to take shape in the air before him – the echoes that filled his ears.

By dint of great effort the Speaker had succeeded in projecting his own image onto the air before him, along with echoes of all those who have gone before him, tapping into the accumulated memory of the Tribe. He felt his consciousness expand with faint ghosts of experience; past lives like layers of bark – his body and physical self only dimly important now. It's nearly there, he nearly has a pattern, he sees the man suspended between two worlds – one the everyday world that he was familiar with, the other so alien that his awareness of it was painful to him.

The connection was lost as the Speaker felt his body begin to go into convulsions, dragging him back to his earthbound self. The drug that had freed his mind and sent it wandering around the paths of the spirit world had strong side-effects. It was this that had made him so cautious about taking it. He struggled, resisting the pull of the physical, but could not regain the pattern he had almost grasped.

After some time the Speaker opened his eyes and frowned deeply. His voice, when it came, was a little hoarse.

"I have found no precedent for this – stranger – that you have seen. I do not think in the memory of the Tribe there has been such an individual in our lands, or if there has then it has not been recorded. I must speak of this to the chief and the elders, so that we can put it before the Tribe. You did well in coming straight to me with this story. You have acted with wisdom, like a man."

Taypi heard this with deep relief. The burden of knowledge had weighed heavy on him over the last couple of days, and whilst the Stranger had slept fitfully in his hammock Taypi had lain awake wondering where he came from, and what he should do. The Speaker's praise, the fact that he took him seriously and didn't treat him like a child, made him feel stronger and more confident. He hoped that the Speaker would want to bring the stranger back to be healed by the Tribe: suddenly he wanted the man to live so that he could satisfy the curiosity which pricked at him like a mosquito bite, insistently reminding him of its presence.

When the boy had left, the Speaker sat cross-legged on the platform, mulling over what he had been told, and calling for many bowls of *masato* and hot cigarettes. It was a good thing that the boy had come to him first – forewarned, he could be calm and decided at the meeting of the Tribe. Knowledge was his power, his only fear that he would not have the answers to their questions. And now, he did not have much time.

The Speaker was of necessity a highly observant individual. He tried as far as possible to be aware of everything that might affect his position, or the life of the Tribe, and to be prepared with wise and considered advice. He did not make all the decisions for the Tribe – but the chief would always consult him on issues of importance, and it was imperative that he make the right judgement now about the fate of the stranger, or he would suffer for it later.

It was only his brain, his phenomenal memory, and his ability to understand and transcribe the sacred scripts and ancient stories that had earned him the position of Speaker. He was not a physically strong person, and had been weak and sickly as a child. This sickness had gone away once he had begun his training as a Speaker – it was as though his soul had been trying to escape the prison of his body, and the fevers and weakness he had been prey to before in his youth were its way of communicating with him. The position he held now was one of respect, and some power, and it was one he would not willingly jeopardise. The only alternative for one of his kind was exile, or suicide, which amounted to much the same thing for the Tribe – for beyond their lands the jungle was unknown and full of danger, and the exiles were not remembered.

He felt frustratingly impotent at the little he had been able to learn; the connection, so brief, had given him a single set of mental impressions, but so fragmented that they could never be joined into a whole picture. As Taypi spoke he had been able to glean far more than had been conveyed by the boy's words alone. The Speaker had picked up images, quick flashes of the scenes he was describing, the smell of the Stranger, the boy's acrid tang of fear, his curiosity. But these tantalising hints were not enough to give him more than the sketchiest inkling of the person the Tribe would have to deal with.

Calling some of the children to him, he gave instructions to the older ones to tell everyone that there would be a gathering of the Tribe that night after sunset.

13. A Meeting with Quentin

One of the few people that the Photographer has not managed to expel from his life is his agent, Quentin. This is not through fondness for the man, but because the Photographer considers him to be a necessary evil. He invariably handles the Photographer's affairs with flair and attention to detail, and never bothers him with trivialities. This leaves the Photographer free to pursue his experiments, free from interruption by galleries, reviewers, publishers, accountants, fans or any of the hundred other irritating people who seem to see it as a God-given right to disturb his peace.

Most of their communication is by telephone, or, preferably, letter – with Quentin under strict instructions not to contact the Photographer unless absolutely necessary. The Photographer's previous successes and the demand for retrospectives and books about his work necessitate a physical meeting occasionally. There are always documents to sign and contracts to be discussed. These meetings are held every three months, and always take place at the Photographer's apartment – and the effort made in concealing all traces of his work is disruptive in the extreme. Yet somehow, it was important that they happened there. He wonders what he would do if Quentin ever found out what one of his most important clients was up to; what would it feel like to kill someone in the heat of the moment, and moreover someone who would be missed, unlike the drifters and vagrants who were his usual targets?

The doorbell gave a rusty clatter, and although the

Photographer had been waiting with fierce concentration for the sound, he flinched involuntarily. For the hundredth time that morning his eyes scanned the room for anything he might have missed, anything that had escaped his vigilance to mar the consummate identity, consistent in its falsity, which he projected for his agent. He reflected that he had many of these personas, donned for every occasion. He was like a hall of mirrors, the endless reflection of himself, but each one somehow warped and untrue. At times like this he used his fractured personality to his advantage, turning one facet to his interlocutor, and letting it shine in their reflected light.

The room was in order. He tried to make his eye a stranger's eye, catch details that his, accustomed to the apartment's sparseness, would miss. Nothing was out of place; no anomalies gave evidence to the scenes that had happened here. The Photographer pressed the intercom for the street entrance, and went to answer the door.

Quentin stood in the doorway, impeccably dressed as always, rolling an umbrella he had used to keep the few drops of rain which had fallen that morning from staining his immaculate suit. He was about the same age as the Photographer but the two men couldn't have been more different. Quentin projected urbanity, a civilised man of business, who never let a deal pass him by. Nevertheless he had his secrets. He was a man who could understand the need for privacy.

Quentin was in his element with the gossip and glamour of the art world. He had long ago decided to become a prostitute to success, resolving that he'd rather be a very successful agent than a mediocre artist – he lacked vision, his eye saw the commonplace, but couldn't elevate it unassisted. This, then, is the man who presented himself to the Photographer: carefully preserved, slim, about 5'9" with slightly hooded dark eyes, arched brows and dark curls with just a trace of grey at the temples.

The Photographer asked him in, and Quentin headed towards his usual chair, setting his laptop, mobile phone and papers around him like a general marshalling his troops for battle. The Photographer had disappeared towards the kitchen, to prepare the coffee with which they invariably started the meetings, and to give Quentin time to put his presentation in order, his usual strategy to avoid any unnecessary small talk beforehand.

As he returned with a cup in each hand Quentin gave him a list of issues they needed to get through in the meeting. They covered these quickly, signing papers, glancing at accounts. Quentin showed him reviews and clippings of his work, most of which the Photographer ignored, and filled him in on the gossip and happenings that hadn't made it into the press.

Throughout most of this the Photographer paid only the most cursory attention, his mind on the work that had been interrupted, the discoveries that would have to wait until later. Much of the time he stared at Quentin, barely listening to his words. The agent had the habit of running his hand through his hair when stressing a point. The Photographer suspected that it was intended to make him look dramatic. The position exposed the veins in his neck, the defenceless nape.

The meeting was winding up when Quentin asked the question that the Photographer had been hoping to avoid.

"People are wondering when your next exhibition is, your public are hungry. They've been chewing over what's there for a while now... they're down to gristle – they want some fresh meat."

The Photographer winced; Quentin had a way of stretching a

metaphor just that little bit too far.

"At least do some interviews?"

He shrugged: "Can't we give them a retrospective?"

"A retrospective of what? The last retrospective? They won't buy it. I don't buy it."

"You'll have to. I have neither the time nor the inclination to pull together a show at the moment. The work's just not ready; it's too important for any distractions. You'll have to put them off with something."

"So you are working?"

"Yes, I'm working."

"On what? At least you could let me know, I'm your agent."

"I can't tell you; I'd have to kill you."

"Very funny. Oh well, at least I can tell them there's some new work in progress."

"Yes, I suppose you deserve a few scraps for the jackals to fight over, if it's meat they're after."

Quentin winced at the inference that he too was a parasite on the great man's work – he like the others when he had done so much. But, then, in the end, it was true to a point. He lacked the frightening intensity that lay just beneath the Photographer's seemingly affable front, the dark vision that infused his work. Nevertheless he pressed on. "And me? Don't tell me you're going to hold out on me too?

The Photographer stared Quentin down, looking at him as he might a specimen on his work-desk but with considerably less excitement, and thought irritably that it was time he went.

They had covered all that was necessary in the quarterly meeting; he wanted to be alone once more to pursue his work – to straighten the chaos that the man's visits made. He looked at him, sitting across from him. This urbane, confident man – who nevertheless was a little frightened of him, who could see in his eyes when he had gone too far.

Quentin shifted uneasily under his gaze – pinned by the microscope glare of the Photographer's eyes, which despite his attempts at levity were flat, devoid of humour or compassion. Finally he deigned to answer Quentin's question, his manner final and dismissive, his voice dangerously low and soft.

"I'm not sure if you, or the world, are ready to understand what I'm working on yet. Certainly not now – perhaps not whilst I am alive. It is a labour, you might say, of blood, ink and tears."

He stared fiercely at Quentin, as if daring him to challenge him. Quentin just laughed nervously and replied "I'll quote you on that if I may. I suppose it can't do any harm, making them wait awhile."

"No. The world has waited a hundred and fifty years for this – they can most certainly wait a while longer. Anyway, I think we've covered everything now. I'll see you in three months."

Quentin was used to these sudden dismissals and so gathered his things together in silence. He looked around the room but as ever it gave away no clues. As they passed the desk he looked at some books that were on there. Much later he was to realise their significance, but at the time the volumes were meaningless to him: Montaigne, De Galle's Phrenology, Voodoo practices, studies in anthropology. The Photographer noticed him looking.

"It's this way out Quentin." His dry tone reproached Quentin's curiosity. They proceeded to the hall, with its profusion of dusty houseplants.

"Well, I guess it's goodbye then, for a few months. I'll call if there's anything that urgently requires your attention."

"I'd prefer to be contacted by letter, as usual. It's been a pleasure Quentin. Goodbye."

Quentin found himself in the outer hall, and the door closed behind him. He emerged onto the street with a sense of disquiet, and with a shake of his head headed for the main road and a taxi to the warm and welcoming delights of Chelsea, and the places where he was known.

14. Tribal Gathering

As dark fell the whole Tribe assembled in the central hut.
They made themselves comfortable on the long benches
which had been built against the sides, men upright, and
women in hammocks with their children cuddled into them.
The only light came from the glow of the fire; their faces
were in shadow. Against the backdrop of jungle calls, which
were so much louder at night, was a low muttering as people
took their places, and there was a constant slapping sound
as each tried to ward off the mosquitoes, sandflies and other
biting insects that swarmed at night. The Speaker waited
on his raised platform until each had settled, and there was
silence. Then he raised his voice a little and addressed his
people.

"You will all be wondering why we have gathered everyone
here tonight. Taypi has a story to tell us and we have some
important decisions to make."

"Whilst Taypi was on his spirit journey he stumbled upon
a stranger in our lands – a stranger unlike any we have ever
met before. He came back here today and told me about
it, because the man is ill and might die soon – and from the
things he has observed, the man's spirit is one of great power.
I have called you all together so that we can decide what to do
since the man lives, or dies, on our land."

There was a stunned quiet for a minute, and then everybody
started talking at once – asking the boy questions, offering
opinions and shouting each other down. The Speaker let
this continue for a few moments and then spoke sharply:
"Silence!"

The hush was immediate. People turned expectantly to the Speaker to see what his verdict would be. There was no hierarchy to command their obedience – merely a faith that in the stories would be the answer to this new problem, and that the Speaker would be able to find it for them.

"How will we hear the voice of the ancestors when you all speak at once? Are you children clamouring for a mother's attention? We must carefully and calmly weigh up this possible threat to our people and decide what is to be done."

He glared around him, waiting for someone to interrupt– but no one dared.

The Speaker turned to Taypi "Tell us!" he commanded, "Start from the beginning and tell everything you have seen."

The Speaker lowered himself carefully onto his mat, and Taypi stood up to tell the story as he had been instructed.

"Since the last full moon I have been in the jungle on my spirit journey, fasting and meditating, and following the instructions of the Speaker. A few days ago I came across the stranger in a clearing – and since it was not yet time for me to return, and I wanted to find out more about him, I decided to watch him for a few days. I held quite still for hours so that he wouldn't see me, and watched everything that he did. I followed him, and saw him eat, drink, defecate. I stayed awake whilst he slept and spied whilst he wrote on himself or the things around him."

"He seemed to be looking for something – muttering to himself and consulting a bright amulet that he took from his coverings. He did not look anything like any of the other tribes that live in this jungle: his hair (what was not hidden under a covering) was not black like ours, and his skin was yellow. I did not recognise what he wore, or the things that he used. There were many things that he did that made no sense to me at all. But one thing I distinguished. His skin was inscribed in a manner not unlike our own, although of much greater extent."

There was a mumble around the gathering at this – and the Speaker prompted Taypi gently – "Markings on his skin? Where? On his face? On his body?"

"As for that, I could hardly tell – for he covered most of his body, from his neck to his ankles. But there were no markings on his face, that I could see, and he had hair upon his head – although thin and greying, like an old man."

The Speaker was silent at this – and seemed to withdraw into himself for a little while – for all the world as though holding a voiceless dialogue. The Tribe, assuming that he was asking the ancestors for advice, held their tongues. This time, however, the silence was for effect: the Speaker had already decided what to do, but wanted it to appear that he had consulted the spirits, and that it was they who had made the decision.

After a few moments he raised his head and looked at the people gathered around him. "Do any of you think this stranger offers a threat? And if so, what should we do, given that we are peaceful people, unlike our violent cousins?"

It was Taypi that answered him, flushed with the adrenaline of speaking, and being listened to by the whole Tribe.

"I think that he is a human being, like us, but from a different place – and that he has come here to learn about our land. I don't know why – maybe because there are more like him. But now he is dying – so I have come back here to ask the Tribe what we should do. I will be responsible for him if we bring him back to the pueblo. I am a man now."

The Speaker recognised the element of bravado in Taypi's tone, but on the whole he approved of the change in him. He had always been an excellent student, and was now coming into his own power. Once again the Speaker was silent, and the whole Tribe held their breath. They heard but barely saw the Speaker go into a spirit trance; knew from the gasping inhalation, the heavy stertorous breathing that followed, that his eyes had rolled in their sockets, and his head would be lolling on his neck as his spirit journeyed. He did not keep them in suspense long.

"I believe you are right, and the spirits are in agreement. We must bring the man back if he is alive, or return to see if he has died. Find the man and bring him back to the pueblo – but isolate him from the people – until we learn more about his sickness. I will find medicine for him, and consult with the spirits and ancestors to see if I can find any precedent for this situation. If he dies we will need to know what death rites are necessary."

The chief of the Tribe had been silent throughout this discussion – he was an old man and looked forward to the day when he would be able to rest, and his spirit would finally cross the great river, and take up residence in this world. This disturbance was unlooked-for, so, as had become his habit, he left it to the Speaker to make arrangements to deal with the situation. At the Speaker's look, he inclined his head and grunted to show that he was in agreement with these plans.

15. Watching the Photographer: 1

Nina cast another oblique look in the direction of the
Photographer, with whom she has become more and more
preoccupied, to the point where she has begun to neglect
the usual subjects of her scrutiny and to frequent the library
at all hours in the hope of seeing him. Whilst she quickly
discovered that his visits are regular enough to set a clock
by, so far he remains a cipher to her – inscrutable in his dark
clothes, his cold glance measuring but not engaging with the
other readers, with the librarians, and with her.

Today she is doing her frumpy actress look – moth-eaten
black wig, velvet draperies, Dame Edna glasses and many-
buttoned black boots. She can barely see him, for he is half
concealed behind a tall and meticulously arranged pile of
books, bent low over a reporter's pad in which he is making
notes in tiny handwriting. He is not so absorbed in his work
that he is impervious to the interest of those about him,
and seems to be making a conscious effort to prevent others
from seeing the notes he is taking. Walking quietly past him
she can just make out the titles on the spines of the books,
creating a signature that she has learnt to interpret. Yet there's
no immediately discernable pattern in his choices: studies
by anthropologists long since gone to dust, ancient anatomy
books, treatises by Egyptologists, photographs of catacombs
filled with the desiccated flesh of my flesh, Victoriana – the
fetishism of death. With these are books on linguistics, the
bible code, the tower of Babel, language, hermeneutics,
Kabbalah, Mesmer, the philosopher's stone, numerology –
even the Rosicrucians get a look in somewhere, woven into
the pattern of this strange man's researches.

She has never encountered someone who confuses her so much, nor who covers his tracks so well, requiring all her stratagems to watch him. Then too there is that nagging sense of recognition: familiar in the sense of someone that you've met sometime, but can't quite place. This is a face she's seen somewhere, frozen in attitude in a black and white photograph. Or is it his black clothes, dark hair, cold eyes and pale, spare frame that makes him seem as though reproduced on celluloid? Then she has it. From somewhere deep in her memory she dredges up a recollection of where she has seen him before, his face ever before her eyes, teasing. The memory goes back to her college days, and to the fine art degree she had read for, but never completed. A photographer, she was sure, but what was his name? She could not explain her growing obsession with him – but this inability to identify him, the disturbing familiarity of his physiognomy, intensified the feeling and the sense of a connection between them. She began discern in his habits special messages intended only for her.

Today the Photographer turns up at the library at his usual time: he seems a man of impeccable precision and inflexible habits. This makes Nina's task much easier – for once she worked out when he would be in the library, she was able to relax the schedule which had kept her there at all hours, and anticipate his arrival to the minute. She prepares for these sessions as though for an assignation – spending hours on her costumes and make-up – for she is invariably in disguise, veiled like a coy bride.

Curiosity cuts like heartburn in her chest – where does he go to when he is not in the Library? Where does he live? What is he working on that drives him to dig up such a strange mixture of volumes, and what is the significance of his obscure choices? Once he has finished with the reference books, he invariably amasses a stack to take home – although how he can read them all is a mystery to Nina, as he invariably returns each one within the week. She can only suppose he is doing some giant work of cross-referencing, collating different branches of knowledge, and creating some kind of index. Watching him, as he seems to absorb light into himself in the dim reading room, bent low over a book, so that the stack before him half conceals his hunched figure, she resolves that she must begin to find the answers to some of these questions, which will never be resolved within the Library's walls.

At precisely 3.30 the Photographer consulted his watch and began to gather up his notebook and pen, and to stack the books neatly for the librarians to return to their appointed shelves. Nina knew this meant he was about to leave, and made her way quickly out of the reading room and towards the exit. She would wait for him on the street.

The Photographer came down the steps with an abstracted air, hands clenched in his pockets, and eyes scanning the stairs before him without seeing them, as if totally absorbed in mulling over the facts and myths that he had been collating in the library. From across the road she could make out his tall figure, and watched him turn and flag a taxi, which soon joined the traffic on the Marylebone Road, and meant that for the moment she had lost him.

Slowly she turned and made her way down into the tube station, and the Northern Line, for the Elephant, and home. Once upon a time she would have stayed in the library until closing time – but now she needed to be alone to think over their silent dialogue.

16. Cab Rage: a Moment of Angst

The Photographer settled himself in the back of the black cab, and gave his address to the driver. The traffic was heavy as always on the Marylebone Road, but the Photographer registered little of the passing cityscape, his mind on the work that awaited him at home, the tantalising fragments of information that he had been able to unearth at the library, and the system that he was evolving based on this research.

You must not assume that just because he had taken a cab today, he always travelled this way – it depended on his mood. Sometimes he would take the bus home from the library, the old-fashioned kind, with an open platform. He would sit at the back and watch the other passengers, and the city going past the steamy windows. He felt both connected and disconnected at these times – both a part of the scurrying London populace and above, outside of it. But today he felt like paying for the solitude and discretion of a black cab driver. Should the cabbie be in a talkative mood, one glance in the rear-view mirror usually stopped attempts at conversation dead.

Crossing London Bridge with its black suited city professionals he felt a sudden rush of anger at their antlike existence – which only confirmed for him the value of his work. He resisted the temptation to pull back the glass that separated him from the cab driver and ask

"Do you believe in free will, I mean do you? Really? Look at them with their pensions and PEPs, policies and endowment schemes, insurance against anything which could possibly happen except, of course, the death of the soul. What price", he felt like asking, "do you put upon the soul?" The driver wouldn't listen of course, inured already to the men with sandwich boards; Jehovah's Witnesses daily knocking

"Do you believe? Do you believe in an inalienable right to dictate your own actions, reactions to the world about you? Do you believe in the consequent FULL RESPONSIBILITY for all possible results of your actions? Does it make you scream, and shudder, paralysed with indecision, crushed beneath the weight of that awful knowledge?" He wanted to howl "Do you believe do you understand?"

He realised that he was sweating, breathing hard, knuckles white and strained. But the taxi driver had not noticed anything, or if he had then he had ignored it with the sanguinity of his kind, and the Photographer spent the rest of the journey in silence, mulling over the next stage in the process.

17. Recordings and Methods

The Photographer returned to his work with relief once the taxi had dropped him off, removing the tapes and the player from the drawer where he had concealed them.

The DAT tapes were neatly labelled, and represented three days of continuous recording, the cartridges changed every six hours. Transcribing them was a time-consuming process, but the Photographer had invested in the most expensive equipment – allowing him to scan through hours of material automatically, taking his verbal snapshots. The machine would stop at the slightest utterance, the smallest piece of the jigsaw that constituted the original language, as the sequestered ones gradually forgot the speech they had learnt to communicate in this society and returned to a more primal language encoded in their flesh.

The Photographer cross-referenced another sound on his card system, and made a copy of the portion of the recording that contained the original sample. Checking his watch he realised that it was feeding time for the latest guest. He went into his small kitchen, and prepared a tray: a plastic beaker filled with water, a bowl of soup and two pieces of toast. They often refused food at first, but even the strongest would crumble after a couple of days in the room, and the dishes would be returned to the dumbwaiter licked clean.

This took five minutes, no more. He crossed the hallway to the door of the room, its all-but invisible frame set flush in the wall. The outline of the hatch was equally indiscernible, and was heavily insulated. Silent enough for the room's occupants who had heard their last human voice. The only sound that escaped its padded walls was through the reassuringly mechanical medium of the tape recorder, divorced from the messy physicality of it all. That and the complete darkness of the room created a sense of isolation that divorced one completely from any awareness of the physical world.

Only when the recordings began to lose any semblance of coherent language did he stop bringing the food each day. All that escaped the room when he opened the hatch was the smell of shit and urine, unwashed body and fear – and the Photographer would stop opening the hatch until his recorders picked up nothing but silence. Then he would open up the room and remove the body.

He was gradually building up a library of these tapes, strange moans and broken words. The positioning of the microphones made them sound as though they were coming from the bottom of a deep well, an oubliette whose occupants were not so much forgotten, as never known in the first place.

18. A Decision is Made

The Speaker awoke at dusk with a raging headache, cramps in his stomach, and a taste of dust in his mouth. A whole night and a day had passed in this world, as he slept. He had spirit-journeyed again, and this time, the connection had not been broken. It took him a moment to connect these sensations with the events of the afternoon, and then the realisation of what he had discovered hit him like a blow in the chest. Everything would change with the stranger who was arriving – but the Speaker could not see how, and he struggled to hold onto the connections he had made before they dissipated.

He became aware that there were several people watching him. He got up and followed them to the central hut, where he found many members of the Tribe. They had been waiting patiently for him to emerge from the fugue state, confident that he would have all the answers, as he always did. This only increased his sense of dread, as he stared at the chief of the Tribe, at the heads of the families, and tried to gather words to describe what he had understood. Nevertheless, he could not lie – he had not been given the language with which to do that. His grave face told his watchers that the news would not be good.

"Brothers. I have looked in the memories of our people, and questioned the spirits of the jungle. I have gazed through the eyes of animals, and studied the patterns of probability. I could not understand much of what I saw, but I know that this man is far outside our experience, and that his people speak a language that has never been heard by our people. His mind is like black water – I could not see into it."

"I have found no answers to our questions, nor could I see our future clearly, or the future of the stranger. I do not even know if he will live or die. Yet one thing came through clearly: everything that we have known will change."

The news caused a rumble of disquiet. In living memory, there had never been a situation or problem for the Tribe that the sacred scripts had not provided a solution for. The Tribe were so used to being able to consult the Speaker, who held in his head the Tribe's memories, and could consult the shrunken heads preserved against the jungle for generations for any information that they required, that the very thought that there might be no answers caused some panic. The Speaker continued imperturbably.

"I do not know if he will survive, but I think we should keep him away from the rest of the Tribe for the moment. I will nurse him with Taypi and his mother until he is strong enough to be taught some of the ways of our people."

"If he lives, we will have to learn to speak with him. If he dies, we have no guide, no words with which to free his spirit, nor any way of understanding the knowledge that we would gain from him. Nevertheless, it may be that we will find some connection with him. For the boy said he is inscribed in our manner, if not in our script, and his spirit was not invisible to me. We will leave immediately."

19. Gerard

It was a greyly humid day – smog low on the pavements and the West End traffic snarling its contorted loops through Soho. The streets teemed with young and beautiful affluence, coy glances darting round the pavement cafés.

The Photographer noted careless caresses, faces and bodies strewn about with metal, fashionable clothes and coked-out eyes. He observed men in business suits, expensive cars, exclusive restaurants. He watched with interest the derelicts, the homeless and the uncared-for populating doorways and lingering on street corners.

"Got any spare change mate?"

The dull voice instantly commanded his attention. From the pavement, frayed cuffs wrapped around grimy knees, a hopeful face looked up at him. His eyes are pleading but also aloof: he's probably asked that question a hundred times today, and his faith in human nature survived a bare week of the West End treatment.

The Photographer decides to become involved – up until this point he could have walked away, and risked nothing. But he feels a need for human contact, for games; for gambling. It has become too easy, too safe, the temptation to break some of the rules he has made for himself too strong. Or maybe it's just that he no longer needs them. He feels attuned to them all, the lost people that he saves, the heads he steals from corpses in the morgue, from the scenes of accidents when he can get away with it. There is a poetry to events that he thinks he has the measure of – the grand controller, the prestidigitator of reality, shaping lives like a clever illusion for motivations both obscure and subtle.

Rules are made to be broken.

"I'm sorry, I never carry change – but I'll buy you a coffee if you want – how about it?"

"Milky, three sugars please – nice one mate"

"Oh it's all right – come and drink it with me – there's a very good place just around the corner."

"I'd rather stay here if you don't mind... I... I'm waiting for a friend; he'll lose it if I'm not here when he gets back."

"How long is he likely to be? Surely you've time for a coffee? I'm a Photographer – I'm doing research for a book on street life. I'd like to talk with you."

"Where's your camera then?"

The Photographer reached into one of his pockets and pulled out a pen and a small notebook.

"Let's just say I'm taking verbal snapshots at the moment – now, how about that coffee?"

The young man is still suspicious, his manner aggressive. "Do you take pictures for magazines and stuff then? Any I might have heard of?"

Deciding at this point not to reveal that magazines in fact ran features on his work (anonymity being crucial to his plan), the Photographer just smiled, nodded, and replied,

"You might say that... I'm freelance – what's your name anyway?"

"Gerard"

"OK Gerard – so – are you going to help me out with my research? Talking to people, first hand, best material... only it's hard to write standing up in the street!"

Gerard considered this for a moment, whilst several things warred in his mind. Abandoning such a lucrative pitch was risky – but the guy might pay him; a hot coffee in a dry cafe was an enticing prospect... the guy was a bit creepy... could even be plainclothes, or on the cruise... Soho a natural stamping ground for nonces.... Still – couldn't do any harm if he kept his wits about him and his eye open for any possibilities.

"All right then." Gerard stood up, shook out his blanket and rolling it up, shoved it in his bag, pocketing the few coins that he kept there to give passers-by the right idea. He shrugged his shoulders, smoothed down his pants and said, "Where's this café then?"

"Oh, not very far." replied the Photographer "it's this way"

The Photographer led the way, walking rapidly and with purpose, his arms swinging, and his black coat billowing around him. Gerard shuffled his feet and followed him with a loose stride, shoulders slightly hunched and hands in pockets. The Photographer turned his head to ensure that Gerard was in fact following him and slowed down a little, continuing his questioning as they walked.

"Where are you from Gerard? You're not from London?"

"No – I'm from Bristol, originally. I've been down here a few months. My mate said he'd get me a sound engineer gig – I've had some training. You know, tape op and that. But he blew his contact with the studio. Some of the kit went missing

– so that's out. Still I thought I'd stick around. See what's happening."

"You don't like Bristol then?"

"No man, I've done that you know? There's too much hardcore drugs down there, too many angry people. Anyway – the West Country isn't going anywhere. There's opportunities down here for someone like me – someone with a bit of smarts, knows the score – mind?"

"But what about your family, your friends – you must miss them?"

Gerard pulled up and looked at him so sharply that for a moment the Photographer thought he had blown it – that Gerard had seen through his gently probing questions, designed to elicit the maximum amount of information whilst giving away nothing about himself. He felt his stomach churn and a tight feeling in his chest, where a fist seemed to clutch and roil. But, unwittingly, he had hit upon a nerve. The fact that Gerard had not even asked the Photographer's name suggested that he was too self-absorbed to notice the slightly clinical manner in which the Photographer was stripping him of information about his home, his background. That was fine with the Photographer. He wasn't intending on giving much away anyway.

"I don't have any family man. Me mam died when I were small – I grew up in a home. I never knew who me da was – not sure me mam did either. I got by. Are we nearly there yet? You said it wern far. I have to get back soon. I've got shit to sort out, mind."

Gerard's jerky voice gave away a tinge of nervousness, and suggested just the hint of a habit. Nothing too serious, but some dependency was conveyed by the way that he spoke.

"No – it isn't – in fact here we are. Don't worry – you'll be recompensed for your time." The Photographer kept his voice steady and smooth, giving no hint of the turbulent anticipation beneath. The important thing now was to gain the young man's trust.

They had arrived at a typical Soho café – the tables in the front facing the street for maximum posing value, those at the back tucked away, to allow intimate little téte a téte's, secretive assignations. The Photographer had been concerned that the staff might not allow Gerard – whose hands and face were grimy, whose shoes were crusted with dirt, and who smelled none too clean – inside, but either they didn't notice or didn't care. At any rate no one tried to stop them. The Photographer chose a table at the back that couldn't be seen from the street, and which was slightly cut off from the rest of the café. He seated himself with his back to the other customers, whilst Gerard took a seat against the wall, facing outwards. He told Gerard to order anything he liked. Maybe he was hungry?

Almost immediately an insouciant waiter came to take their order: an espresso for the Photographer; a hot chocolate, a large Coke, several sandwiches and a cake for Gerard, who was bent on taking full advantage of this free lunch ticket. As the waiter walked away with the order, Gerard asked sharply: "Got any fags?" The Photographer didn't smoke – had not anticipated this eventuality. Spotting a cigarette-vending machine at the far side of the café, he dug some pound coins out of his pocket and handed them to Gerard, telling him to buy himself some cigarettes. Gerard manoeuvred himself out from around the table – nearly colliding with the waiter who had returned with their order. As he fumbled the coins into the machine and squinted at the various brands on offer, the Photographer watched him and thought about the ritual to come – not a ritual in this case, but a departure – for Gerard was different from the others, more aware, sharper. A change from the drifting human wrecks for whom, the Photographer believed, death was a release, and the means to free the potential in their souls. Gerard had something in common with them – living as he did on the borders of society; and as such might not be missed for a while if he were to disappear, nor looked for too long. His youth made the Photographer a little uneasy, but he seemed to suspect nothing.

As Gerard came back to the table, the Photographer carefully rearranged his features so nothing of his thoughts would show. Gerard sat down and laid into his sandwiches with the gusto of someone who hasn't eaten properly for several weeks, washing it all down with huge slugs of Coke alternating with hot chocolate. The Photographer let him eat in peace for a few minutes and then carefully, casually asked him:

"Gerard, you've got good bones, you could be quite photogenic. I'd like to take some pictures of you, for the series that I mentioned, on street people. I'd like you to come over to my studio. Naturally I'll pay you for your time – what do you think?"

Gerard looked at him for a moment, considering, hand grasping the chocolate glass, his jaws still working on the sandwich. Their eyes met. The Photographer saw nothing but an interminable boredom there.

"Sure man, just say the word."

20. Watching the Photographer: 2

From across the street, Nina sees him stop and turn to look at a young homeless guy panhandling on the kerb. She can't hear what they're talking about, but after a couple of minutes the beggar gets up and follows the Photographer down Dean Street.

She's been following him for a couple of hours now. A morning's patient waiting outside his flat rewarded by his decision to use the bus to go up West; and now they're in Soho.

Nina is surprised to see them go into a café together; the Photographer seeming very tall and spare next to the young guy who she can see now is skinny, and slightly hunched. She follows them in and takes a table near the middle with her back to them. She can't see them, but can just hear some of what they are saying to each other.

She hears chair legs scrape, and then the homeless guy is walking past her to the cigarette machine. He passes so close she gets a noseful of the stink of him, fumbles money into the machine, and then heads back to the table. Meanwhile, a waiter comes up and takes Nina's order of a hot chocolate, Milan style. She bends over the book she has taken from her bag and strains to hear what is going on at their table.

She can't hear much except the clattering of cutlery and glasses; agony. She risks a quick glance. The still and upright back of the Photographer is as though graven in stone, and the homeless guy is tucking into sandwiches and an array of drinks. She looks down again, and then catches a few words from the Photographer. He is inviting the guy back to his apartment. She hunches down further over the book as they pass her table and leave the café. Nina knows where they are headed, and makes no move to follow now.

Since Nina had started following the Photographer outside the library her dress sense has changed. She still adopts a succession of disguises from her bottomless costume trunk, but she has toned down their flamboyancy; she doesn't want to be noticed. Her aim is to blend in; to become part of the surroundings.

A hat, of course, is required. Today: a cloche in a conservative colour; a long dark coat that conceals anything beneath; flat shoes to hide her height. Ah Nina, God love you. No one would look at you twice.

21. Bringing the Stranger Home

Taypi led his companions unerringly to the place where he had left the Stranger the day before, and when they were a few minutes away from where the Stranger had pitched his camp he motioned to them to stop and wait for him to scout the situation. Since his discovery of the Stranger, and his transition from adolescent to adult, Taypi had made a pact with himself that he would take responsibility for the man and the task of healing him from his illness. With infinite care and silence he threaded his way through the vines and trees and grasses that twined thickly together around the little clearing until he could see that the Stranger was lying in his hammock just as he had left him. Taypi did not think the Stranger would be in any state to attack him, but took great care to ensure that the crack of branches or the rustle of dead leaves underfoot would not give his approach away.

As it happened, there was little need for such caution. The stupor of the Stranger was so profound, so wrapped about with hallucinations, that even had one of the giant anacondas embraced him in its tightening coils, he would probably have been smothered unawares. Taypi called softly to the others to come near. The Speaker approached the hammock with the unconscious Stranger lying in it and took his first – long and measuring – look at this intruder.

The Explorer could not at this moment have looked more different to his former self – his once strong frame rendered fragile by age and under-nourishment, his skin yellowed and translucent from the fever that was consuming him. His clothes, from his weeks in the jungle, were tattered and filthy, and hung on his diminished frame in rags. He smelt strongly of himself and damp, and open sores covered the parts of his flesh that were visible.

Every so often he would stir and mutter – his eyes twitching behind his closed lids or opening for a short time to stare sightlessly before him. The Speaker did not at this moment doubt that he was flesh and blood like the Tribe – and that he did not have long to live. It was not just the glimpse he had had of his mind during the spirit journey: the man's physical condition particularly convinced him, for spirits were not prey to the fevers and illnesses that killed mortals, and would not be so covered with sores and bites.

Of course, they were very cunning. A spirit could have disguised itself in this way, and let itself be carried unresisting and seemingly unaware into the heart of their land, where it could cause all kinds of mischief. However the Speaker had confidence in his ability to banish such evil spirits and strip them of their earthly manifestations or pseudo-bodies – and did not think such a creature would put itself at such risk, however cunning it might be.

No, this was definitely a man, like themselves but completely foreign to their experience. A quick glance was enough to show him that fact, taking in the strange coverings, the height and shape of him, the bags and bundles that he had strung from the trees around, that no doubt contained more strange and inexplicable objects. This man obviously came from a place entirely foreign to their experience and comprehension, yet populated by people like himself. It would be important for them to learn as much about him and about his people as possible, in case more followed this lone traveller.

Concluding his observation of the Explorer, the Speaker drew back and spoke to the others quietly.

"Taypi you were right: this before us is definitely a man, and no spirit. We have no time to waste if we are to save his life."

Taypi and Aymara had already come to the same conclusion. Aymara handed the Speaker a gourd containing black water, which she had brought especially as the Tribe believed that black water could cure fever, and a soft piece of leather, which he dipped in the water. He dribbled some of it onto the Explorer's lips and rinsed his face, before laying the cool leather on his forehead. The Explorer stirred a bit and mumbled, but did not wake. The Speaker continued this treatment patiently – in between settling back on his heels and looking at the man speculatively. He could not tell yet whether he would live or die. But the fact that he had survived this long told of an indomitable spirit. Time would tell, and the jungle is a great teacher in the art of waiting.

22. Bringing Gerard Home

Gerard and the Photographer took a black cab to the Photographer's apartment. In the cab the Photographer noticed how Gerard's cheap sweatshirt clung to his back, outlining thin shoulder blades; the skinny hips encased in grimy low-slung jeans, with a strip of greyish skin showing. He felt a great wave of disgust wash over him, for this man who seemed to care nothing for his life, living on London like a parasite clinging to the back of an elephant. He was bright-eyed and cocky, and talked continually, apparently blissfully unconcerned whether the Photographer was listening or not. After a while the Photographer tuned out both his words and the heavy sweetish odour, which made him suspect that he had not bathed in some time. He wondered if the cab driver had noticed the mismatched nature of his passengers – but then reflected that London cabbies are trained to ignore pretty much everything, and anyway he'd his hands full trying to negotiate the heavy traffic around Westminster and Parliament Square.

Gerard was quite aware that the Photographer's guard was down. And also sure, by this point, that the man had asked him back for sex. It did not for one moment occur to him that he actually wanted to photograph him, but he was happy to go along with his fictions. They dovetailed rather nicely with some plans of his own. Whoever the guy was, he didn't seem strapped for cash. Who knew what equipment he might have stashed away in his house? Gerard knew that if he could get a few quid together, he could vanish beyond this man's ability – or that of the police – to track him down. All of this, however, rested on his act now. He strove to appear innocent and stupid, and tugged the Photographer's sleeve

"I love that wheel man, it's poetry"

Gerard's touch broke into the Photographer's reverie, and instinctively he flinched. Masking his irritation with difficulty, he looked across at Gerard, then followed his pointing finger with his eyes

"What's that?"

"The wheel – you know, the London Eye, whatever it's called. It's fucking class: you been on it?"

"No, I'm afraid I haven't had the pleasure."

"Me neither. Bet it's fucking cool though. I mean, you're up there for forty-five minutes, hundreds of feet above London – suspended like a fucking fly in a web. I bet it's amazing. I bet the views are fucking awesome. When it's not raining, of course. Fat chance of that in London, though. Call this a fucking summer?"

"Hmm?" The Photographer, not really listening, let Gerard rattle on. He didn't think that too many people would miss this one. His kind dropped out of the scene all the time, sucked in by the spider's web of London, a quick trip they never returned from. So much potential wasted by the cruel city, a grinding wheel that never stopped turning. The Photographer saw symbolism in this, as with the other elements of the day, and the meeting, and the journey back to the flat; they would all be recorded and correlated against the picture he was beginning to build up of Gerard, and his place in the collection.

"I mean – you can fit twenty into one of those cars. Twenty people flying around up there. You could have a party, or a wedding for fuck's sake – you could have a murder up there.

I bet it's pretty cool at night. You could write a book about that: Murder on the London Eye. Doesn't it make you want to take pictures of it?"

Gerard was spaced, talking fast and frenetic, eyes fixed on the wheel as they crossed the bridge and headed for Waterloo. The Photographer felt a familiar twinge of relief as they left north London behind, and remembered that he was supposed to be putting Gerard at his ease.

"No. I don't do much of that kind of work any more. I've been working on a number of... portraits. Why I want to use you. People's heads tell you a lot about them, if you know how to read the lines. The whole of human existence, encoded there – just waiting for someone with the right eye to bring it out."

"You got one of those china heads with all the markings on, like they have down in Camden market? What's that they call them?"

"Phrenology models – developed by Franz Joseph Galle, end of the eighteenth century – but that's a much abused approach – crude science at best. I don't believe that you can tell people's personality as easily as that – although it's been convenient for some to lend it credence."

Gerard shrugged at the Photographer's use of the word 'credence' – it meant little to him.

" So how come you know about that shit man – you been reading up on it?"

"Phrenology interested me... for a while. You might say it had a bearing on my work. Systems, numbers. It survives even now. Did you ever assume that someone was weak-willed because they had a small chin, or intelligent because they had a high forehead? And how often were you right?"

"Yeah – I get what you're saying. Still sounds pretty dodgy to me though – like all that stuff and that they're doing at the moment; cloning sheep and that? I saw something about that on the telly a while back – people will be able to design their children, like kitchens. It seems like everyone will be the same – I mean you're hardly going to have a kid that you know will end up being a murderer or a moron are you? So what you're saying is you think you can work out everything about someone, just from looking at their head?"

"You'd be surprised, Gerard. You'd be very surprised."

The two of them sat silently in the back of the cab. Gerard felt canny to the Photographer – a harmless eccentric, easy touch. He was pretty sure he could handle him. The Photographer ignored him for the moment, mulling over the next stage of the plan. He had managed to persuade Gerard to come back to his apartment for a shoot, and to continue their interview there. That he had achieved this astonished the Photographer – but Gerard's initial suspicion had transformed into an ingratiating friendliness, a rather pathetic eagerness to please, after the sandwiches and coffees, and a few carefully phrased sympathetic questions.

How strange – to be that naïve? Or trusting? Or was it a simple arrogance that nothing could happen to him? Of course, he could be planning to rob him once they got home – attack him in his own apartment, and then nick any money or valuables that he could lay his hands on. As if reading his thoughts, Gerard piped up again.

"So, what's your gaff like then?"

"We'll be there in a few moments."

"Bet you've got loads of stuff in there. Loads of cameras and lots of your pictures like? Bet you take pictures there all the time. Do you have one of those rooms, all lit up red with the photos hanging off washing lines?"

"You mean a darkroom?"

"Yeah. Man, I reckon that's half of it. I mean anyone can take a photo – but the skill's in the developing, all the chemicals and that."

"There's an element of the chemist in what I do. You have to get the balance just right, or you'll ruin the picture. So long as you stick to the formula, you're pretty much guaranteed the right results though."

"Scuse me gov'nor – what end of the street did you want?" The cabbie pulled back the window and slowed the cab at the end of the Photographer's road.

"Here's just fine, thanks"

The Photographer gave the cabbie a note and jumped out of the cab. Gerard got out too, and stood looking expectantly at the Photographer from the kerb. Without comment, the Photographer strode off down and across the street, stopping, and turning into a mansion block half-way down. Gerard hurried after him, and reached the entrance just after the tall spare man stepped inside, door swinging in his wake. Gerard caught the handle and went in after the Photographer.

Inside, a dingy hall greeted them – an old-fashioned wrought-iron lift making the dark space seem cramped. The Photographer ignored the lift and inserted a key into the lock of one of the ground floor apartments. Opening the door he stood aside and motioned Gerard inside.

Gerard stepped through the door into a small hall space

dominated by a huge rubber plant, lit only by a heavily shaded bulb. The Photographer reached behind him to pull across a heavy velvet curtain that completely concealed the door, and motioned Gerard through to the rest of the flat, following him inside.

"My study's just here." He opened one of the dark-stained doors that lined the hall. "I'll be through in a minute, Gerard, make yourself comfortable."

"Sure man," Gerard replied, and went through.

The Photographer's study was quite large with long windows from floor to ceiling, set at regular intervals in the thick walls. It would have been bright and airy, but heavy curtains cut off outside light. The only light in the room was artificial – deep shadows cast by Anglepoise lights, walls covered with bookshelves, framed and unframed photographs and old lithographs hanging in the spaces between them.

Only a few pieces of furniture relieved the severity. The straight-backed black mahogany chairs, an ebony table and a spare, unornamented desk gave the room an ascetic feel, heightened by a floor of highly polished inky boards with no rugs to relieve its starkness. The general effect would have been pure monochrome if it weren't for the dusty houseplants that grew everywhere, cramped and twisted even with the relatively high ceiling – their huge leaves casting strange shadows on the walls. The lack of a central light and the use of many small sources of illumination gave everything in the room multiple shadows, frozen fingers clawing the corners.

Gerard settled on the edge of a chair, and scanned the objects and furniture around him. The unfamiliar environment made him feel flat, distinctly apprehensive; his plans in the car unrealistic and absurd. The flat was completely silent, and he wondered what had become of the Photographer, and whether there was anything worth nicking in the room. He couldn't see anything particularly valuable and portable from where he was sitting – he'd probably need to turn the place over to find anything worthwhile.

"Coffee, Gerard? Two sugars is it?"

The Photographer's voice made Gerard jump guiltily – it sounded as though he was right behind him. He decided to sit tight for the moment and see how the situation panned out. "Yeah man, churze."

In the kitchen the Photographer worked with deft and practised skill. He had already reckoned Gerard for about ten stones, and prepared a dose that should lay him out for a good few hours – far longer than he needed, but always better to be on the safe side. In the meantime he would allay Gerard's suspicions by setting up the interview, the shoot – pandering to his vanity. It always amazed the Photographer what power the camera gave him; they would do anything, subject themselves to any indignity, he sometimes thought, for the sake of the picture, the shot.

Subtly the Photographer assumed another of his many personas, the trick hypnotist, his power total as his victims willingly give up responsibility and control to him. In this frame of mind he strode back into the study and handed Gerard his coffee with a flourish, then laying a blank notebook and a pen on the table as if in readiness for an interview.

"Sit there for a minute, Gerard, while I'm setting up the equipment. You'll probably want to move then so that I can shoot you."

"Ha ha – that's funny – it's a whole different language this photography lark, isn't it? So how long you been doing that then? What's that you're setting up now?"

The Photographer didn't reply immediately, and Gerard watched as he set up tripod and camera, fiddled with a light, positioned a chair just so. In the back of his mind was the thought that now was the time, now was his chance to clock the guy and clear out of here with his stuff. But his curiosity was stronger: he wanted to see how the kit worked first. Then he could take that too, and fence it a little more knowledgeably. He had this situation. He was master of it. Certainly he could afford to wait a little?

The Photographer appeared to have finished setting up the equipment. He made a final adjustment, straightened up and looked towards Gerard.

"All ready now. If you'd like to come over and sit in this chair, we can begin. I'll probably be moving around, taking shots and making notes – just talk to the air in front of you, that should do."

Gerard got up to move to the chair he had indicated. He noticed, as he stood, that he felt a little dizzy. Probably just the after-effects of the drugs he'd taken the night before. He threw his shoulders back and walked across the room. A screen had been placed behind the chair that he was to occupy. No details to identify the room the pictures had been taken in. Gerard was suddenly reminded of having his picture taken for the identity parade.

"Going to give me a number to hold then too are you?" He motioned to the screen with a grin to indicate that he was joking. The Photographer looked puzzled for a minute, and then replied slightly more sharply than intended.

"Don't be foolish – the screen's to cut down the glare from

the lights, so I can get good clean pictures of you. Just relax – I'm a professional, remember."

This last an attempt at humour – he'd had a shock there, the reference to the number as if the boy knew that he'd be part of a sequence. But of course he was just referring to a police station. Who knew how many times he'd been in one? Not too much longer now – distract him so he doesn't feel the effects too soon.

"Right, we're ready to begin. I'll just take a few preliminary shots, to get the range. Just relax, look normal. That's it. OK, now turn your head a little to the side. Tell me Gerard, what are your ambitions? You're obviously not going to be on the streets all your life, clever chap like you?"

"I don't know. I used to think I wanted to be a pilot – before I found out about the navy, basic training, all that. I couldn't take it – bastards shouting at you all day long. So I quit"

Gerard shook his head as if trying to clear it

"I quit, and you pretty much" he was tailing off, fading visibly now, lids dropping with the effort of keeping his eyes open "know," he lost the battle, "the rest." His head dropped to his chest, and he slumped a little to the side.

The Photographer emerged from behind his camera and stood looking at the young man, head cocked a little to the side. When he showed no more signs of movement the Photographer walked up to his chair and laid his hand on his loosely clasped fingers. There was no reaction. He lifted one of Gerard's eyelids, checked out the slack iris. There was no doubt about it. He was out cold.

23. Fever

The Stranger sweated out his fever under the care of the Speaker, Taypi and his mother, Aymara. All three were protected to the best of the Speaker's ability by the designs that he had pricked out on their skins using a large thorn, and by special charms that he had made using the teeth and claws of caiman guardians of the spirit. It wasn't much, but it was the best that the Speaker could do against the danger he felt but could not name.

On the third day the fever broke. Aymara observed that the Stranger's sweat ran freely, and that his skin cooled to the touch. His brow was merely warm and somewhat damp, rather than as hot as a stone that had been left in the fire. She began to hum a song of thanks to the spirits of water and air, for healing the man whom they had all thought would soon die. The stranger would be weak for many days after the fever had abated, and it was possible that his spirit had been so drained by the fever that he would never regain his full strength; but it now appeared that he might live.

She herself felt as weak as he looked. The last couple of days had been exhausting. Someone had had to stay awake to ensure that the Stranger did not become dehydrated, and to be ready in case he died. What sleep she had had was snatched and interrupted by his shouts and ravings; the fever made him call out and talk to people that they could not see, in his strange guttural language. At other times he thrashed loudly and had to be held down, a stick between his jaws to stop him biting off his own tongue. The Speaker said that he was arguing with the spirits who had taken his body whilst his soul was out wandering, and who now refused to relinquish it.

One sound in particular recurred with some frequency. They took this to be the name of the spirit that was invading the man's body, and the Speaker said that this meant that he would be likely to recover. Since he knew the name of his tormentor he had at least some power over it, and would be more likely to drive it out of his body. She saw now that the Speaker had been right, for the man lay in a deep and natural sleep, and she could afford to leave him for a little while.

With Taypi's help she had stripped him naked, so that she could apply cotton soaked in cool water from the river to his hot flesh, and treat the ulcers and bites that festered on his torso and limbs. The clothes that they removed had astonished them – they had never seen metal or such finely woven cloth. Since they did not want to cut through the clothes, they patiently worked at the fastenings, marvelling at the workmanship of his belt buckle. Although it was basic and un-ornamented, it was nevertheless a source of wonder to a people who made any tools that they needed with palm bark, leaves, bamboo, wood and stone.

He had covered his body with many layers – beneath leg coverings they found an inner layer of soft, yellowed material, tightly encasing his calves and thighs. They wrinkled their noses at his smell; it seemed as though he had been wearing the same coverings for many weeks. His top half was wrapped in more layers – a continuation of the inner leg coverings covered his skin up to the neck and continued on his arms almost to the elbow. Above this he wore another, looser covering of lighter material and above that a heavier covering with many pouches, most of which were fastened. Although his face was nearly as dark as theirs, when they had removed all of his coverings they discovered the rest of his body to be of a dirty whiteness, blotched and discoloured with sores and with the marks of old scars. They were astonished to see that he grew hair on his body – his legs and arms were covered with long wiry hairs, and on his chest formed a thick curling mass over the breastbone, which was greying like the hair on his head. They guessed that he had not eaten properly for many weeks, for his body was emaciated and his ribs prominent.

The Speaker guessed a number of things about his culture that were to surprise the Explorer in the coming weeks. From the number and complexity of his coverings, the protective leather which covered his feet, the material in which he concealed his whole body, he conjectured that the stranger had a terror of coming into contact with the natural world, and that his skin must be very delicate. For this reason they had laid him in a bed of extremely soft fibre, which they had removed from the inner bark of trees and shredded so that it was as fine as raw silk. They surrounded his bed with smoking hornets nests – to drive away flies and other pests and slathered a paste made from lemongrass and termites on his skin to repel mosquitoes and sand flies. These were the same measures that they took to protect the skin of new-borns and very young children, whose tender skins and fresh blood were more susceptible and attractive to parasites.

Once the Speaker discovered the Explorer's books, he sat and stared for many hours at the markings and small sketches that the Explorer had made. The Stranger was a fair draughtsman, and the Speaker marvelled at the washed-ink drawings that seemed to capture the very essence of birds and plants that he himself was familiar with. The tattoos of the Tribe were in some senses representative of the world around them – but in a far more ritualised and formal way. Each symbol corresponded to a system of classification of the multiple species with which they shared their land, and by which they identified themselves from birth to death. Since their concept of time was synchronous, a person might have many different names throughout their life, to describe life stages. However, these life stages were united by the self of the individual, which was continuous.

In one of the pages of the small books the Explorer had represented 'bird' – but for the Speaker even his faithful renderings of the plumage of one of the innumerable species of parrot provided only the barest hint as to which he was referring to. Their own tattoos would have included the cries of the bird, the time of day or season at which it was observed and, if it was heard to utter any human tongue, of what it spoke. It seemed to the Speaker that the Stranger must have a very limited awareness of the jungle – which confirmed Taypi's description of what he had observed in the days before the Stranger's collapse.

The Speaker thought hard about all of these things, and spoke at length with Taypi and his mother – mulling over the old stories and essaying trances to find out what the Stranger's arrival meant. At length he came to the conclusion that since he was far from his people, and travelling with very few possessions, the books must contain (like their preserved heads) a copy of the experiences of his ancestors. Maybe he was writing down both what he remembered as he walked, and what he observed of this new country for his descendants – both on his own skin, and on the bundled skins he carried with him. This much they could discern from memory and talk around the unconscious figure of the Stranger – but had no way of confirming the truth of their suppositions. They began to wait with increasing impatience for him to wake from his stupor, and to discuss whether they should use a stimulant to rouse him if he didn't come to on his own. In the end they decided to be patient – even their weakest stimulants might be dangerous in his feeble state.

The Speaker felt the moment that the Explorer decided to come back into the world. His intuition was soon confirmed by a change in the man's breathing, and the gentle fluttering of his eyelids. The connection was still tenuous, and the Speaker knew that he was returning from far away. He could feel the effort of will the Stranger was making to open his eyes, and saw the tips of his fingers and his toes twitch, as if he were relearning the limits of his body. A tiny vein in his temple throbbed.

The Speaker sat patiently, watching the signs of returning consciousness, and was rewarded some time later when a crack appeared in his eyelids; the eyes that were revealed, for a brief moment, were as blue as the sky. They opened again, and the Stranger winced as he strained to focus in the diffuse sunlight; again they closed, and his nostrils flared, as thought the visual stimulation had proved too much and he had decided to concentrate for the moment on sound alone.

Just then Aymara returned. The Speaker turned to her and spoke quietly.

"His spirit has returned; he is back in his body. He is even now listening to the sounds of the jungle, and I sense his mind is awake."

Aymara smiled, and they both turned back to the stranger. His blue eyes were open again, and staring fixedly at them, alight with a strange fire. The Speaker caught and held his eyes, and tried to penetrate to the man behind the gaze. He felt the Stranger trying to do the same. At length he sensed the the man becoming uncomfortable with the intensity of his gaze, and dropped his eyes. When he looked again the Stranger's eyes were shut; his slack features told the Speaker he had lost consciousness again.

"Water, please."

Aymara heard the stranger rasp out these words, and although she didn't recognise the sounds, the stranger's cracked lips, the way that he ran his swollen tongue around them, told her that he was thirsty.

She gently poured a little water into the man's mouth, and saw in his eyes a look of trust and quiet joy. Whatever the others of the tribe might say when they took him to the gathering, Aymara felt in her heart that the Stranger posed no threat.

24. Recuperation

May?

Could it be that I have found them? Oh sublime discovery! Strength fails now; will write more as I am able.

May 10th

I feel a little stronger. Much to record! My hand still shakes & I am too weak to walk, but at least I can grip this pen & commit my recent experience to paper.

I do not know the date, but certainly many days have fled since these people rescued me. I think that it is already May, so the 10th will do for a guess. I woke some days ago, feeling as though I had returned from the very borders of the Styx, only to find myself face to face with a native of a type never before recorded. Yet I guessed he was a Chaman, for I sensed he had great knowledge.

He was completely bald, and his scalp and face were covered in tattoos. His frame was small and wiry, with a huge round belly that jutted proudly over the brief piece of woven fibre that was wrapped around his hips, and tied around with bark. His feet were splayed, short and wide with spatulate toes that spoke of a lifetime of climbing and walking in the jungle. His skin was coppery, where it was not covered with tattoos, and his eyes, set in deep folds of skin, were the eyes of a jaguar, tawny and piercing.

We stared at each other across a gulf – each full of questions, yet with no common ground between us. I had the impression that he could see facets of my mind, my thoughts reflected back through the deep pools of his eyes. I could read but little from his expression, save a curiosity as strong as my own, but for my part I was suffused with a sensibility of relief & trust.

With the Chaman are two others: a young boy & an older female who I took to be the the boy's mother. I can see no signs of habitation, except for the obviously temporary low lean-to wherein I find myself. Who are these three? Can they be all that remain of their Tribe, or perhaps they are living apart from the rest?

I have more questions than answers & the interminable motion of my thoughts exhaust me. I must sleep now.

May 15th

My pen wanders on the page & my writing is barely legible; slow & enfeebled. So much time lost & who knows how much remaining? Thank God they were kind enough to rescue my belongings. No babe was ever as happy to see his mother's breast as I was to be reunited with my books.

I am full of a thousand impressions of these people, half-gleaned from some kind of strange insight or mental link that I share with the Chaman. I cannot conceive it in our terms, but maybe the theories of Mesmer hint towards his powers & provide the closest lexis in our terms to describe them.

Their language is fascinating, though as yet unintelligible to me. It seems to consist of sound and gesture. Its nuances are rich & the people so expressive that I find I can almost understand them – but that understanding is elusive & fleeting.

They are a small people, but very strong & wonderfully agile, though all less than four feet in height. Their costumes are simple & utilitarian & cover only their groin area, though they seem clothed head to foot by the intricate tattoos that are most elaborate on their heads. Of their philosophy I have learnt even less than their language, but they seem a gentle people & have certainly shewn me nothing but kindness & the most civilized welcome.

For my part too I have tried to share some small benefits of my limited kit with them. Observing Taypi making fire by a most laborious method, I showed him how to use my tinderbox. The sulphur matches, flint & tinder most astonished him & also the Chaman, who examined them very intently, before handing them back almost reluctantly. His delight knew no bounds when I made him a present of a spare that I carried in my pack. He gave me a long look indeed before tucking them very carefully amidst his many pouches – as if to ask what motive I had in making him such a gift. I gave back as level a look as I was able, for I had not the words to say that the tinderbox was a small enough exhange for the life they have most certainly saved.

I cannot doubt the Chaman is very knowledgeable about medicine, for he has pulled me back from the very brink of death, but I think even his powers are limited in the face of my malady. I have had fevers before & survived many & all. But now I sense that central organ without which no body can persist is diseased & will fail before long. I have chest pains & struggle to draw breath. Even now the iron bands constrict my breast. I had not thought my doughty heart would betray me so.

This journal is almost certainly now written for Posterity. I shall not survive it. I do not have much time & feel a terrifying urgency to capture what I can of these unique people. (Possible name...Capo: head, Scripti: writers? Can such bastard Latin be forgiven?)

May 17th

I awoke this morning with the agreeable sensation of one who has found his journey's end. Of the boy & the woman there was no sign. I surmised that my kind hosts were busying themselves in collecting provisions from the Jungle & had left me to sleep until my natural inclination woke me. Of the Chaman likewise I could discern no trace.

Left thus to my own devices, for the first time since my fortunate rescue by the persons above mentioned, I performed a brief toilet & now apply myself to this pleasant task – namely committing to my journal the incredible experiences of the last few days.

Who can describe the feelings that fill one's breast when at last perceiving, after the many hardships & trials described in this account, the object of a journey so arduous as to all but result in the author's death? To find, when almost all hope has been lost, that one was justified in one's belief in the existence of such an enlightened & magical people, despite the incredulity of all one's peers? That they not only exist, but seem to possess powers of communication undreamed of even in our so-called enlightened age? Imagine!

But I am getting ahead of myself. I can only blame the wonder & confusion of the past few days on this outpouring of words. Permit me but a moment & I will compose myself, as befits the chronicler & attempt to convey in detail the essential points of the people amongst whom I now find myself.

I am not unusually educated for a man of my age & station. A gentleman of leisure may be an anthropologist, ornithologist, palaeontologist & lepidopterist at the same time. Some months ago I read Mr Darwin's account of his voyage on the Beagle, being an account of the lands he travelled through & the people he met. But Darwin's interest is all for the flora, fauna, geology & he is blind to the depths of the native peoples. He finds them disappointingly primitive, describing them as almost bestial. I take a completely different view – to me it seems as though these people are angelic, *uncorrupted by the worship of science & the pursuit of material things. Even the scant few days I have already spent in the company of the Chaman, the boy Taypi & the woman Aymara have shown me a people who conduct all their relationships in an enlightened & humane manner. I suspect that their knowledge of the properties of the plants & other substances in the Jungle dwarf the clinical knowledge of most doctors I had been acquainted with in what is rapidly beginning to feel like my former life & hint at a similar level of development in other areas. In short I feel that I have stumbled across Eden. My reader might dismiss these impressions as the products of a disordered mind, but I am confident that they will be borne out as I grow to know the Caposcripti better.*

25. Shibboleth, Language; the Secret Room

The relationship began again as unfinished words;
rough shibbolim passed between the sterile medium of
the microphone, trapped behind the padded walls, the
soundproofed door. Between them they explored new
languages – the vocabulary of sustenance, of abstinence, of
delirium. The Photographer never counted the conversations
he had with his subjects before they enter the room: those
were merely the words of one of his personas, assumed for
the sole purpose of seducing the subject, of gaining their
trust for the few short hours it took to make them his forever.

He has amassed a considerable knowledge, by now, of the
drugs that are still used in certain areas of the Amazon basin.
Through patient sifting through the descriptions of certain
substances used by the Caposcripti and related in the old
man's notebooks and through questioning a network of
Colombians and Peruvians, with whom he has cultivated a
relationship, he has obtained the necessary substances and
learnt how to prepare them. In London you can find anything
if you look long enough.

By far the most interesting of these drugs, for him, was
Ayahuaska. The term 'Aya' in Quechua means 'Spirit' or
'Dead' and 'Huasca' means liana, vine or rope. Literally
translated 'the vine of death', its stem grows back on itself
to create a braided rope that stretches high into the forest
canopy, where it blooms invitingly with white, pink or
lilac flowers. This root is mixed with other substances –
for example *chacruna* – by shamans in the Amazon region
to reach visionary states. He was sure that this was the

substance, by a different name, that the Caposcripti had used to escape the lie of this reality and discover the true language, the actual names of things and of themselves. He had had to travel to Brighton to find a shaman who would perform the Ayahuaska ceremony for him, but it had opened the door to a world he had not known existed. Once, his eyes had seen only the surfaces, forever frozen images and moments, juxtapositions and visual statements in the lens of his camera, on glossy, on matt, on silvered paper; on the reels and reels of celluloid that still didn't tell the full story.

And then he had had that strange journey, a journey into himself where he left his body and opened his mind to terrifying visions of a place he thought he would not return from. Perhaps sensing the canker in his soul the Shaman had sung him a dark song, tantalising glints of some strange language, a music that resonated but whose pattern and meaning he could not quite grasp. The shaman had purged him of everything that was in him, the drug causing the Photographer to retch and gasp and vomit until it seemed that his very stomach would be expelled through his unwilling oesophagus. He felt emptied, hollowed, and gradually he didn't feel anything at all beyond the thoughts that seemed to follow each other beyond his control, logical and inevitable as a string of pearls, through the voided chambers of his mind. And as each memory, each realisation clinked into place in the magic lantern of his awareness, he felt a click of resolution, and they disappeared, as if the events and things that they described had been once again unmade.

He was afraid to go back down that route again – accepting that maybe in the end the sacrifice of himself might be required to learn the original language: but not yet ready to give up ego. But others could also discover the glimpse that he had been given of the sacred language. He took them so much farther than he dared go himself, and at the last stole from them what they had found in that other world.

He thought of these people more as avatars than victims – finding the secrets for him, lending their voices to the babble that he would then decode and absorb through the ceremony of shrinking their heads. Metempsychosis. All that they were would become part of him; a faceless Jesus surrounded by light.

The Photographer couldn't describe the way in which he thought at these times: it was as if he had discovered a different mode of expression – a language that manifested meaning, somehow revealing the history of everything – encoded at the moment through multiple mediums. He hungered for the language that created merely through description. Writing, photography, sound recording: at the end of the day they were all just different mediums for information, which can exist in any form. The message was there somewhere, a signal fragmented through the noise of many media. This is what they had all been looking for, the alchemists, the Templars, whether searching for the grail or the philosopher's stone. But they had all been wrong. It was not a thing, nothing concrete. The thing that gave power was language, was an idea. And it would be his.

26. Ayahuaska

May 20th

For the first I will permit myself the singular, but, I think, deserved, honour of giving to these people a name – for they are so isolated in their Jungle home that they have never before encountered any but the neighbouring savages. These neighbours they rightly avoid, for the habits & customs too horrible to describe which they daily practice – the least of which is cannibalism. These people whom I have the honour to have encountered first amongst my race, I will henceforth refer to as the Caposcripti, or 'head writers' – for the ingenious tattoos with which their faces & sometimes their entire heads are covered. The designs are so intricate, each one so unique, that I cannot help thinking that they represent a kind of language & that the tattoos themselves are stories.

Having dispensed with the first prerogative of the explorer, that of naming & classifying what he discovers, I will attempt a methodical description of all the aspects of these people's lives that I have so far been able to discover – although I do not doubt that there remain still a multitude of their wonders for me to discover in the course of my stay with them. The first of these is, naturally, the ceremony involving Ayahuaska, which the Chaman took it upon himself to perform for my benefit. I do not think it has been the privilege of any stranger before myself to observe the preparation of this substance & even less to participate in this type of ceremony. Mr Darwin speaks of the Fuegians that he discovered off the Coast of the Americas, but had he been so fortunate as to acquaint himself with the Caposcripti, he would not suppose that all of the native peoples of this continent were nothing but savages; Indeed I have experienced the greatest courtesy from my hosts that one would suppose is possible outside of a London drawing room – far greater than some of the drawing rooms it has been my misfortune to enter. But enough of this – it is not of London, of back-stabbing & false courtesy that I wish to speak to you now, but of the ceremony which took me to the mouth of the black river & of the language that I found there.

This morning I was shaken awake some time before dawn. In the gloom I could just make out the shape of the Chaman, outlined against the fading stars. I shook off the sleep & the remnants of a confusing dream of home & pulled myself painfully to my feet.

The Chaman waited somewhat impatiently for me to put on my boots & hat & then motioned for me to follow him, moving silently & gracefully on bare feet down one of the more heavily used paths that led to a plantation of manioc. Despite the tight band of pain that constricted my chest, I stumbled after, tripping over roots & wondering what the purpose of the journey could be.

We reached the field of manioc in a few minutes & the path ended in a confusing network of runs through the plants. The Chaman cut straight through, whilst I followed as close behind as I could manage in the near dark, cutting past the bole of a huge tree, climbing over its massive draping roots & heading up a steep muddy slope onto higher ground. The Chaman seemed to glide over all these different surfaces, whilst I struggled behind, beating plants out of my way & grasping the long vines that hung everywhere for balance. It was getting light very quickly now, in the way that it has here & the Chaman gradually increased his pace. I battled my pain & weakness & followed as best I could, for I didn't dare lose sight of him, lest I might become lost.

Suddenly the Chaman darted off the path that we had been

following & when I caught him up, I saw that he was pointing at a giant woody liana vine with shiny, dark green leaves; long smooth ovals with pointed ends. He ripped off part of one of the leaves, crumpled it in his hand & thrust it under my nose. The leaf smelled strongly herbal. It was slightly reminiscent of bayleaf, but with something darker & more bitter underlying it.

The Chaman crouched down on his haunches & began to dig at the ground beneath it with a sharply pointed stick he had stuck through his waistband. Once he'd uncovered the roots he sawed some off with a large catfish spine & slipped them into his bag, carefully wiping off the dirt that clung to them. Straightening up again, he looked at the light coming through the trees & continued back along the direction we had been following with great rapidity. It was only by sticking close to the Chaman's heels & placing my feet exactly in his prints, that I was able to discern a path at all. I certainly would not have sworn after we had been walking for half an hour or so that I could have found my way back to the camp very easily on my own. As always I had my instruments on me, but they are of little use when paths are rarely straight & direction changes all the time. The Jungle is so dense that you could pass within ten feet of a pueblo & not even know it was there, unless the sky was clear enough to see thin lines of smoke from their fires – if you were fortunate enough to find a rare break in the canopy.

In fact it is a miracle that I found the Caposcripti at all. Of course in the end it was they that found me.

The Chaman continued gathering various leaves, roots & seeds from the plants, picking up banana leaves & balsa wood bark as he went & making neat parcels of them which he tied to his waistband or slipped into his bag. Some he handed to me to smell or taste, indicating by gestures & words what they were used for. I began to get a hint of the meaning of some of the explanations, but others mystified me completely. One plant with lethal-looking red & black berries went into the same pouch as the liana roots that the Speaker had found earlier, but I couldn't make a connection between them. I realized that the Chaman was trying to teach me something important & felt a great frustration at my inability to grasp their language.

One word the Chaman kept repeating was 'so'-om-wa-wai-yajé' – have decided to assume for the time being this means 'medicine'.

Eventually I realized that we were nearly back at the camp, as the route we were following became more recognizably a path, with logs laid over streams & muddy patches of land & a well-used appearance. I judged it to be about mid morning, from the heat & the sun, which although lighting the Jungle in patches, was not yet directly overhead. The Chaman continued, his pace unvarying, until we reached the campsite.

Once there I sank gratefully onto a log that served as a chair. I was still weak from my illness & the gruelling walk had left me drained & sweating. That new sensation afflicted me again; my chest felt as though bands were being drawn ever tighter around it. It seems my fears are true & my heart is at long last starting to give out.

The Chaman did not appear to be much affected by his exertions & whistled Taypi, giving him quick instructions. In the meantime he began to build up the fire & to grind & shred the leaves & seeds & other ingredients he had gathered in the Jungle, muttering in a low, almost singing tone. He mixed some of these with a dried & twisted root that he had ground to a fine powder in a coconut shell, using a stick with a rounded bole at the end as a mortar.

By this time Taypi had returned with vessels containing water from the river. The Chaman took one of these & poured a few drops into the coconut shell, singing a wordless song as he did so, until he had reduced the mixture into a thick dark red paste, with an acrid, leafy, earthy smell.

He scraped the lot into a pot he had hung over the fire & poured the rest of the water over it, stirring until it had dissolved completely in the water. Once he was satisfied he began to shake a bunch of leaves tied together (which I had assumed to be one of the ingredients) so that they rustled like rain & to whistle & sing gently over the pot. He remained like this, stirring & adding water for the rest of the day. The mixture was reduced, diluted, reduced & diluted until I estimated that the Chaman had evaporated several pints of water from it & it was viscous & dark.

When the Chaman finally lifted the pot off the fire & set it aside to cool the brew was smooth & thick & the dark red of arterial blood, with the consistency of cream. I was very hungry by this point, as I had eaten nothing since the previous day, but the Chaman had not broken his own fast & only offered me a little water to drink. When I got up to leave, he motioned that I should stay where I was & pointed towards the pot cooling beside the now banked fire. He sat silently & meditatively, banking his jaguar eyes beneath heavy lids, knees & feet forming a triangle, on the upturned side of which his folded arms rested. He seemed a figure carved in amber, tattoos etching complicated figures which made the features upon which they were carved appear as immobile as stone & as inscrutable as a statue.

It was well past dark & I had dropped into a light sleep when the Chaman tapped me on the shoulder. He held a lighted taper in his hand, which had been dipped in fat & I could just make out two sitting mats facing each other on a flat patch of dirt in the middle of the clearing. Two bowls, a pile of rolled dried leaves that looked like small cigars & the bundle of leaves that the Speaker had been shaking over the brew were laid out between them. The smaller of the two bowls held the distillation, now reduced to about a pint of thick liquid & the larger was empty.

The Chaman motioned to me to sit on one of the mats & lit one of the cigars with his taper. Once he was satisfied that it was alight, he blew out the taper sharply, leaving us in darkness & began to circle the area around the mats, stopping at a number of points to blow sharp blasts of smoke & shake his bundle of leaves. When the circle was complete he pointed to the sky & to the Jungle forming a circumference of dark verdure around the clearing & made a gesture of warding with his out-turned palms, as if to say 'nothing from outside can enter here'. He picked up the large pot, which was empty & held it up to his mouth, miming the act of vomiting & pointing at me, grinned quickly. I felt a moment of doubt, realizing that I would be required to drink the noxious brew which the Chaman had spent that day preparing, but I have sampled many strange drugs during my travels: Chinese opium, Mexican peyote, the Bhang Lassi of Northern India. Perhaps the effects of this distillation would not be so very different. The Chaman smoked quietly for a few minutes, whilst I listened to the sounds of the Jungle around us – the tree frogs, cicadas & birds all calling in counterpoint to one another – & wondered what would happen next.

The Chaman produced a drinking cup & poured some of the mixture into it. He blew smoke over the surface of the liquid with a sharp whistling sound, before handing the cup to me to drink & throwing back his head as if to mime finishing the draft. I drained it in a few swallows & only then had time to reflect how unpleasant the taste was. It was as bitter as wormwood, with a deep earthy, musty undertone that spoke of ancient caves. It was in other words unspeakably foul.

The Chaman nodded approvingly & poured a cup for himself. He then rubbed lemongrass into his temples, chest & neck, filling the *air with its sharp citrus smell & began to shake the bundle of leaves so that it made a sound like rain & to whistle a haunting melody.*

I realized that it had started to rain heavily; flashes of lightning lit everything for a moment & were followed by huge peals of thunder that made the ground vibrate. Each time the lightning struck I was temporarily blinded & the darkness surrounding us seemed even more impenetrable afterwards. Seeing this, the Chaman reached out & closed my eyes with a gentle hand. I felt my head & my limbs grow heavy & my heart slow, along with my breathing. I could still hear the Jungle sounds & the Chaman's voice, but they were joined by a buzzing like a swarm of bees in my left ear. The Chaman was singing in a kind of falsetto, with perfect control of pitch & timbre, so that his voice rose & fell like a bird swooping. I didn't understand the words he was singing, if they were words at all, but I began to see pictures behind my closed lids.

At first the images were just flashbacks to things that I had seen over the past few weeks, my mind retracing the journey until I was back at the beginning of my trip. But as each scene flashed through my mind's eye it felt as though I was emptying my memory; the events no longer felt real, I no longer felt real & the world that I thought I remembered just a convenient fiction, a dream I was awaking from.

I found myself standing on a dark riverbank with no sensation of body. I felt the presence of spirits around me & could not explain how I knew that they were the spirits of jaguar, of caiman, of the Caposcripti who had passed forever into this world & those who were visiting it. I perceived these beings as light; gaseous shadows against the black river. I was aware of sounds, a language comprehended, but whose meaning escaped me & which reminded me of the liquid tongue of the Caposcripti.

I realized that the river before me was a portal to a different world,

or a different aspect of the world that I normally inhabited &
felt a compulsion to cross the water, the voices felt but not heard
encouraging me on. The need warred with my growing dread,
the fear of what was on the other side of the bank. Hades, the
underworld & the dark boatman of the Styx. I suspected that it
was a crossing I might not return from. All of a sudden the fear
filled me & became a huge nausea. I was aware of the Chaman
shoving the bowl into my hands as I retched & retched while tears
streamed from my eyes & mixed with the sweat from my brow.

As I vomited I felt that all of the fears & prejudices, mistakes &
sins that were on my soul were being expelled along with the bile
from my stomach. My throat became a conduit for the darkness in
my spirit & I felt lighter & lighter, as if I was no longer a weight
on the mat I was kneeling on. The vomiting was stopping now, with
only the occasional spasm sending me grasping for the bowl. The
Chaman was blowing sharply through his teeth & I noticed that I
couldn't hear the buzzing of bees in my left ear any more. Feeling
gradually returned to my arms & legs, although I still felt dazed &
unreal. The effects of the drug were beginning to wear off & with it
the river & the things I had seen & heard, which became misty, like
memories of having once known something.

The Chaman looked at me curiously & motioned to me to go to
sleep. I went to my hammock & lay down, with my mind buzzing
& alert – but five minutes later I was in a deep slumber.

Now it is afternoon & I have slept the morning & half the day
away. There are only a couple of hours until dark. The sun is low in
the sky & my sleeping place is in deep shadow. I had a raging thirst
& it felt as though my bowels had turned to water.

Once I had refreshed myself, I returned here to try to capture some
detail of that evanescent experience. I wonder if it will ever be

repeated?

May 21st

When I had finished writing in my Journal yesterday, I looked up to see the Chaman, watching me with an unreadable expression in his eyes. Wordlessly he handed me a bowl full of masato & I was so thirsty I drained it all. I patted my stomach & put imaginary food into my mouth to indicate that I was hungry, but the Chaman just shook his head & gestured for me to follow him. We returned to the hut where the Chaman made me sit down & seated himself opposite.

We remained like this until dark. I shifted from time to time to relieve the pain of my cramped limbs; the Chaman remained completely immobile. As the sun was going down the Chaman picked up a bowl that I had not noticed previously. He poured some of its contents into a smaller bowl & handed it to me.

I was not surprised to discover that it contained more of the dark red liquid that the Chaman had given me the night before & felt a moment of disquiet. I was not sure I wanted to be faced again with the black river of my vision. But the Chaman was insistent & so I drank again & listened as he began to sing & waited as my body was taken over by the sensations that I remembered from the previous night.

But this time it was different. The Chaman changed the tone of his singing; he began to sing sharp dissonant staccato notes, rattling the leaves furiously & dancing around me, plucking me with his hands. The buzzing noise in my ear returned, increased so that it sounded like a furious hornet & I suddenly felt a wave of nausea grab me. I groped wildly for the empty bowl, was sick until I thought there could be nothing left in my stomach & then more, until I was sweating & shivering & had retched until my throat was sore, on my hands & knees over the bowl. Now the Chaman changed yet again & began to whistle a fresh & gentle melody, until I had recovered & composed myself again.

The Chaman lit another of the cheroots & began to blow smoke over my head & around my body. I felt his gentle hands on my eyelids, closing them & heard the soft shuffle of the Chaman seating himself opposite. This time I didn't feel the effects of the drug wearing off – they intensified, until I had an uncanny sensation of seeing & understanding everything that the Chaman was singing about. I saw plants & animals that I had seen in the Jungle, but with a new recognition of their properties. I saw reality layer upon layer, so that I felt I was peeling its essence like an onion, each skin a casting-off of illusion, confusion, to the centre where there is only truth & calm. The Chaman was singing directly to my soul, in words that transcended language. I saw the faces of the Caposcripti, some seemed to recognize & some I was sure I had never seen before, appearing before me in a long succession. In their faces, in the ideograms that covered their cheekbones & spiralled around their crowns & foreheads, I began to read the history of the Tribe & in the procession of souls, the birth of language.

I found myself once again on the bank of the river – its waters still & black. This time I knew I must cross, for the Chaman was trying to show me something by returning me to this place. I suspected that he would keep sending me here until I understood the lesson. I had to remember this was a dream river; there must be a way to get back. But it seemed so real & there was such a palpable sense of menace from it that still I hesitated. Finally I could stand the tension no more. I moved towards the river, understood that I was floating over it into darkness & silence. I began to lose my frame of reference, myself, memory, language. My brain was whirling & making sense of nothing. I forgot who I was & found myself making sounds that I couldn't understand & that had no meaning. I would have been *afraid that I was lost, but I no longer remembered that I had come from anywhere.*

There was no doubting that I had gone far away, into myself & past myself, until only the thinnest link connected my spirit to my body. It was the Chaman that brought me back across the dark river. He changed the rhythm of his song yet again & began calling me back to him, reminding me that he was alive, calling me back to an awareness of myself. At first it was just a faint echo – heard as though from miles away. Then it began to get louder & I felt a tugging on the fine thread that disappeared across the dark river. As he sang I understood his words, as though I had known the language all along & had merely forgotten it for a while.

> Listen to my song; is not our world beautiful?
> Come back from the dark river; it is the first soul,
> Let not your spirit be eaten, for the first soul is hungry,
> He is the eater of worlds.
> He has swallowed the spirits of our first fathers, all those that have left
> But that world is not for us.
> Listen to my song, this music is a medicine for your mind;
> The draught you have taken is strong, the knowledge of us
> Listen to my song, return to us now,
> Remember, that language you had forgotten –
> Do you remember it now?
> Now, I think, you will begin to understand a little,
> it is only that you have forgotten,
> and need to be reminded.
> Now, for now has always been,
> and will be, the lie of the everyday
> is momentarily confused
> Can you can see reality, taste the bitter core?
> Bring knowledge back from the dark shore…

The ceremony is over.

*I heard those words, spoken as a hypnotist would to his subject &
realized that once again the tide of the drug had receded, leaving
me light-headed & my limbs tingling. But the world around me was
once again as it had been & I was no longer connected to my body
by a thin cord, but wholly inhabiting it. As I sat thinking about
these sensations I heard the Chaman's voice & became aware, with
a sense of unreality, that I could understand him:*

*"Go & sleep, my friend. Today we have found a common language;
tomorrow you will begin to learn the true history of our Tribe."*

May 23rd

*It seems to me that far from learning a new tongue, I have gained
the ability to decipher Babel – for that surely is what the speech of
these people would sound like to the uninitiated. It seems that they
possess the power to communicate, having neither vocabulary nor
grammar, but purely a 'translating engine' or organ that enables
them to comprehend directly to the heart of their interlocutor's
meaning. That this is somehow connected with the extensive system
of tattoos with which they are covered seems most evident to me. It
is also the result of a series of initiations, of which at present I have
been afforded only the haziest indications, but one of which the boy
Taypi was engaged upon when he chanced across my unconscious
form.*

*I too have undergone an initiation, through the agency of the
Ayahuaska, which the Chaman (who I shall now refer to as the
'Speaker' for that is his function in the Tribe) administered to me &
the ceremonies that followed.*

*The reader of this journal may find this difficult to credit – but
I have only to use as an example the effects of drugs well known*

to the civilized world, such as Opium & Hashish to shew that this is possible. Having said that, it has not been recorded that these substances are capable of producing the complete shift in my perceptions that I have experienced at the hands of this Chaman. The drug & the chanting of the Speaker opened a door in my mind & the mesmerising power of his eyes & his song took me on a journey to what may be another country & forever changed me.

That this was some kind of test I am quite certain; although I do not know what behaviour was expected of me, it seems that I have passed the bar, for tomorrow we go to find the main settlement of the Tribe.

27. Headshrinking: 1

With time the Photographer has been able to refine his methods, so that the ceremony allows him to distil a much purer language from the subject than was previously possible, thus increasing the power that he gained from the ritualistic tattooing, subsequent decapitation and final reduction of the subject's head.

The reasons behind this ceremony and the preceeding isolation of the subject were complicated, and entangled within the private philosophy the Photographer had constructed for himself. From the story of Babel the Photographer had surmised that we had not lost our capacity for natural language – it had merely been confused. The ceremonies and methods he had developed were drawn from the old man's journals, and then refined by the research that the Photographer himself had carried out. That this original language had given extraordinary powers to its speakers, the Photographer did not doubt for a moment. The secrets of the philosopher's stone, of the animation of golems and of zombies, the building of great edifices and the control of minds were all bound up with natural language: a cipher that he intended to unlock.

Over the years the procedure has been refined and he no longer uses a razor to remove the hair, the eyebrows and lashes. Depilatory creams make the process far less messy, and there's no chance of damage to the skin.

Through a method of trial and error he has found a cream that doesn't affect the action of the chemicals that he uses for the rest of the process. It claims to be 100% natural and

Ayurvedic and is neither cheap, nor easy to get hold of – supplied only erratically by a mail-order company in New Delhi. He sometimes thinks it's ironic that in death their skins are softened and pampered so much more than when they were alive, and at such expense.

Next he prepares the tattoo needles – black India rubber ink because it is traditional and will not fade with the heat or humidity. He lays them out in a prescribed order – by size and so that they will come easily to hand when he needs them. He does not use a tattoo gun – the process must be entirely manual.

Through all this the subject's expression is totally blank. All lines have been smoothed, and all emotion erased before rigor mortis set in. The eyes have been closed, giving the face a peaceful look.

In the beginning he had stolen some of the heads from mortuaries – or bribed hospital attendants to let him have them – whichever was easier. However he's found that some parts of the process work better if the subject is alive – so he's taken to obtaining fresher specimens.

He has laid out about him his notes, transcriptions from the tapes, and one of the journals. Scattered in among the old man's notes on life with the Tribe, and their customs and language, are his thoughts on a variety of other topics – ranging through developments in nineteenth-century medicine and other branches of learning – mathematics, the natural sciences, physiognomy, phrenology. Much of the thinking seemed dated compared to the advances that had been made in the last hundred and fifty years, especially in the areas of neurology and linguistics, but the notes about the Caposcripti provided a framework for the inscriptions that form the next part of the process.

The smooth and expressionless head is now ready for his ministrations. Sometimes he photographs it at this stage – a side shot perhaps, an art shot, the light angled to create a false profile. These seductive and vulnerable portraits adorn his darkroom – colour and shadows bleached in the red light, as he sits with templed fingers, contemplating their anonymity.

This could go on for days.

28. Meeting the Tribe

May 24th

When I awoke this morning it was to see Taypi, Aymara & the Speaker packing up the camp & supplies. I looked questioningly at the Speaker, who indicated that I too should pack up my belongings, as we were going on a journey. I did as instructed & within a short time the campsite had disappeared – only a scorched patch of bare earth, trampled vegetation & some cut palms that had been used for the lean-to remained & these traces too would soon disappear.

I knew that these preparations were a prelude to our return to the main settlement & could hardly contain my excitement at the thought that I was finally to be taken to the Tribe that I had come such a distance to find. Over the previous days of my recovery I was at first too weak to take much interest in anything & as my strength increased my attempts to communicate with the Speaker & Taypi had been frustrated by our lack of a shared language. As I have already described, the Ayahuaska ceremony has created a strange bridge of language that enables me to understand a little of their speech – but my joy knows no bounds now that I am to be given the opportunity to experience their culture at first hand.

Whilst I have not learned the Caposcripti language overnight, the ceremony does seem have given me an uncanny ability to understand when Taypi or the Speaker speak to me & retain the vocabulary that I hear. It is just as the Speaker promised; it feels as though I am merely remembering something I have always known rather than learning a new language.

We set off just as the sun was beginning to cast pools of light in the forest & followed a winding path through the Jungle. The Caposcripti were setting a slow pace, but I was still very weak & was forced to concentrate all my energies on just keeping up with the party, with little energy or leisure to reflect on the people I would meet there or the direction that we were travelling in. Within a very short time I had completely lost my bearings & wonder at the Caposcripti's ability to travel through the Jungle by invisible landmarks, continually doubling back & going around huge obstructions, but with no sign of hesitation in their direction.

The Jungle was very silent – although I could hear the occasional cries of birds & the sound of tree frogs there seemed no breeze to disturb the leaves of the plants. The only animals we saw were insects & the occasional parrot or toucan flying overhead.

As we walked I noticed that the Jungle was changing its character. We travelled through an area where there were huge trees with little but dead leaves underfoot, where the secondary canopy grew at a height of twenty to thirty feet above the ground, on the trunks of trees to a more dense Jungle which had obviously been cleared, planted & then allowed to return to the wild. The Speaker explained that these were fields that had been let go fallow & that we were entering the Caposcripti lands proper. It was not much further to the pueblo, but apart from the altered character of the vegetation there was no sign of human habitation – even the cuts on the trunks of rubber trees looked as though they could just as easily have been made by the claws of the puma as by people collecting the gum.

I was forced to store up many questions because of the rate at which we were travelling, which left me little time for composing them. I forced myself to be patient, however, as I knew that many things might be self-explanatory once I had had the opportunity to observe *the Tribe further.*

I was hot, thirsty & beginning to wonder how much further we would have to walk in the stifling heat when the Speaker stopped & held out a hand behind his back, so that Taypi & Aymara stopped too & I almost collided with them. They stepped to the side & the Speaker turned around to face me. He examined me critically for a couple of minutes & then pulled a seed from one of his ever-present pouches. The seed was about the size of an acorn & a deep russet brown in colour, studded with small spikes. The Speaker bit the end off & spat it out. He then took a blow dart from another pouch & inserted it through the hole he had made. He worked the dart inside the seed for a minute or so & when he removed it the tip was coated in a bright red paste.

Approaching me he wiped the sweat from my face with the back of his hand & then began to draw intricate designs on my forehead with the blunt end of the dart. I submitted to this patiently – and only wished that my looking glass were not tucked away in my shaving kit so that I could see the designs the Speaker was drawing. I wonder what relation they bear to the patterns that cover the Speaker's own visage?

Satisfied with his work, the Speaker stepped back, holding my arms (he couldn't reach my shoulders with any comfort) & examining me critically. He gestured over his shoulder with a jutting thumb & I realized that we were only a few moments away from the main settlement. Within a very short time I began to see plantings of manioc & bananas & pineapples that had evidently been directed by the hand of man. As we crossed these cleared areas I suddenly caught sight of a palm-thatched roof amidst the greenery. We had reached the outskirts of the pueblo.

May 24th – *Evening*

*– Interrupted earlier. We continued on past the dwelling. It was
more of a shelter than a house: palm trunks supported a roof
thatched with dried fronds & the complete lack of walls allowed me
to see into every part. There are many such dwellings in this part
of the world, where it never gets cold enough to prevent the breezes
from passing through. The floor was of packed dirt, which extended
for a few feet to each side of the structure & waist-high platforms
had been built around the edges of the floor, which I assume are used
for sleeping. All sorts of objects are hung along the beams of the
house, which are much used for storage, leaving the floor quite bare
apart from a few bits of detritus – coconut shells, plantain skins &
fish bones, which had not yet been swept away.*

*I only had time for the most cursory glance before we had passed
the house. The Speaker continued in his usual determined fashion
onwards towards the rest of the pueblo. More roofs began to show
amidst the gardens of banana plants that almost completely
concealed them & the path we were following had been beaten flat
& wide by the passage of many feet. Aymara & Taypi disappeared
without warning down a fork in the path & we two continued
on until we reached a cleared area. The hut in the middle was far
larger than the rest, with low benches along the sides rather than
the sleeping platforms. The Speaker swung himself up onto the
platform, with a fluidity that belied his jutting belly & reached
down to grab first my pack & then my wrist. I was full of relief
when he told me that we could rest there a while. The sweat was
dripping down my face, stinging my eyes & causing the red dye to
drip down off my chin onto my chest. I did not dare wipe it off, but
thought I must have presented a rather clownish aspect & was glad
of the opportunity to take stock & breath.*

*The Speaker was silent & looked thoughtful, gazing meditatively
at the ground until a woman walked up slowly, balancing two red*

& white clay bowls. She handed the first to the Speaker, who took it carefully & the second to me, keeping her eyes lowered & trying not to stare at me, but unable quite to restrain herself. The Speaker stirred his bowl with a finger, before tipping it towards his mouth & taking a long swallow. I followed his example & also took a good draught, much refreshed by the sour masato, (to which I have now become accustomed, but was certainly not to my taste at first. It is reminiscent of sour milk, but not quite as bitter, with a watery texture & fragments of white pulp floating in it. It is somewhat fermented & imparts a cheerful fuzziness, enabling one to forget tiredness).

As we sat there various members of the Tribe found an excuse to wander up to the central hut, to see the stranger that Taypi, Aymara & the Speaker had brought back. Most seemed relaxed & curious, peeping at me with bright eyes; but others seemed to have misgivings & stared at me with hostility. A few stopped to speak with the Speaker for a while, but none offered to join us on the benches in the central hut, so that after a while I began to feel as though I were some exotic animal on display. From time to time the woman came to refill our bowls with masato (which continued to give the scene a most unrealistic air & relax me more than I would have been otherwise) & I was content to sit & examine the people that were wandering past as intently as they were inspecting me.

In between I studied the hut where we were sitting. It was subtly different from the dwellings that I had seen in other parts of the Jungle. Like the house it was constructed of palm trunks, with a roof of interlocked leaves & branches – but here the beams were bare of the objects that had cluttered those of the houses. The only things hanging on them were strings of beads & seeds looped around in long strands & strung with birds beaks, catfish spines & feathers. At one end of the platform a fire had been built in the dirt from whole trunks & large branches, arranged so that the end of each was in the centre of the fire. It was smouldering now & I surmised that it was always kept burning so that a source of fire was invariably to hand.

As the afternoon wore on to evening & the brief tropical dusk gave way to darkness people began to come & seat themselves on the long benches & on the hard-packed ground. Taypi returned & sat himself next to me, which delighted me as I have grown to like the boy, who is cheerful & friendly, always has a smile for me & seems to take me as his personal responsibility, watching out for me in the Jungle & showing me what is good to eat & what isn't. As it became completely dark the hut filled up with people & the fire was built up so that I caught glimpses of their tattooed faces in its steady glow. They talked to each other in low voices & seemed altogether very grave.

Once many had gathered, the Speaker cleared his throat loudly, causing an instant hush in the quiet babble & began to speak. I have been learning the language rapidly since the Ayahuaska ceremony, so I was able to pick up references to myself in the Speaker's remarks & understand that the Speaker was relating to the Tribe how they had found me & nursed me back to health. I gazed around, trying to read the faces of those assembled. I have seen little in Taypi & Aymara to suggest that the Caposcripti are an aggressive people; still less in the Speaker, but I do not know if my three companions are typical. Still I remembered the mistrustful looks of earlier & knew that the Speaker, although he had the authority to overrule any dissenters, was seeking to win them gently with his words. For my part I was silent, but wished earnestly I could win their approval. I want more than anything to be allowed to stay in the pueblo & learn their ways.

After a time it was Taypi's turn to speak. He stood up & spoke with gravity, as if mindful of a new status. I cannot help but think of him as a boy – he seems so youthful – but it is clear that here he is a man. He has consistently displayed the presence of mind typical of someone far more advanced in years. I wonder what happened to his father? I suppose he must have met with some accident.

But I digress – indeed my mind wandered as Taypi finished speaking & I suddenly realized that the Tribe were looking at me expectantly, as if waiting for me to add my voice to the meeting. I stood up & looked over to the Speaker for some hint of what was expected of me. The man's face was inscrutable & I realised that no help would come from that quarter & this was part of my test, necessary if I was to mix with the Tribe.

My brain was in chaos; a whirling vortex of impressions. Such was the disorder of my thoughts that I could barely have expressed myself in English & whilst I had begun to understand fragments of their language, I was little equipped to frame pretty expressions in it. I cast about for any words that would let me convey my relief that they had found me, my desire to learn from them & to teach them about my world; but my mind was empty. The words wouldn't come. I knew a moment of blind panic, unable to remember even a single phrase, whilst the massed faces of the Caposcripti fixed on me, tattoos swirling in complicated patterns in the dim light of the fire & wreathing their eyes. At this moment they seemed a people completely alien, with whom I would never be able to connect. Then I began to speak, in a halting tone, broken English mixed with odd remembered words from their language, sounds clawed painfully from my memory.

I spoke for maybe a minute or two, but it felt like an eternity & those few souls gathered might as well have been a multitude. I stopped & gazed around me, at those sitting in judgement on the stranger in their midst & began to sense I had won them over – or the Speaker had – I saw welcome in their eyes.

I have just looked up from my work of writing this to discover that I have amassed a small, but silent audience, whose eyes have been following my every pen stroke. I must present a strange sight to them, crouched over my book, cramps in my hand from gripping the quill pen, knuckles white against its ivory shaft. Their eyes are round with curiosity as to what this stranger is up to. I shall show them some of the small sketches I have made whilst writing this of their pueblo & ask if I can draw them.

29. Watching the Photographer: 3

She is watching him, concealed as always, and alert for any sign that would indicate he is aware of her surveillance. It has become a habit, this constant anticipation of another's movements, or a game that they are playing. Sometimes she thinks that perhaps he has known all along of her interest in him, and is leading her a merry dance, as though to test her dedication, his every act a challenge to her intelligence and determination.

Watching the Photographer has become an escape from herself – she has become nothing more than an eye, a conduit for this clandestine and silent relationship. She has no doubt that the relationship exists, that they share something. Why else would he pretend not to notice her constant presence when it must be obvious to him? His very silence is an affirmation of their connection. Even now in the busy street he carries an air of isolation about him, an inwardness that suggests deep motives.

Nina can't help comparing him to all these people in the street, unconscious, unreflective as sheep, going about in their herds, always following each other around. Cannon fodder. When she has let them in, tried to share some of what goes through her head, her thoughts and fantasies, they shy away, unable to take her measure. She's seen it many times – the slightly scared look in their eyes that rapidly becomes resentment. If she met some people more on her level… but that didn't happen, even at college. She was too far out-there for the cosy art students with their received ideas; all those protests about things that were so fucking meaningless in the grand scheme of things. Clever but empty executions that gave rise to the kind of circular conversations that made them sound intelligent, serious – then going out and getting coked out of their heads, feeling down and dirty on speed, hanging out in trendy bars, all the right hair cuts, combats and second-hand nighties, clothes worn for their irony factor, so cool they didn't need to care, thinking that they made a difference, ignorant gobshites. Course most of them could afford it with their Home Counties parents, the overseas students slumming it for a while in 'gritty' London. Thinking about it gave her a bitter taste in her mouth.

Wait – now where has he gone? Squinting (she ought to wear glasses) she spots him. He's wandering off. She hurries, on the other side of the street, keeping up whilst pretending to check out the window displays, concealing herself behind the milling pedestrians.

Still thinking about her life, worrying at it like a sore tooth. She'd like to think she comes across as enigmatic and interesting. If she's honest with herself she probably just appears morose or patronising. At least, where she is now, the lowest level, the lowest ebb, surrounded by the dregs of society, there isn't much to challenge her. It's easy to be anonymous and keep her interests to herself. To float – and occasionally to provoke – safe in the knowledge that her victims won't remember her or will be in too much of a drug haze to be freaked by her questioning. Because there must be more. There must be more. There fucking has to be – doesn't there? There's a lot more to the Photographer than meets the casual glance, the average observer. She's worked this out from watching him closely, even now beginning to gain some idea of what that is... something... repulsive – but interesting? Whatever it was it would force her into a choice. Complicity or rejection.

He's crossing the road now – coming in her direction. With a flutter of adrenaline in the pit of her stomach she ducks into a bookshop. Was she ill? Could she stop? She told herself she could quit at any time - this strange habit, which had begun as casual observation in the library. Or was that true any more?

When she was not watching him, she devoted her energies to finding out more about his background. Every and any bit of information, no matter how trivial, was grist to her mill, once she had finally dredged his name from the rat-trap of her memory. The web supplied her with the name of his agent and finally his address.

His movements tended to the predictable. She had already remarked his clockwork visits to the library – now she discovered that the same almost fanatical punctuality extended to other areas in his life. Service washes every week at exactly the same time, for example. But no deliveries to his flat. He seemed to discourage people from going there – "a very private person" said his agent. Yet he sometimes brought people back, furtively. She didn't see them come out – but then it was often late at night, and she didn't hang around that long once it looked like he had retired for the evening – not much to watch except heavily draped windows with hardly a chink of light showing. Draped in the daytime too – which was odd, but not (given the kind of people she lived with) that unusual. Probably didn't want his neighbours knowing about his… lovers? She wasn't sure. It didn't quite add up.

His agent had said there were no new exhibitions in the pipeline, when she'd phoned up posing as a journalist from one of the Sunday papers – and no chance of an interview. He didn't give them – and "what paper did you say you were calling from?"

No luck there – yet he was certainly researching...
something.

This afternoon he had visited the British Museum. She had
followed him from gallery to gallery, almost losing him in
the maze of artefacts, as he had lingered particularly fondly
over the South American collection and gone straight from
there to the Egyptians, giving only the most cursory glance
to what lay in between.

Dodging him in and out of the sarcophagi felt like some
strange courting ritual, glimpses of him bisected by the
open caskets, their occupants laid out like some anatomical
display, thousand-year sleep disturbed by the rude eyes of
tourists and schoolchildren. Perhaps this was the revenge
of those uncounted slaves who had died constructing
the monuments that would keep the Pharaoh's remains
inviolate, hidden from mortal sight. Was it a fascination
with death that sent him to study the mummified remains
of these ancient Egyptians, to scrutinise the Alexandrine
stones? As if satisfied that he had found what he was looking
for he turned on his heel and had begun to make his way out
of the museum.

He was gone now – hurrying, she caught a glimpse of his
coat, heading down the back streets towards St Martin-in-
the-Fields. She saw him vanishing into the Crypt, waited a
few minutes: five, ten...

It had been surprisingly easy to find out where he lived.
She had (briefly) worked at a photo developer's, for the
money and the free materials, and therefore knew that he
must be registered with the Photographer's Guild, and that
they would need an address for the registration. She had
looked him up on the register, and there he was. The ease
with which she'd done it, the practised and methodical

way in which she'd uncovered this and other details of his existence was slightly intimidating. It was as if she were discovering another personality – a woman who could patiently watch, and follow, and uncover and worry away at the truth until she has discovered everything there is to know about her quarry, wrung them dry. But where would it end? Everything must have a beginning, middle and an end – that's what you're always taught. But what happens at the end?

He must have found a seat by now. A large dark espresso and his ubiquitous notebook on the table before him. She could run the risk, now, of finding some nearby alcove where she could watch him unobserved. She walked down the steps, opened the door and stepped into a whitewashed underground café, a big self-service counter, cash desks, tables tucked away in alcoves and in between arches. All around black and white photos, playbills and posters advertising classical concerts. A quick coffee before the opera darling?

She saw him and turned away, the movement instinctive now, his position plotted. She queued, ordered, paid, grabbed a plastic tray and found a table where she could pretend to bury her head in a magazine, watch him from an angle, half glimpsing his notebooks over his left shoulder. She had noticed that he often sat with his back to a room – automatically denying the possibility of human contact.

Nina knew that there would come a point when they would no longer be strangers, and the following, the watching – the stalking if she was honest – would have its natural conclusion. They would have to meet, if only to confirm the complicity that already existed between them. Is complicity always unspoken? She knew that inevitably she would create some pretext, in due time things would be so arranged – by she or the other self that was beginning to seem almost autonomous, so as to bring them face to face. How then would he represent her, a Dali with his Gala, a side of meat and a telephone?

30. Headshrinking: 2

The Photographer's kitchen was one of the smallest rooms in the apartment, more reminiscent of a laboratory or a surgery than a place for the preparation of food. It was inhumanly clean and glittering, with surfaces and cupboards sheathed in antiseptic stainless steel. Along one wall he had installed a giant Aga some years before, modified according to his own specifications. Along the other was an unusually long drainer with deep round sinks set flush in the metal.

Hidden away behind the immaculate surface, in a myriad of drawers and cupboards, was the accumulation of several years of research, minutely organised and tucked away, catalogued and sorted, so that if you opened one of the cupboards you would find racks of glass tubes and jars filled with mysterious substances, rather than the expected ketchup, tinned soup and tea. This drawer contained rare substances procured from his South American and Caribbean agents, this a selection of knives and scalpels, forceps and catgut; that one notes; and in yet another hanks of hair, desiccated skin layered like tissue paper with sheaves of intricately drawn designs for tattoos.

The refrigerator would not, at first glance, give you any clues as to the purpose to which he sometimes put it – its usual contents a bottle of wine, a few camera films, and the inevitable gentleman's relish, relic of some ancient hamper. The sole clue, perhaps, is the lack of a central shelf, leaving enough room to store a polythene-wrapped head in each of its stages of preparation.

The Photographer was half-way through the process that

would reduce the head to the size of an orange, and provide him with another fine piece to add to his collection. Naked of hair and minutely inscribed with characters, it rested on the stainless steel worktop in readiness for the next stage. On the Aga was a large pot that had been filled with water, and simmered for hours with roots and dried plants until it had reduced to a watery paste.

The latest subject had proved problematic, and provided little for the Photographer to work from. He had starved himself rather than eat the food prepared by the Photographer – food that had been mixed with drugs designed to intensify the effect of the dark padded chamber, of 24-hour-a-day silence and isolation, of timeless incarceration.

He had proved resistant to all these methods: the relationship stillborn, holding his secrets inside. Perhaps it had been a mistake to take him – but it was too late to go back now. There had never been any question of his release. For 28 days they had carried on an invisible battle, and finally the Photographer had won, had heard on his tapes the pleas for release gradually giving way to an endless mumbling, a litany of life whose vocabulary had become diffused until nothing but a long susurration had issued from the spinning reels. When he had opened the room he had found only Gerard's emaciated corpse, his feather-light form, the smell of fear and faeces. In some essential way he had escaped, had stolen away, and left the Photographer no closer to the solution.

Still, they all went in the end – and perhaps even Gerard who had clung so hard to the lie had something to add to the pattern. The Photographer smiled with grim satisfaction at the thought that if nothing else he would contribute his energy to the apartment, flesh to kilowatts, body becoming a shape in ashes in the hot coals of the Aga. Dust to dust, ashes to ashes – dirt we are and to dirt will we return. The body is nothing – the mind is the temple of the self. His head will hold all that there is of him, all there already, his life his knowledge – just waiting for the needles to bring it out. Done now.

He's fed enough now to the hungry Aga to keep the temperature constant for a few hours under the giant cauldron that had once been used for boiling puddings. A visit to one of the catering shops in the Edgware road, armed with a set of precise instructions, had furnished his cooker with the necessary modifications, the Aga equipped with a large deep hotplate which he uses to heat black sand whilst the head is simmering on the other ring. Flesh falling from the bone. Tender as a well-broiled ham.

The Photographer lays Sabbatier knives, medical scalpels and long pins ready on the sideboard. Rolls of absorbent cotton and lint are lined precisely in front of him, behind a tripod that has been modified so that he can use it to support a head. All is ready now. Right tools for the job. Ritual observed but modernised. And why not? Is this not after all the twenty-first century? He had a feeling the old man would have approved – well, possibly.

Deftly he lifts the head out of the pot with a set of long shining tongs, and stands it on the tripod. His critical eye notes that it has survived the first stage of the process remarkably well.

Surgeon's gloves and surgeon's grace – the neat incision from crown to nape, the scalp rolls back easy as the skin on a Sunday joint. He lays it out on the pile of sand, which moulds to the shape of the face and supports it whilst he deftly trims the fat, razors the attachments to the bones. Gently now for the bridge of the nose, fingers trace eye sockets, and the sharp blade follows them almost lovingly, teasing, pinching, rolling, rubbing the recalcitrant flesh. Quickly now before it cools too much. The skull comes away clean and blanched. Stack it on the shelf with the others – he'll deal with that later.

Trim the neck, remove the flesh inside with a sharp scraper, preferably with rounded edges. Remove the fatty excess, the slight jowls. Smooth and cauterise slightly with a hot stone. He imagines describing this process. What had the old man felt the first time he watched it? The black sand packs in smoothly, hot and dry, moulding to every hollow.

Sutures prepared, butterfly stitches hold the flaps together, quick tacking ready for the neat seam. Lovely bit of needlework there. Practice makes perfect.

Standing back he admires his handiwork – but only for a moment. Turning and smoothing the hot skin, flat stones heated on the back shelf of the Aga. From here on he's entirely faithful to the ritual – even if the stones are from the beach at Brighton rather than some Amazonian riverbed, they're suitably smooth and rounded. Soft pads of cotton absorb the sebum leaking from the shrinking pores. Lips sewn shut. Fine needles hold eyes and brows and nose in shape; redundant acupuncture. There's a symbolism to where they're placed. He's done some research on Chakras. Always struck by the parallels between these ancient cultures.

The first batch of sand has already cooled, compacted and cemented slightly with the fatty juices that it has absorbed. Gently he scoops it from the shell, delicate and flexible as a deflated balloon. The head has already become somewhat smaller, but retains its shape. It's going well so far. He gathers up more hot sand and pours it through the neck hole.

The rhythmic motion of hot stones smoothing the planes of the face, sculpting the death mask, the shibboleth. The tattoos become a black tracery of etching on the dark skin, taking a shine like mahogany, upon which rich beads of grease appear as the head desiccates, and are wiped away.

The Photographer has great faith in processes, carrying out the most intricate plans, step by step, performing each necessary element with care, and attention – the pleasure of watching as all the elements come together to form the perfect pattern. Ideally he would like to control everything, pinpoint everything in existence with omniscient accuracy, fix it in its place in the divine order. From this perspective every situation becomes a weighing of the odds, a balancing of all parameters – a Euclidean curve of potential and possibility.

In the journals, in the Explorer's meticulous recording of the Caposcripti's practices and beliefs, he can sense a kindred spirit. What are the Caposcriptan tattoos if not graphs mapping the individuals' journey from birth to death; forking lines suggesting avenues of possibility to be explored? Playing with life, and playing with patterns. Language, *Logos*, the word, creates and destroys. Say something and make it so. The grand author. The architect. What was there for God to fear in the tower of Babel?

And so he measures and marks, describes and makes so, weighs the odds and continues his grim business – each addition to his gallery a strategic pruning of the messy tree of life.

Within the Photographer's plans there is no room for deviation. Because if the word is fact, is a making, it is also logic; the hard truth of the percentage. And how can it be that the Caposcripti, with their thorns and berry juice, drugged visions and wandering descriptions of the moon, the stars whose children gallop across the sky – can have grasped so complex a pattern?

31. In the Pueblo

May 28th

Time passes rapidly here, yet has a curiously suspended quality. You could set a watch by the rhythm of the days, the dusk that invariably falls at six pm sharp, the rapid descent into dark, the creak of the bullfrogs calling for rain – even the showers fall regularly. Yet all of this conspires to make me feel as though I am outside time – now that I am no longer endlessly travelling there is little to tell the days apart & only my journal to remind me that I have already been here a week.

This morning, as usual, I was woken by Taypi to eat with the family & watch them prepare for work with the crops. The Caposcripti cultivate many plants & herbs for their use, yet so gentle is their tread upon the land & subtle their husbandry, that you would little suspect that many of their plantings are the result of cultivation. Yet when I saw Aymara harvesting pine-apples from what at first I took to be a wild thicket, I realized that they had been carefully seeded so as to provide a convenient source of the fruit; & were of a variety plumper & sweeter than the 'wild' pine-apples I had eaten during my travels.

Earlier I had another painstaking language lesson with Taypi. He is amazingly patient with me, but it is slow going. I am beginning to understand that much of the meaning is conveyed through sub-vocal expression & furthermore can be inflected by the body decoration & language of the speaker, so that the tattoos of the Caposcripti create for each of them a peculiarly unique & intimate vocabulary. This explains why the Ayahuaska was able to create such a strong

impression of comprehension in me; by enhancing the visual &
empathic powers, it enabled me to understand that part of the
cipher I am now struggling with.

The afternoon has passed much as any seems to in the pueblo;
watching the men drinking masato & talking, sketching &
scribbling. At dusk there will be hunting & fishing & fires stoked
to cook the evening meal – a mess of fish & turtle's eggs, stewed
with bananas, yucca, cassava meal & cilantro. I feel peripheral
to most of these activities – an observer whose help would only
inconvenience. I am content to watch & write & shore up my
strength.

May 30th
Cold sweats & shivering last night, also premonitions & bad
dreams that left me wakeful.

Much recovered by morning. Went on an early foraging trip with the
Speaker in the woods around here. Language skills are coming on,
but I still cannot tell when he is mocking me. A deep one.

May 31st – a trip with the Speaker
My skin retains a jaundiced tint, despite the good food & rest
that I have been enjoying here. I can see the Speaker looking at me
with a doctor's eye & he too understands that my recovery is more
apparent than real. It adds a sense of urgency to my work here, for
my weakened heart would not long survive a relapse of the fever.

Last night he shook me roughly awake in the black dark of the
hours between midnight & dawn, to accompany him on one of his
rituals. He seems to carry out most of his occult duties at night, or
in the very early dawn. On this rare occasion it seemed I was to be
allowed to participate. Up until now I have been barely tolerated
as an observer, often at such a distance that I could hardly discern

what was happening in the dead of night. I would hazard a guess that there are other ceremonies about which I have no information at all & which my very presence would pollute.

They leave frustrating gaps in the framework I am beginning to develop about the Caposcripti, but I dare not ask the Speaker about them. He keeps a distance, treating me with a formality that transcends his near nakedness, the tattoos that cover him, the pouches & charms all hung about his person. Perhaps they even contribute to the air of authority that makes me feel somehow clumsy in his presence; ignorant & strangely defenceless. That, or his curious tawny eyes, which seem to look right through me & take me back to the dark places in my head that I first visited during the Ayahuaska ceremony.

He has not invited me to drink the bitter broth again. In part I am grateful for this, since I'm not sure I want to return to that dark place. & yet… sometimes it seems that there is so much that I will never be able to understand otherwise. Much that I see leaves me with more questions than answers.

June 3rd

Another language lesson with Taypi; they are getting much easier now & we have established a great rapport, mixing English & Caposcripti (for he has started to learn a few words) to achieve an almost perfect communication between us.

I have not described this boy – but he is certainly as handsome and proud a specimen of the Caposcripti as you could wish for. His candid eyes are set within a whorl of tattoos that cover his face and continue up across his scalp, shaven but for a long tuft of hair that has been left to grow at the back. It is a beautiful face, the young skin taut and stretched over high cheekbones, the proud bridge of his nose; all dark with the patterns of the Caposcripti, so that he

seems to look out from behind a striking mask. It would terrify
and bemuse the people of Western society, who can not see past the
'savage' exterior, so different to their own unadorned faces, to the
knowledge within. All they would see is a bloodthirsty savage, like
the Jivaro. It seems a shame that all the people of this region should
be tarred with the same brush.

Taypi is as full of curiosity about Europeans as I am about the
Caposcripti. He has introduced me to everyone in the pueblo &
explains the complicated relationships between the families that
make up this tribe. There are other tribes, he says, but contact is
rare, maintained by Speakers who travel around the Jungle & send
messages by knocking on the roots of huge trees, the sounds thus
produced reverberating for leagues around. This method is also used
for contacting or locating the other settlements. For, he explained, it
is not unusual for a whole tribe to move if there is a serious disaster
or bad omen, or when the rains come, causing the rivers to rise by
the height of ten men.

Our exchanges have fallen into a pattern, whether walking in
the Jungle or talking in one of the palm shelters in the pueblo –
composed not so much of words but of gestures & objects, of show
& tell. In return for lessons in the tongue of the Caposcripti, the
naming of things & the customs & taboos to which they adhere, I
have tried to explain Western culture to Taypi. This was far more
difficult, as he lacked any context for most of what I told him &
thus developed some very strange ideas about the people on the other
side of the big lake. I could see him making pictures in his mind that
were completely different from those that I was trying to describe &
the more I searched, with my imperfect command of the language,
for parallels, the wilder & more unlikely the pictures became. There
some other things Taypi simply would not believe – for example that
there were places on the earth where night never fell at certain times
of year, whilst at other times it was dark for months on end.

Only the existence of my musket, my watch & telescope, the maps that I carry with me & sundry other instruments such as my thermometer gave weight to my crazy claims. I tried to teach him about the Equator, convince him that the earth wasn't flat, outline the distribution of the continents, the orbits of the planets. But at this his incredulity knew no bounds and he would not be convinced.

The Speaker watches these lessons with interest. But he never contributes. I don't know if it's because he denies the existence of the outside world, or does not want to lose face by looking uneducated in the mysteries of the world. For sure his sharp eyes miss nothing & I'll wager he's taken in every detail of my descriptions & the documents & instruments that I use to illustrate them.

June 6th

Whilst the Speaker doesn't accord me any particular respect (much the contrary in fact; I still have not managed to penetrate his reserve), the rest of the Caposcripti seem to perceive me as a Chaman in my own right; especially since they often see me writing in the books that I keep so carefully wrapped up against the humidity of the Jungle. Frequently I look up from my writing to find myself ringed with Caposcripti all staring at me from a respectful distance. At first I found it unnerving to be the subject of their constant scrutiny, but now I am well used to it & able to ignore them completely, or stare back at them with equal frankness. I have less contact with the women, who seemed to be almost a tribe in themselves, as do the children, who run around in packs as soon as they are old enough to leave their mother's side. However through sign language & careful questioning I have been able to pick up a lot about the foods, medicines & other areas that the women hold under their iron sway.

These people have forgotten nothing, it seems, since the beginning of time; all captured both by their rich oral tradition & by the catacombs wherein they store the heads that hold the sum of tribal knowledge in the form of the rich symbolism with which they are enwreathed. The women showed me cures for many illnesses, as well as the medicines that prevent malaria, yellow fever, dengue & other maladies for which I could ascertain no name in my language. I wonder how they would resist the yellow fever, chicken pox & common cold that have decimated so many other tribes of these regions? I have no wish for the greater part of man to find these people too soon. The longer I spend in their pueblo, the less do I relish some missionary trying to convert these people with their customary fervour; the Speaker knows these risks too & it is this that causes the greater part of his reserve towards me.

June 7th

I am fast running out of paper & must fill in my observations in any tiny bit of margin or other white space. In this & many ways the journals have begun to feel like a metaphor for my own life… much detail being added in at the edges, but the main narrative ended. I have almost reached the last whole and unwritten leaf of paper in this book. From now on my notes shall continue as marginalia; the final page I shall conserve until I can write no more. To him who shall come after. I will send the boy with my books if he will take them. I pray he will convey them to Iquitos for me.

June 12th – 'The Fairer Sex'

The women prepare & grow much of the food for the settlement, as well as making red & white coarse-glazed pottery & jewellery, which the Caposcripti prize highly. Their workmanship is astonishingly precise despite the coarseness of their materials. When I asked them what had informed their choice of shape & construction they gave me to understand that the patterns were passed down from generation to generation through the tattoos which adorned their faces & bodies & that differed from those of the men. Women have their own secret knowledge, their own ceremonies, passed down from mother to daughter & across the female hierarchies within the Tribe.

Women hold a special place in the Caposcripti hierarchy (in so much as such a thing can exist in a people as scattered & fragmented into family groups as they.) They hold the secrets of medicine & crafts, create new lives & give names to things & to people. For the Caposcripti a person does not really exist unless he or she is named & the unnamed are vulnerable to having their spirits stolen by those who have left & to being possessed by demons & the spirits of animals. It is especially dangerous for a woman who is with child to associate with the unnamed, or with the recently deceased. Possession is taken very seriously by these people & they take no chances with those that they perceive to be vulnerable. Infants are therefore given their name as soon as possible after the birth & the mother is isolated from all but her closest female relatives until the child has been safely named.

June 15th – Choosing of Names

The choosing of names is not an exact science, but follows a system of belief & symbolism as complex & inflexible as the periodic table. New-borns are particularly closely observed to see if they express a predilection for any specific plant or object. The position in which they sleep, the sounds that they make, whether they cry or smile are all correlated against complicated criteria which enable the women to plot the path of the individual & so give them the name that will be with them until death – unless some accident or event befalls them that changes the nature of their life or temperament.

The Caposcripti firmly believe that the shape of the new-born's skull will tell of the future make-up of the individual & it is this that controls the first of the tattoos that are inscribed upon the young child's naked crown – before the skull has even had time to harden completely. It forms the basis of all the inscriptions that follow – spiralling out from the centre like the branches of a tree. The tattoos that follow coincide with key events in the individual's life & might include the names of children & ancestors, the occasion of the first hunt, the name of a mate, the transition from childhood to adulthood. When the heads are preserved, great care is taken to ensure that these tattoos remain intact, for they contain the whole history of the individual & remain as a testament to their existence & accomplishments, as well as a blueprint to learning for future generations.

Time

The Caposcripti do not measure time. They live simultaneously in the past, present and future, which they read in the rings of trees and the scales of fish. 'Morning' is not a distinct parcel of time, but a collection of descriptions, or concepts, each linked to a specific moment and aspect of the jungle – each with its own name, and all existing simultaneously in a series of parallel dimensions. Thus there is the bird time – when the innumerable varieties of parrots and other avian life try to outdo each other with their calls and screeches – the dew time, the sun time, the sleep of the night creatures, the waking of those who walk by day.

Such is the language of the jungle – a language infinitely more subtle in its gradations than ours. For when the sky is rarely visible through a canopy of green; when looking up will distract your attention from the snake in the undergrowth; and time is measured by the calls of birds and frogs, the diurnal journey of the sun and moon become irrelevant.

June 16th – Caposcripti Writing

I have so far been able to put together only the most rudimentary lexicon of their script, but from what I have been able to glean it is made up partly of representations of the natural world – birds, insects, snakes, monkeys, jaguars, trees & other symbols of deep significance to the Caposcripti; inscribed in relation to more abstract symbols which appear to represent time & emotion. It is a complex system & made more so by the subtlety of the Caposcriptan language, in which all things are delimited by their relationships as well as their properties; describing something, they make it so. The juxtaposition of tattoos can tell someone who knows how to read the script everything about an event – like a window into the past, a dark glass that reflects back & illuminates the present.

It is a culture of the mind astonishing in a people whose mode of living is so simple as to render hardly imaginable its development & the prodigious feat of memory it entails. Evidently preserving the language in the form of tattoos on the head ensures the continuation of the language – but only a fraction of the symbols are inscribed on each individual, with the Speaker responsible for that ceremony. I can only wonder if these people are born with some innate knowledge – for whilst I have been applying myself most assiduously to learning its grammar & inflexions I know that I have only the most rudimentary grasp of its complexity; much of its subtlety escapes me.

June 20th

I am in the grip of evil premonitions: darkness threatens me; chills grip my bones; I have horrible dreams. The worst of these is that I will die here & that this chronicle will be read by no eyes but mine; preserved for a while, perhaps, by the Caposcripti, but destined, finally, as perhaps they are destined, to be consumed in the hungry maw of the Jungle. I am much troubled with bouts of coughing & I am having trouble breathing, as well as pains in my chest. I had not suspected that my heart would prove such a faulty engine at the last!

I fear that I am in a race against time to record the Caposcripti tongue & it is imperative that I think of some way to transport my journals out from the wilderness to those that can make use of them. I know it for a certainty that I will never leave this place & that my wanderings over the wide world are to end here. There is little time.

32. A Meeting at the Pitt Rivers

The Pitt Rivers Museum is a dark cavern of a place. The walls are wood panelled, giving on to a high and gloomy ceiling, an impression of dusty drapery, exotic statuary hanging from the roof beams.

Large old-fashioned display cases crowd each other, fighting for wall space. No question of touching the exhibits, which are locked away on shelves, or fixed to walls, stuffed with objects pilfered from around the globe, and thrown together according to theme, so that African masks rub shoulders with Eskimo carvings and plastic children's toys. In a large wall-side display, a mummy, its cask positioned to show the mouldering wrappings of an Egyptian princess (perpetually 27) is accompanied by a 1950s x-ray of her skeleton, hand-labelled in faded ink. Other cadavers keep her company – from Mexico, China, the Capuchin catacombs; religious relics, miraculously preserved finger bones. It's strangely gruesome – the distance normally felt between civilisation and the 'savage' reduced by the juxtaposition of artefacts from times ancient and modern, dust shrouding the clash between East and West, and equalising all.

The cases march in neat rows, some shrouded with dust drapes. Dark wood and heavy velvet dominate the large chamber, preserving its Victorian feel. A security guard is asleep in his chair on the high gallery, accessed by a double staircase, which runs across one side of the room. Had he been awake, his position would just about have allowed him to see into the narrow aisles between the cases in the centre of the space. The rest of the chamber is concealed beneath the overhang of the mezzanine floor and the spaces along the walls feel almost like caves.

The cases themselves are nearly impenetrable: the glass thick and slightly dusty, the artefacts inside filling them so that it's impossible to see through them, even obliquely. Although the Photographer has been here before, the dusty maze nearly defeats him; he's beginning to wonder if the collection has been moved, or sold off... and then, almost without warning, there they are.

As with the other exhibits, the heads have been culled from a bewildering variety of cultures: Africans, South Americans, Haitians, islanders and mainlanders crowd together tightly on the glass shelves. Bleached skulls laced with garlands of thorns bare their teeth, brushing against the scalps of North American Indians, suspended in clusters with their long hair hanging down.

At the far end of the case the shelves have been given over entirely to the shrunken heads, mounted on thin poles, chins jutting, lips thrust out and fastened together with long ceremonial cords hanging down. Mentally the Photographer compares them to his own efforts – the lips invisibly sewn with gut from the inside, skins burnished to a high gloss, tattoos picking out the bone structure, spiralling around the naked crowns. These heads are not beautiful objects – misshapen and blackened, with long matted hair and pained expressions. They are the faces of those that have died in agony, been taken as the spoils of war.

Hand-lettered cards explain their origins and describe the trade in shrunken heads that started when the process was discovered in 1897; the Tsantas traded for guns and beads and whisky, the high demand which helped to decimate the tribes around the Jivaro's territory. Even though the Photographer has read the cards before, and probably knows more about the process than the curators of the museum, they still exert a fascination on him. There's something the Jivaro were missing – an awareness of the human body as an art form, the connection with the sublime made the Caposcriptan heads and expression of their own spirituality, capturing the soul of each member of the Tribe.

It's not hard for him to picture the scene where the heads were made. The Indians retreating from some battle, building fires and smoking the heads on their way back to camp, the process stretching out over days as they travel through the jungle, and in due time driven by western demand: heads hunted to order, trophies decorated with shells and beads – as if the head itself were not enough. The Photographer comes here to remind himself why he is doing what he's doing. It redresses the balance. Looking at the heads he feels a kind of sickness in the pit of his stomach, revulsion for these objects, the fetishism of death. Yet he cannot look away. It feels as though there is a silent communion between them. Complicity.

33. Last Days

June 28th – The dark horseman rides near

June 28th – The dark horseman rides near
I have not stirred from my bed for three days now. Flesh fails, and
whilst my spirit remains strong, I must come face to face with the
reality of my own death. & the possibility that all that I have learnt
of the Caposcripti will die with me – the meticulous notes eaten
by the hungry Jungle, to be followed soon after by my bones, until
nothing is left but a memory in the minds of people who have every
reason to conceal themselves from the eyes of their fellow men. This
is not a new thought – it has dogged me even before I found the
Tribe, tormented me when I lay helpless with fever in the days before
the Caposcripti rescued me. But to die now, when I have reached
my goal & amassed such a priceless store of knowledge about their
culture… to die now seems cruel indeed. It is this that creates such a
paralysis of indecision within me. As I weaken I am sinking further
into a deep melancholy, 'My head aches and a drowsy numbness
pains my senses, as though of hemlock I had drunk.' Keats? I know
not any more.

July 4th

July 4th
The more I think on it, the darker my thoughts turn, and this in
turn feeds my illness, so that my intimations of death are rapidly
becoming a self-fulfilling prophecy. I rest twixt the twin horns of
dilemma. Even if I were to work out some way to get my notebooks
out of the Jungle, I know that the Speaker will prevent the discovery
of the Caposcripti if he can.

Comparing them to the society back home, I cannot help but agree.

I think of other tribes in the Amazon basin, the rape of lands &
people in the name of sugar, of gold, of coffee, of rubber, of guano
& all of the other rich pickings to be had on this endless continent –
the slavery, the waste of lives, the cultures lost in the scramble for
power, land & wealth. Can I in all conscience reveal the location of
a Tribe who up until now have managed to keep their very existence
a secret? It seems certain that if the journals are found then others
will come to look for the Caposcripti. & they will find them,
without a doubt.

There is always the chance that the Caposcripti would be discovered
anyway – that my desire to hide & protect them from the wider
world will be futile, a kind of vanity, as if by keeping them hidden
I am in some way responsible for their existence. I had after all
initially hoped to reveal them to the world as my protégées. I find I
cannot bring myself to conceal what I have discovered completely.
Still I shall shroud their location in enough secrecy that they shall
not be discovered just yet.

The Caposcripti carry not just the fragments of the original
language, that curses Western man with a sense of his own
incompleteness & sends him wandering around the world like Ahab
in search of the missing pieces, but a full blueprint of it, stencilled
on their own skin. Comparing their language to English, or for
that matter any that I have ever heard or read is like comparing a
black-and-white sketch to its original. Like Plato's forms or ideals,
our own language is but a pale reflection of that of the Caposcripti.
As such I am in a hopeless position – there is no way I could hope to
capture the subtleties and nuances of the language by recording it
in my own: but my meticulous transcriptions of the symbols which
they used might be enough to give someone a clue about what I have
discovered, enough to enable them to try to rebuild the lexicon. I will
not reveal the location of the Caposcripti: that little I can do to try
to preserve them as they are for at least a few generations, but I can

try to keep their language alive if, as seems almost inevitable, they are to be destroyed by contact with my own people. I cannot bear to imagine that their language should be diluted, contaminated and eventually lost completely to them.

I am filled with memories of my long life, which seem more real than the Jungle around me. I spend my hours in long reveries, only to wake with a start, feeling disoriented & forgetting where I am & how I got here. My thoughts are filled with a kind of lucidity that I have never experienced before. I feel as though I am entering the final stretch – the dark river of my visions beckoning me. 'The paths of glory lead but to the grave.'

July 10th

I am resolved to ask Taypi to deliver my papers. I shall furnish him with letters of introduction, and what little store of gold I have left. I know it will be a long journey for him, and perhaps it will destroy him. But I cannot but think that the Jungle's hazards will be least of his troubles. What will the mestizos that infest the river's banks make of one so young and proud, and moreover unlike any Indian they have seen before? The Caposcripti never leave their lands, yet I must wrench him from the bosom of his people and send him forth into the belly of the beast; what kind of monster am I that could so lightly contemplate setting him upon a perilous journey? The instinct for self-preservation that is all that is keeping me alive now.

July 11th

I have been with the Caposcripti long enough to witness birth & death; to begin to know them as people & understand the harshness of the life that they lead. It is not pretty. Death is no stranger to these people, yet they seem strangely fatalistic even if the victim is a child. It is accepted. Nor do they spend energy on creating visions of life after death, creating false utopias, heaven or hell.

The Caposcripti do not die, they merely leave their bodies to decay, whilst their spirit lives on in the spirit of the jungle & on the tattoos passed on to their descendants. It is for this reason that proper death rites are so important. For spirits can be angry as well as benign. They have the power to possess the bodies of the living if the rituals are unfinished. I have witnessed the ceremony for young & old alike.

The ritual begins with decapitation. The head is severed from the body with sharp stones gathered from the caves & shrunken to the size of a man's fist; the body left in the jungle for the ants & teeming insect life to do their swift work. I have seen the corpses suspended in the trees, flesh swollen & split; retched at the smell of corruption. Ants removing every trace, even the bones broken down over time, lost in the thick humus of the jungle floor.

This is what will happen to me too. My bones will decay, my body will be eaten by the jungle. I am long past any illusions. Nothing but my head will survive – shrunken & mummified – preserved by a process already documented in my journals – themselves mildewed & stained, pages half-rotted & eaten by termites, marked by the corpses of flowers & strange butterflies, petrified fragments of the landscape.

Time now to close those notebooks off, to complete, in so much as is possible, the chronicle I have written. & to remove those essential clues that would lead to the Caposcripti's discovery by someone less altruistic than myself.

I must write letters for the boy & for my family. Letters of introduction, of passage; letters of recommendation & explanation. I know it will not come as any surprise to my circle of acquaintances when I do not return from this latest expedition: they count it little short of a miracle that I have returned from other such journeys in the past. The surprise, if any, is mine. I somehow did not expect this ending. Life has finally caught up with me.

July 14th

I am all preoccupied with plans & contingencies, prey to dreams & visions, so that I can hardly tell what is real any more. The letters are written, though I fear the penmanship is poor. My hands shake as though I have palsy, and it is all I can do to make out the characters against a deepening gloom that I know is my vision darkening. I shiver constantly with a cold in my bones that has naught to do with the temperature, for the atmosphere is as stifling as ever. Aymara has done what she can to make me comfortable; but how can any man rest who is staring that final long sleep in the face? Still – all is ready now. Aymara tells me that Taypi is mending nets & will be back when the night birds start calling. On him all rests. I know no one will write of my death, but the Caposcripti will preserve my head in the Jungle's depths – it is too much to hope that someone will find it years in the future. I am resolved to lay this heavy task on Taypi. Dark, so dark...

34. A Mission for Taypi

For some days now the Explorer had not stirred from his hut. The sun was high in the sky and normally he would have been up and about since dawn, waking with the rest of the pueblo and sharing breakfast with Taypi and his mother. On any other day he would be found wherever there was activity, with his ever-present journal and quill.

But all that had changed now. For days he had not joined the family for their meals or sat talking to the men as they squatted on the platform drinking masato and discussing the fishing or the portents of the stars, or the messages of the drums from other tribes living in the Amazon basin.

Taypi was mending nets down by the river when a little boy called Rimiki came breathlessly towards him.

"Taypi – Aymara says you must come now – the Explorer would speak with you."

Taypi immediately laid down the net and followed Rimiki back to the hut. He found the emaciated Explorer lying on his palette, with bundles of paper on his chest. His eyes were closed and he looked as though his spirit only tenuously inhabited his body. As Taypi approached his eyes opened, and gradually focused.

"Taypi, you came."

The voice of the Explorer was hollow and reedy, as though already coming from a dead man.

"Taypi. There is something you must do for me."

"Of course – I would do anything for you."

"You must undertake a journey – a longer journey than you can imagine, travelling far from your people for me. I would not ask this of you, but you are the only one who can help me now."

"A journey?"

"Yes, Taypi – a journey to my people. I will die soon. I can feel it and my dreams speak to me of a dark future. But I cannot leave this place without sending a message to my people. They must not lose my history, for then it would be as though I had never lived. You must deliver it for me."

"Do you mean your *tsanta*? You want us to return it to your people?"

"It is not my *tsanta* that you must deliver – for they would not be able to understand your language, or the ways of your people – but the story of the last days of my life and of your people, and of this place, which I have recorded in my notebooks. I wish that my people might have them to remember me by."

It took the Explorer a long time to get these words out. He stumbled over the syllables and several times stopped for breath. Taypi could barely make out his request, delivered as it was in a hollow whisper – but he understood that he must help him.

He was not surprised by this appeal – understanding that the Explorer's people would find in the notebooks the history of their relative's life that would have been lost to them otherwise. To lose the record of a life was like losing a part of the people, which was one reason why the Caposcripti preserved their heads so carefully. But he could barely imagine what would be required to carry it out. He was silent for a long time whilst he thought of the long, long journey to the Explorer's lands, a journey undreamt of by his people. Yet he would do that and more for the Explorer, whom he had come to love as one of his own family.

"I will do as you ask, but how can I find your people? You told me that they live far away, so far away that the sun cannot reach there and it is always cold. Surely it would take me many years to walk there?"

"Yes, that is true. However you would not need to travel to my country: there are some of my people closer to here, living where the great rivers meet. You could take my notebooks to them, and they would send them across the great water to my country. Will you do this for me? I trust you above all others to make this journey."

"Since you ask me I must do this for you, although it will be dangerous, and I never travelled so far from my people, or for so long. I will go to the Speaker and ask him what preparations I must make for this journey."

The Explorer gave a start, as though he had drifted into a reverie. Taypi looked at him anxiously. He pulled himself visibly together and fixed Taypi with his piercing eyes.

"I have already told the Speaker about this, and he has given his blessing. I wanted to ask you in person before I become too weak to do so. The spirit river is calling to me now. I can hear them talking on the other side."

Then his voice weakened again and he lay back, closing his eyes. The instructions that followed were delivered in a flat monotone, as though rehearsed.

"I have maps and instructions for you, as well as messages for my people, which I will give you before you go."

"You must leave as soon my body is cold, and do not tell anyone where you are going. Especially Aymara. The Speaker and I are agreed on this. Your mother would worry too much. The Speaker will tell her that you have gone on a spirit journey."

"But how can he tell her that which is not so?"

Taypi's smooth forehead crumpled as he struggled to get his head around this concept. He was an intelligent young man, but lying was completely alien to his nature. The Explorer was quick to dissimulate, having had years more practice.

"It will be so: the journey will complete your passage into manhood, which was interrupted when you first discovered me in the jungle. When you return you will have learnt enough to take your place amongst the Caposcripti as a leader of men."

The Explorer pulled himself painfully up onto an elbow.

"I have no more strength now. Will you do these things for me?"

Taypi nodded silently. The Explorer let himself fall back onto the palette with a grunt of pain, and closed his eyes again. His features fell into a slack repose, and Taypi could see that the effort of their conversation had drained him of what little strength he had left. For himself, he wanted to be left alone to consider the magnitude of the task he had been set.

35. A Conversation with the Speaker

The Explorer may have lied to Taypi, but the Speaker would not be so easily gulled. As soon as the Speaker saw Taypi, he knew what was worrying him, and what the Explorer had asked him to do. The boy's mind was like a clear pool to him; and he immediately sensed the new depths and troubled eddies that the Explorer had created.

He said nothing to Taypi, but went at once to see the Explorer. He found him writing, as always; his crabbed hands moving feverishly and almost independently of the withered frame that seemed almost too frail to support the weight of his arm.

"You are making your preparations for death."

It was a bald statement of fact. The Explorer's head turned slowly and he looked at him, as if trying to divine whether the Speaker had guessed his arrangement with Taypi. The Speaker continued.

"You wish to send Taypi on a most unwise journey. I know well the dangers in store for him amongst your people."

The Explorer tried to speak, and was wracked with a fit of coughing that left bloody bubbles on his lips. At last he was able to draw breath again, and he rasped out a question.

"Did he tell you?"

"There was no need. I would not be Speaker if I could not read these things. I have known for some time that this was in your mind."

The Explorer was silent, but the Speaker read shame in his eyes, coupled with a hint of desperation. The Speaker continued:

"You wish him to take your records to your people?"

"Yes."

"I must think on this. Taypi must be prepared."

The Explorer was incredulous

"Then you will let him do it?" The shock left him struggling for breath, and he was again twisted with wracking coughs.

"It is not in my power to forbid him. But I have grave misgivings. I am sure that no good will come of the journey."

The Explorer felt the Speakers eyes dissecting his soul. He knew that more was expected of him.

"I respect...the wish of your people...to remain alone here. I could not knowingly...put at risk a people...who have shown me much kindness."

"It was not kindness that caused us to save you from the jungle."

The flat statement punctured in a moment the whole lie of the Explorer's being, and revealed to him the wisdom and fragility of the people he had described as 'most noble savages' in his journal. The man before him was under no illusions, was in no way ignorant of the society that the Explorer had exiled himself from. It was almost as though he looked through the Explorer at the whole of his race, massed in ranks behind him. There were the wars, the death and the enslavement of human beings. There were the thousands of tiny miseries daily inflicted and borne. The Explorer felt dirty.

His eyes implored forgiveness, but received none.

"The Caposcripti are a good people."

"And yours are not. I have understood much that has not been spoken from your descriptions of your homeland and the people that bore you. You are in flight from them, but your spirit yearns to return. This is only right and natural. If the records that you have made are not returned to your people you will disappear, it will be as if you had never been. We will perform the death rites for you, but your head will not be preserved with those of the Caposcripti who have journeyed on to the next reality. What then will become of your history?"

The Speaker tilted his head to one side, and the Explorer sensed that he was playing with him.

"I promise you... there will be no clue in my records..." He broke off again to cough violently, and the Speaker noticed more blood spotting his lips and chest – "...or in the messages that I send to my family... that could bring anyone to this place... or enable them to find your people."

"And is this one of your not-truths?"

A sudden flush hit the Explorer's pallid cheeks. "No! It is my word!" He fell back, trying to catch his breath and failing, and the Speaker felt his heart fluttering arhythmically, like a bird that has been poisoned.

The two men held each other's gazes, in a silent stand-off. Finally the Speaker sighed wearily.

"For us words cannot describe that which is not so, yet you twist our language and make it dance to a strange and terrible music. Still Taypi will go, for I see the truth in your eyes if not in your speech. You will not knowingly betray us. I will go now and speak with him, and help him to prepare for the journey you have laid upon him."

The Speaker turned on his heel and walked away, his shoulders a little bowed as though they weighed heavy. The Explorer was exhausted by the intensity of their exchange and fell back on the platform, closing his eyes.

It had taken the greatest effort to sustain all those lies in the face of the Speaker's preternatural sensitivity. The journal was full of descriptions of the Caposcripti – every detail of his existence with them had been meticulously observed, every symbol of their intricate language had been inscribed somewhere on its pages. But no clue, he was certain, could lead anyone to the exact location of the Tribe, still less to the hidden caves where the heads of the elders were preserved, inscribed with first Word, the whole language of the first men which the rest of humanity had lost. Those secrets would die with him, and salve his conscience for the vanity that would send Taypi out of his world and into hell.

As the Explorer lay there, he felt again the shortness of breath and irregular fluttering in his heart's rhythm that signalled the onset of one of the attacks he had come to dread. He tried to regulate his breathing and relax into the sensation, which had sometimes seemed to help the attacks before. But this time the symptoms intensified, and he was suddenly gripped in terrible agony; at the same time feeling like some great weight was pressing on his chest; as his lungs flooded with blood his body thrashed spasmotically. His ears roared and it felt as though his brain was being starved of oxygen. The Explorer experienced this as a series of flashing lights and a feeling that sections of his experience were being closed off, like a series of doors slamming shut behind him. Finally there was nothing but darkness. And then there was nothing at all.

36. Watching the Photographer: 4

The trip to Oxford had been a whim. Nina had been following him, as always, and that lunchtime had jumped the barrier at Paddington, as he walked in his usual rapid and distracted way along the platform. She had hesitated only a moment before choosing another carriage a couple down, where she wouldn't be seen. Once the train had got underway, and he had had time to find a seat, she had made her way down to his carriage and taken up her quiet vigil.

He seemed distracted. She wondered whether his destination was Reading or Oxford – the only stops this train made. And what he would be doing there? A meeting? Possibly – she would have to wait and see. He didn't seem to have any friends, and his agent handled all his business (her mind flashed back to Quentin – something hidden. The man had been unconscionably disconcerted over the information requested about his client. No, he wasn't an easy man to contact. A meeting out of the question.)

The train stopped at Reading. The Photographer made no move to alight, but merely stretched his long frame as the woman across from him got off. He gazed into the middle distance, seeming oblivious to his surroundings, deep in thought. So they were going to Oxford.

That made sense, given the Photographer's penchant for libraries and museums. She had followed him to the British Museum, dodged him through the great stacks of the British Library. Perhaps he was visiting the Bodleian? She had never been to Oxford before, but had heard of the famous collection.

Finally the train had reached Oxford. She nearly lost him leaving the station – the front was wide open, and she had had to wait until he was almost out of sight before following him down the street he had taken. They had reached the Museum of Natural History, crossed through the high light chamber with its wrought iron filigrees and dinosaur skeletons, when he disappeared down the back and she had come into the dark chamber that housed Pitt Rivers' artefacts.

A balcony or mezzanine floor ran along one side of the room, overlooking the display cases. She had gone up there, and watched him from above, seen him wander restlessly through the narrow aisles as though searching for something; and then, seem to find what he was looking for. He appeared to relax into a different state as he stood rapt by the contents of a certain case near the far end of the room. He stood there as if in communion with something. She sensed that that whatever was in the case was very important to him, and was the key to this mysterious man, the journey a kind of pilgrimage for him. If there was ever to be a time to approach him, it would have to be now. The checkerboard of cases stretched out below her, inviting her participation in the game. She had gone down to make his acquaintance.

"Excuse me – sorry to disturb you, would you happen to know the time?"

The question jerks him out of his reverie – unexpected here where there're so rarely other visitors; he can count those he's seen when visiting on the fingers of one hand. He spun around, as if shocked by tazer, from his position in front of a case containing many skulls and tiny shrunken heads.

She has never been this close to him before. Never stood face to face, measured herself against his bulk. He's a little bit taller than her, seeming massive with wide shoulders, the trademark long black coat; his dark hair. Cold, cold eyes.

"Four thirty-six."

"Oh, is it that late already? – The museum closes at five. What do you think of it – it's a crazy place isn't it? Fascinating. These heads are a bit gruesome."

She trails off in the face of the Photographer's enquiring glance. What does he see?

- Seen her before somewhere? Where? That hair – rings a bell.

"Sorry – am I distracting you? So do you know much about them? I'd be interested in anything you can tell me. They're not very well labelled are they?"

Definitely seen her somewhere before. Where. Think. Play for time. He can sense something important happening.

"They're from South America. *Tsantas*. War trophies of the Jivaro Indians mostly. Those that aren't fakes, of course. There was a bit of a craze for them in the twenties – you could buy a shrunken head for about $25 in those days, and have it sent by mail order. Pitt Rivers located a number of them for the collection."

A slow-dawning gleam in his eyes. The situation feels fraught as a game of blackjack, each card turning slowly, raising the margin of risk.

"Really? And do they still practise it? That's astonishing. I'd be fascinated to learn how it's done. I suppose you live in Oxford, and are terribly knowledgeable about this kind of thing? They're so small! Are there any bones inside?"

Her questions seem fairly innocent but something tells the Photographer that there's something not quite right. The girl seems slightly nervous; she's babbling – like someone casting around for something to say, spinning out the conversation for some reason that's not clear to him yet. And asking him about the heads: coincidence? Can't be. She must know something. And if she knows, does anybody else? Has he been fooling himself that he's invulnerable, that his actions are sanctioned by some higher code? Or is there something else, synchronicity, serendipity, that's caused this meeting? Apart from themselves and a sleepy guard on the balcony the museum is deserted. If there'd been anyone else there, would she have asked them the time instead, would they be standing now testing each other with this ostensibly banal conversation? He frowns slightly, but answers her question, buying himself time to think.

"No – London – but I try to visit the Pitt Rivers if I happen to be in Oxford. And you – do you live here? Do you always talk to strangers in museums?"

"Umm, not – not normally. I'm down from London too, just for the day – but I happened to have some spare time and museums fascinate me. And you looked as though you might know about the heads – I don't know what made me think so – perhaps the way you were gazing at them – as though you knew the history of each one. I'm so sorry if I've bothered you?"

She must know. Have to find out. Could she have told anyone else? Could she be silenced if it were not already too late? Not the same, killing someone like that. If she knows she'll be suspicious, on her guard. Think. THINK.

"No – not at all, although you did give me something of a start. This place is usually deserted apart from the odd school party."

"Look – they're about to close the museum, and I've got to

get back to London on the five-ten. We can talk on the train if you're going back too?"

"That would be wonderful if you're sure I'm not imposing"

"Not at all – it would be good to have some company on the journey. I can tell you all about the *Tsanta's* too."

They left the dark room and came back out into the atrium. Nina had a sudden impression of light and space after the gloomy intimacy of the artefacts rooms.

The Photographer led them on a winding route through the colleges and narrow cobbled streets of the town, so that within a couple of minutes she was completely disoriented. It was dark and cold, and a kind of mist hazed the street lamps, throwing the doorways into deep shadow and giving a feeling of desertion to the narrow alleys. Nina began to feel a little nervous, and studied the broad dark back of the man who was walking rapidly a couple of paces in front of her, so that she had to hurry to keep up with him, occasionally stumbling on the uneven cobbles.

Why was he playing along with her game? After so long spying, watching, observing every public aspect of this man's life, without ever having made his acquaintance she was a little thrown find herself following him down a dark Oxford street, about to spend over an hour in his company on the train. And who knows how much further?

His response had not been entirely as expected. He had neither brushed her off nor seemed to know her – his look reflecting the polite interest of a stranger. Somehow, she had expected a shock of recognition in his eye – that she should have been so intimate with him over the preceding weeks, and he have no sense of her, was startling.

Yet this was apparently the case. The Photographer had not spoken since leaving the museum and she followed him obediently – wondering if he knew that she had been his constant shadow, that this would be the second train journey they would share that day.

When they reached the station the train for London was standing on the platform. The Photographer made straight for the first-class carriages, and chose an empty compartment with a sliding door. The rest of the train was crowded with commuters, but she noticed, as she had before, that the Photographer seemed to carry an air of solitude with him. They sat down facing each other in the compartment, still silent. With a whistle the train departed for London.

37. Journey back from Oxford

Nina sat opposite the Photographer, the grey scenery rushing past the window forming a temporary distraction, the carriage quiet and deserted apart from the two of them.

After days of hiding, watching and constructing narratives in which they were connected she found herself at a complete loss for words. Those cold eyes, now turned on her, stifled the conversation in her throat and unnerved her. She felt as nervous as a teenager on a first date. In person his presence was even more forceful, almost hypnotic in its intensity. Unable to hold his gaze she looked down, wondering if the gesture appeared coy. Beneath the table their feet were mere inches apart. She had never been this close to him before.

Still the Photographer said nothing, merely examining her with his eyes, twin gimlets pinioning her in place. Was this his manner with his subjects? Was this the technique that enabled him to strip the artifice from the image, exposing the hidden corruption beneath the trappings of society? She sensed that she would have to go carefully here. Neither could make reference to her surveillance of him. He had his own agenda.

His opening gambit made no reference to their relationship, nor showed that he was even aware of it. He quickly assumed the persona that he had decided to use with her; the artist discussing his work, and shot her a leading question.

"So tell me about yourself – where does this interest in long-dead cultures spring from?

"I went to art college – studied photography. I've always

been interested in the representation of the body after death, mummification and all that. So I read around a bit more than was strictly necessary. Actually, I've got a small confession to make. I know who you are. I recognised you at the museum. You're S... Some of your work was on our curriculum at college. I did kind of ask you the time because I'm a big fan of your work. And then when I saw you standing there, I guess I just felt like I needed to make a connection with you. That sounds really cheesy."

Nina kept her tone deliberately light-hearted.

"And of course it just occurred to me that I didn't introduce myself. I'm Nina." She held out her hand, somewhat self-consciously, for him to shake.

The Photographer surprised her (and himself) by leaning over the outthrust hand and placing a dry kiss on its back. He paused a minute to inhale her scent. Lifting his head so that he was only a few inches away from her, he drawled, "Charmed I'm sure".

As he said this she could see him watching her, intently, as though searching for the slightest signs that would tell him she was lying. Was that a tremor in her eyelid? She tried to keep her gaze level and continued in a rush.

"I think it was all that work with the body and perspective, all those shadows on the glass. It said something to me about truth, and lies – which aren't untruths, but different versions of reality. Like most photography today is trying to be topical – but it doesn't need to be about events, or people, because at the end of the day they're all just accidents. Does that make sense? I've thought so much about this stuff, but it's hard to explain it."

The Photographer looked away out of the window, as if

considering, his profile fuzzed into double outlines by the train window. Then he turned quickly, as if he had decided to play her at her own game.

"Ah – so you've seen some of the old stuff. That's all done with now. My new work is a big departure. I've been looking deeper. Imagine. Perhaps there is a real truth, and all the interpretations you talk about are just veils concealing it? Has that possibility occurred to you? I'm trying to show that each of these versions of reality is a lie that we are awaking from. Maybe this world is a mass hallucination, and we need to be shaken back into ourselves – and that is why we have languages upon languages, proliferating as the human race fragments, and mass communications that just raise the level of Babel, the confusion. Maybe we need to cut through all that and realise that it's a drug, an opiate – that there is a single language out there that is the key to the single truth that we are powerless to comprehend? How would you go about finding that language?"

What was he asking her? She sensed that this conversation, so incongruous with the situation, was in fact a code that he was inviting her to break.

"That depends on what language it is you're talking about. A visual language?"

He shook his head. "Not necessarily – I think you would need to induce a certain state of mind to comprehend it though, a state where you could see and hear things differently."

"You mean with drugs? I don't know. I'm not sure if I agree with that. You always think you've discovered the secret of the universe and then when you come down it's all just chemicals, organic soup. Isn't it funny, all this time I've been making up my own interpretations of your work – and now we seem to be talking completely at cross-purposes? So what are you working on at the moment? You haven't shown anything for a while, have you?"

"Funny, my agent keeps asking me the same question. And I always give him the same answer: sorry, I can't tell you, I'd have to kill you. Luckily he appreciates my sense of humour."

She smiled at his joke, and waited for him to continue.

"Anyway, I'm working on a series of portraits – you might say they're visual representations of verbal snapshots, observations of the subject over a period of time. I'm piecing together a language out of patterns. It's hard to describe. Maybe you'd like to see some of my latest work? No one's seen it yet. I'd be very interested in your reaction."

"I'd love that. In fact I'd be honoured, if you're sure you don't mind?"

"No, not at all – in fact if you're not doing anything later, maybe we could go straight back to my place? I'm sure I could rustle us up something to eat as well."

Enough. She had to do it now; the days and weeks of watching from doorways – not just the Photographer but others as well – had come to fruition in this, she realised.

Was it about sex? Nina looked at the Photographer suddenly with different eyes. She'd always imagined hers was a cerebral obsession; following and observing, and extrapolating, and creating a perfect picture of the subject. Suddenly she wondered: is all this driven by biology? Do I just fancy him? The offer of dinner made her pause, and she searched his expression for a subtext. The Photographer in his turn wondered if he had gone too far in his attempt to portray the genial host and come across as a lecher.

Both went a bit red in the face and they were quiet for a

while, on the last stretch of the journey to London, each thinking their own thoughts. The Photographer sneaked quick looks at the girl as she looked out the window, evaluating her pale skin, the freckles that scattered themselves over her hands and face. He could see in her glance that she was used to concealing her thoughts – and wondered whether she was a consummate actress, with a reason for accepting his invitation so quickly or just, as she said, a fan of his work who had jumped at the chance for an exclusive preview. Either way, she was his. It was not his way to choose a victim after so accidental an acquaintance, but he was beginning to reach a dead end with the vagrants and drop-outs that were his usual targets. Gerard had been a new beginning; a break from routines which were becoming stale, without providing any real insights. Yes, she would do nicely – but first he needed to find out a few more things about her.

"Do you live alone? I find solitude concentrates the mind wonderfully when I'm trying to work. I suppose that makes me a bit of a loner, but then perhaps you need to be completely alone before you can see clearly."

"Yes – well, kind of – I live in a squat with a bunch of other people, but you could hardly describe it as communal. They pretty much take pains to remain anonymous. I think I prefer it that way – no one keeping track of your movements. People think you're odd if you like to be alone too much, I find."

"The vast majority of people seem to think anyone who isn't exactly like themselves is odd – perhaps it consoles them for their lack of originality. Anyway – here we are."

The train was pulling into Paddington, lights shining over the empty platform, the old station like some pre-war cathedral, with its glass roof and wrought iron supports. They stood up ready to alight and fight the crowds on the platform. Stepping off the train the Photographer ignored the other passengers and strode purposefully in the direction of the taxi rank with Nina in tow. They could hardly get home now quickly enough to suit him, and as soon as they were seated in a cab he began talking rapidly. Nina wondered if he were nervous.

"It will be interesting to see what you make of what I've been working on lately – to get your perspective on it. It's a bit of a departure for me you see, and I suspect it's not the kind of thing that will appeal to any kind of mainstream audience."

"I'm not sure that I'm exactly typical, but I'll do my best. It's not every day a famous photographer asks my opinion! So where are we headed then?"

"South London, my apartment. I've got my studio and darkroom there. Hopefully it shouldn't take too long – looks like we've just missed the rush-hour."

Lights flashed past the windows, vehicles rushing past each other, crossing lanes, swerving at the last possible moment. They had left Marble Arch behind, and were speeding down Park Lane with its ballrooms and Ferrari showrooms; Hyde Park stretching dark and emptied along one side.

They drew up to a traffic light and the Photographer gazed into the darkness whilst Nina studied the windows of the Spy Shop, and thought about bugging the Photographer's apartment.

Inside she felt tense with the knowledge of something born on the journey from Oxford, a change in their relationship. Up until now he had communicated with her by tacit messages, signs that she had read in his behaviour whilst stalking him. But now they were in direct communion – and still he persisted in pretending that there was no connection between them, treating her with the politeness of a stranger. She felt his presence as a physical touch, a sensation on her skin, a tingling between her legs as though his fingers were resting there.

38. At the Apartment

The Photographer was feeling far less nervous now – realising that at the end of the day she was not that different from Gerard. The two of them, on the surface quite dissimilar, had more in common than had first appeared. Both were equally disconnected from the world, border-dwellers, and therefore vulnerable. He dismissed his concerns about anyone noticing her disappearance, and settled comfortably into the routine that he had developed over long practice.

She trusts me, he thought, fingers templed under chin in a gesture common with him – she trusts me like the others, she sees this personality, donned like a disguise just for her, and thinks I've given her a glimpse of the real person.

They crossed the river, drove down dark streets glinting with damp, and arrived, rain misting the pavement with steady drizzle, at the Photographer's apartment.

He paid the taxi off whilst she waited on the pavement, nervous in this familiar street and pretending that she didn't know exactly which block was his, recognise the stale smell of the hall. Behind the door was an apartment she could only guess at – the heavy drapes had concealed even the slightest glimmer of light, the slightest gap through which its contents could be glimpsed.

The Photographer opened the door for her and bowed ironically.

"Welcome to my humble abode."

Nina forced a smile.

He pointed her towards a chair, and left the room – "I'll make us some coffee." Nina sat down restively, then jumped up and followed him. He was bending over the counter, fiddling with the coffee machine.

It was a small kitchen; bachelor sized, with an incongruously large stove, an Aga or somesuch, along one side. A quiet step brought her to him. She reached out a hand and touched his cheek. He froze as she moved her fingers slowly down his jaw, and fitted herself into the hollows of his back, holding him in the cage of her arms. She was just tall enough to lay her head on his shoulder and whisper in his ear.

"It wasn't just a fascination with your work that made me approach you in the Pitt Rivers – you know that, don't you? You feel it too? Isn't that why you really brought me back here?"

The Photographer was completely rigid. It hadn't happened quite this way before – this was not part of the program. His thoughts flew around the network of rules that he had built for himself like rats trying to escape from a maze – her slight breasts pressed against his shoulder blades. Her touching him. The seconds passed, he stood there frozen. What to do: was this some kind of game? What was her strategy? What should be his?

He dropped his hands and grabbing her wrists, spun around and ducked out of the circle of her arms. Her eyes were level with his, but there was no fear in them.

"Please don't. Let's talk about this. Maybe you have the wrong idea about all of this, There's nothing mysterious about my motives, I just wanted to talk to you. Here, I haven't finished making the coffee – why don't you wait in the sitting room, and I'll be through in a minute?" He kept his tone level, calm and conversational. She had to buy this. He kept his back to the counter whilst she took the step that brought her to the door. He didn't think she would have noticed anything. It was all part of it.

As soon as he was sure she was following his instructions, he shouted through to the other room.

"Milk and sugar?"

"Just black please, two sugars."

He stirred the powder into her coffee, and brought the two cups through to where she was sitting.

Nina was perched on the edge of a seat looking pensive and uncomfortable. All good – he could take the upper hand. He handed her the coffee and took a chair facing her, but not too close. She took a sip of the coffee, grimaced at the temperature and put it on the floor to cool a little. Not enough of a sip for the sedative to work... The Photographer felt tension spring in him, his nails cutting into his palms. He forced himself to relax, fingers uncurling. He placed his hands deliberately on his knees, where she could see them.

"You don't have anything a little stronger do you?" She smiled at him, slightly mocking. She was playing with him. He should never have brought her back. He wanted to kill her there and then, lunging across the gap that separated them to wrap his fingers around that slender thoat, but kept his voice level.

"What's your poison?"

"Oh anything; I'm probably pretty much immune to most of them by now: Whiskey for preference."

The Photographer stood up and went across to the cabinet where he kept spirits and tumblers – mostly for effect, since he didn't drink himself. "Is Jamesons OK?"

"Sure, that's fine."

She brought the cup across, balanced carefully so as not to spill the hot coffee. As she moved the Photographer caught himself noticing things about her, little details; despite her height she had a childlike quality about her, a slight gawkiness perhaps contributed to by her long limbs. He sensed bravado, and curiosity. Awareness of these things made him somewhat nervous. It didn't do to become identified. It made everything that much more complicated; but there could be no going back now.

The Photographer poured a judicious shot of whiskey into the cup, the liquid swirling up almost to the rim. For a few moments they were just a handspan apart, and then he capped the bottle, stepping back to replace it in the cabinet. Nina stood there for a few moments, sipping the coffee to give herself time, and walked back to her chair, once again balancing the cup precariously. As she sat down her eyes looked a little glazed, and she grabbed at one of the wide armrests to steady herself. The sharp eyes of the Photographer missed none of this – but it would be far too early to feel the chemicals only now entering her bloodstream, the whiskey, sugar and strong coffee concealing the taste of something sharper. He took small sips from his own cup, watching her over the brim.

The hot liquid was cooling, and Nina was conscious of a hollow space in her belly that had not been filled since the day before; her eating habits had always been irregular to say the least. It was to this that she attributed the slight feeling of dizziness; the blurred edges that made the room seem slightly unreal. As she looked up over the rim of her cup she was aware of the Photographer watching her. Was his gaze unnaturally intense? It seemed that his eyes were bright with anticipation of something, but also heavily guarded. The whiskey would explain the slightly rough taste to the coffee, the warmth in the pit of her stomach. But not the strange feeling that started in her groin and made her feel as though all her muscles were relaxing involuntarily.

Nina stood up and took one step towards the Photographer. Another. She felt heavy, as though walking at altitude, her feet blocks of concrete somehow attached to the ends of her legs, her consciousness riding high and looking out from the windows of her eyes. She took another step, which barely reduced the distance between them – although she could have sworn that they had not been sitting that far apart. The black shutters closed in fast until she was looking at the Photographer down the length of a tunnel, and she felt herself falling.

When he saw the girl lose her balance the Photographer sprang up from his seat and threw both arms around her. Grunting with the effort, he lowered her carefully to the floor, adrenaline powering his muscles So she was just like the others – just as trusting and stupid...

Nina felt his hands grasping her arms, the hard fingers digging into her soft flesh. She felt him seat her back in the chair, and lie her head on the rest. She wondered if she had fainted, but suspected that he had spiked her with some kind of drug – the rest of her body felt as distant as the moon, although she could hear him breathing.

She felt straps, smooth and cool, encase her wrists and ankles, and a part of her mind panicked – but at the same time it didn't seem that important. Another strap crossed her chest and then she felt her head grasped firmly in his large hand as another went around her neck, and he fumbled with a head-clamp. It was too late to stop him now. Her only hope was to make it appear that she was helpless as she seemed.

The Photographer had some preparations to make, preparations that would normally have been a preliminary to bringing a victim back to the house. But this one had been too unexpected, throwing everything awry. Too much could be forgotten, essential stages left out. He bent down and pulled an eyelid back – did he dream it, or was there some resistance there, the slightest flutter? No – the eyeball was rolled back in the socket, glazed and unseeing. Good.

He went back through to the kitchen to assemble the tools for the first stage, preparing her for the tattoos with which she would be marked; the story of her journey out of life.

39. Death Rites

The body of the Explorer lay on the pallet. In death and stripped of his clothes his wasted frame was laid bare, crisscrossed with a tracery of old scars. He looked fragile and impossibly ancient, as if a hundred years had passed and served to mummify him; yellow skin stretched tight over his once large frame. The Speaker looked at the corpse dispassionately. The spirit of the Explorer was long gone, banished as his heart gave out and left his body an empty husk. Their main task now was to ensure that his spirit was sent on its journey with proper ceremony.

The Caposcripti death rites are long and protracted, and can take up to eight days and nights to complete. If it were not for the fear that if the Explorer's unquiet spirit would roam the jungle, tricking the unwary, and looking for a new body to inhabit, then there would be no question of taking the trouble for a stranger. The Caposcripti are not a sentimental people – they cannot afford to be.

The Explorer was decapitated with his own machete, and his body taken into the jungle to be disposed of. The Speaker carefully threaded a length of thong through his mouth and down through his open throat, and then strung it above the fire. The smoke would keep insects from devouring the head before the Speaker had finished his preparations. He would be gone for two days, which he would spend gathering the required plants, meditating and fasting – purifying himself for the ceremony ahead.

He left instructions with the Tribe for a large quantity of smooth stones to be gathered from the river, of varying sizes but as round as possible. They also collected many baskets of sand and began to make preparations for a feast. They laid a bed of sand on a cleared patch near the river, and built up a big fire with wood and brush, which they lit through the use of several flat stones, some tinder and a dried branch. On top of the fire they laid large round pebbles from the river.

When the Speaker returned just after dawn he was carrying a large pot fashioned from the reddish clay that was everywhere beneath the jungle floor, and hardened in the fire and sun. He placed this on the ground, filled it with water, and began to drop in stones that had been heated in the fire. After a short while the water began to steam and bubble, and the Speaker carefully removed the stones with a pair of wooden tongs. Then he picked up the Explorer's head and placed it in the pot. He lit one of his hot cigarettes and blew smoke over the pot, all the while chanting and whistling invocations to the Explorer's spirit. The surface of the water was soon covered with a greasy scum, as the Speaker kept adding more hot stones to keep the water at an even temperature.

After half an hour of this treatment he removed the head from the pot and placed it on a pile of sand, which had also been heated with the stones from the fire. The first stage of the process was complete, the skin hung slack and greasy from the bones of the Explorer's face.

In order to shrink the head to the size of those that the Explorer had occasionally seen since he had been living with the Tribe, the skull had first to be detached from the skin. The Speaker achieved this with the utmost care, first shaving all of the hair from the head, and rubbing the whole scalp with a paste made from charcoal and herbs.

Once the head was completely hairless, the skin was removed from the skull by making a long incision with a sharpened palm knife, from the crown to the base of the skull down to the bone. The skin was then turned back on both sides and peeled from the bony structure with great care.

The Speaker carefully severed the connections to eyelids, ears and nose, working quickly and precisely to ensure that the skin was as little damaged as possible by this process. This tricky part of the procedure completed, he removed the entire skin from the skull, leaving it naked save for the blue eyes, curiously denuded now in their bony sockets, and the Explorer's few remaining teeth.

The Speaker turned the skin inside-out, and scraped the fragments of flesh and fatty tissue from the inside with the edge of the knife, following this by applying a pungent smelling paste and rubbing it in well. This done, he turned the skin right side-out again and, carefully laying the head face-down, cushioned by a mat of moss, filled it with hot sand. Another Caposcripti handed him bamboo needles and palm leaf fibres (which the Tribe also used to make hammocks, ropes, hand axes and fishing lines). He used the sharp needles to push the palm fibre through the skin until he had sewn up the mouth and stitched the eyelids closed. Small bamboo spikes were inserted in the eyebrows and the bridge of the nose to stop the features from dropping. He plugged the nose and ears with soft fibres. There must be no return gateway for the man's spirit.

All of this was carried out in perfect silence, with only the sounds of the jungle and the occasional crackle of the fire to break the spell. Even the children of the Tribe, normally playful and noisy, were completely mute and still.

Once the Speaker had finished, he held in his hands a slightly smaller version of the Explorer's head, strangely youthful and peaceful in death, the deep lines and wizened skin smoothed by his ministrations. The Speaker communed silently with the head for some time, marshalling his thoughts and preparing the death chant with which he would free the Explorer's spirit. Then he began to sing the history of the man since he had been with the Tribe, and what little he knew of his life before.

The fire was banked up with fresh fuel, to heat the sandy bed upon which it had been set. In the shimmering heat of the flames, the Speaker was sweating freely, and the miniature thermals created by the blaze distorted the air, causing his tattoos to twist and shimmer with a life of their own. He threw herbs on the fire to give out a thick billowing smoke, and swapped the hot sand for stones, which he rolled out of the empty shell so that they rattled in counterpoint to his chanting. The stones got ever smaller as the head reduced, until he was inserting tiny pebbles into the opening that had been left in the neck hole, rattling them around like dice in a cup. Time and time again the cool, slightly greasy sand was poured from the head, and hot smooth stones rolled around the inside. Flat stones were rubbed all around the outside, sliding easily over the smooth skin, for the contracting pores continually oozed fine oil. The Speaker continued this process throughout the night, until his voice was hoarse and his eyes raw with smoke. By the next morning the skin was as smooth and hard as tanned leather, the head itself the size of a grapefruit. The resemblance to the Explorer was quite extraordinary – every feature was preserved, and the deep lines that had marked his face had faded and refined until they they were a bare tracery, on deeply tanned skin the colour of mahogany.

The clearing was bright with the rays of the morning sun, and the mist rising from the jungle mingled with the smoke from the fire to give everything a pearly quality. The Speaker hung up the head by its thong and sat back on his heels. At last they were safe from the spirit of the Explorer, whilst he was free to be reborn, having cast off the shackles of flesh and breath.

40. Waking Up

When he returned she was just as he had left her, almost as though asleep with just a faint line of drool on the corner of her mouth and the slack features to tell the truth. He laid the ink, the needles and the long straight razor on a small table that he had placed next to her chair for that very purpose, and leant forward to feel her pulse. The dose he had given her would normally have been enough to keep her under for a few hours, but she had drunk just under half of the coffee that he had given her, and the sedative would surely be affected by the whiskey that had been mixed with it. Her pulse was slow, with just the hint of a flutter, her breathing light and regular. To the tattoo ink he added just a touch of curare – hardly one part in the thousandth, but sufficient to prevent the muscles from twitching, and to anaesthetise the skin.

These preparations were just a series of sounds to Nina, half felt and reconstructed in slow motion. She heard the click of scissors, felt their cool blades against the nape of her neck, felt the softness of shaving foam, the precision of the blade following the contours of her skull, the fingers cupped in the hollows above her nape, the hair falling to drape across her fingers, the rough touch of a towel, the new coldness of her unprotected crown. A brief respite. A dawning terror. And then the thousand-fold agony of the tattoo-gun, a million needles piercing her skull, the spreading numbness oh god the blood dripping down her temples, like the thorny crown oh my god he is crucifying me, and the Photographer, intent on his work branding her with the first of the skeins of language, like a dark arachnid praying mantis needle following the places his fingers have caressed feeling and stealing the heart of her.

She knew he would certainly kill her.

She had lost all sense of time and movement, but it felt as though the night was well advanced. She wished she could open her eyes, but it felt as though she couldn't even conceive of movement. What the fuck had he given her that had paralysed her so?

She would certainly die. Death – the word was like an alarm bell returning her to herself, her heart somewhere in the far country of her body leaping in shock – and – is that a tingle in my toe? From the vibration she judged the Photographer to be somewhere around the back of her head, the whole area numbed so that she felt nothing more than a dull ache, silence but for the regular tenor of his breath and the buzzing of the needle. She guessed him intent on the pattern he was creating. Unlike a hairdresser he had not provided any mirrors so that she could view his work from behind oh god my hair…

Don't panic.

Think.

The steady pressure of the needle was to the left of the nape of her neck – he seemed to be heading down towards the top of her spine, and Nina concentrated on willing her circulation to return, willing movement to return, anything so she didn't feel so powerless, so removed. She was becoming his – he was reshaping her in some image of his own – she would no longer be herself, but something other, please god was that a tingling in my eyelids, flutter, can he see? And her whole body numb, like a giant shot of Novocain – was that a twitch in my finger?

Suddenly the pressure was gone, as if he were standing back to examine his handiwork. Walking around her like she was a model. Oh my god not my face, please not my face. Still not accepting that she would actually die. Still a part of her believing that she would escape this.

To her infinite relief it seemed like he was taking a break – she heard his heavy footsteps receding and the click of the door closing behind him. She could definitely feel sensation returning to her body, along with movement – although she hardly had the strength to move a finger. Experimentally she tested the bands he had used to strap her to the chair. They seemed to have some give in them – it felt as though if she concentrated she might be able to free one of her hands at least. But how much time did she have before he returned?

Her left arm felt as heavy as lead, but at least she was able to move it. Slim hands and years of wearing tiny bangles allowed her to arrange her fingers into slim cylinders, so that her hands became slender extensions of her wrists, the practised twist of the thumb-joint into the Venus mound, skin slippery with blood. He had obviously been careful to leave the ties loose enough to allow circulation, perhaps so he could judge by the colour of her nails whether she had gone into shock, and had not expected her to regain consciousness for some time. Now she had one of her hands free, and her ears strained to hear whether he was coming back to the room…but it seemed as though he was leaving the house – was that the clicking of the hall door closing behind him? Her right hand was free and she concentrated on freeing the left. It was a painfully slow process – she still felt weak and disconnected from her body, but the knowledge that he planned to kill her was enough to help her find reserves of strength that surprised her.

Got it.

She began to work at the strap around her neck, hands bloody and fingers encountering the ridged tattoos he had left on her scalp and down the back of her neck – the shaved skin where once had been hair.

The neck strap was fastened with a buckle which the blood made slippery and difficult to undo, but a few moments of sweating and it came free. The effort got her circulation going, and she began to feel sensation returning everywhere to her body, pins and needles and cramps shooting up her thighs and calves. The waist strap had no blood on it; removing it was the work of seconds. She bent over and started to undo the straps at her ankles, head throbbing and blood dripping from the fresh tattoos with the effort, ears straining to hear if he might be coming back. Then they too came away.

The harsh ring of the telephone nearly killed her with the shock – but when it continued without stopping she realised that she was alone in the house – unless he just wasn't bothering to answer it. As she stood up she felt waves of dizziness almost causing her to fall – but she was free!

What to do next? Escape? Should she leave and go to the police, turn him in and tell them what she knew? But a part of her recoiled from this – she had never trusted the police. And then the sound of the hall door opening again decided her, a shot of adrenaline straight to the heart; fury and terror. Picking up the heavy chair that she had been tied to she tiptoed quietly to the door, and waited for him to come through it as she knew he would, to check on her. As the door opened she brought the chair down with all her force on his head. Surprise and shock chased each other across his face and then his eyes turned up in their sockets and he fell heavily to the floor.

As the rush of adrenaline left her, blood loss and exhaustion took their toll. Nina felt the world go black for a second time.

41. A Journey for Taypi

Taypi set off before dawn on the first leg of the journey that would take him to Iquitos, and the men in the iron ships that would transport the journals back to England along with their cargoes of sarsaparilla, rubber and guano. No one was awake to see him off except the Speaker, who gave him blessings and charms to ward off evil spirits, and furnished him with the Explorer's machete. The Speaker's face was impassive as he reminded Taypi of the instructions of the Explorer, and added some of his own. Taypi was to follow the river (which the Explorer had told him was called the Pongo) downstream until it fed into another huge river, called the Amazon. The Explorer had told Taypi how to construct a raft, and suggested that this would be the fastest and safest way to travel downriver. With the last of his strength he had begun to teach Taypi a few words of Spanish, to add to the English that they had practised together, so that he would be able to communicate with any Mestizo, or settlers, that he met along the way. He was mindful that this might be risky, as many of them had good reason to fear the warlike tribes such as the Jivaros, who regularly carried off and killed settlers on their lands. He told Taypi that he should be sure to make plenty of noise when approaching a settlement, and wave the piece of white fabric that he had given him. War parties always approached silently.

To this the Speaker added admonishments to avoid any other tribes that he might find along the way, and return to the lands of the Caposcripti as soon as he had discharged his promise to the Explorer.

Taypi travelled light: his only luggage was an oilcloth parcel containing the journals and letters of introduction that the Explorer had given him, a string hammock that doubled as a bag, and a pouch containing roots and herbs in whose use the Speaker had instructed him. His step was springy as he travelled through familiar lands, going over his instructions again and again until he could have recited them in his sleep.

It was the first time that Taypi had left his people since the journey that had led him to discover the Explorer. Then Taypi had been a boy, full of the desire to prove himself a man. This time he felt the heavy burden of adulthood and his promise to the Explorer weighing on him, and he was full of misgivings. Nevertheless there was enough of the child still there for him to feel that he was setting out on a great adventure, and he was confident in his ability to deal with anything that the jungle might throw at him. His fears were more concerned with loneliness, which could drive a man to lose his judgement, and about the spirits that might try to entice him from his path, for they were jealous of life.

He rubbed *anato* and *uruku* into his skin to repel the mosquitoes and sand flies that swarmed everywhere, and doggedly followed the stream in its long journey to the great water, as the Explorer had instructed him to. He subsisted on guavas and on the many different types of nuts and fungi that he had learn to forage from a young age, and occasionally speared a fish or discovered a cache of turtle's eggs on the sandy beaches of the river. He was healthy and strong, and fell victim neither to hunger nor illness, but after a while the solitude began to prey on him.

On the edges of his vision he could see the jewelled dances of hummingbirds and butterflies, and began to discern patterns in their flight that spoke to him of the Caposcripti language. He wished that the Speaker was there so that he could ask him the meaning of these things, or the Explorer, who had his own theories to explain their dances, all bound up with the way that species changed over time. He had explained many new ideas to Taypi, and told him of the naturalists who had travelled the great continents of the Americas and written down their observations. Maybe Taypi would meet one of these naturalists on his journey, and he could give him the package that the Explorer had entrusted to him. For although he was fired with the enthusiasm and the curiosity of the young he did not think that he would want to live for long amongst the Explorer's tribe – even after this short time his people's absence was like a pain in his spirit.

Although the Explorer's head had been reduced according to the Caposcripti rituals, Taypi feared that his unquiet spirit would seek him out from the afterworld if he did not carry out the promise that he had made. The Explorer's lips had been sewn shut with the sacred chords, but Taypi still saw them struggling to shape those final words in his dreams. No, no matter how long the journey, or dangerous the way, he could not fail in the task that had been set him, or he would be like the Wandering Jew that the Explorer had told him of when he was well, doomed to walk the world forever.

After a time the river became too deep and swift to wade in, and Taypi decided that it was time to make a raft. The Explorer's machete made this task much easier, as it was far sharper than the palm knives of his people. Although he had never constructed a raft before (the Caposcripti rarely used them) he had been told how it was done, and knew which creepers were good for binding, and how to weave palm fibres to make a rope. He bound the trunks of balsa trees together and cut himself a long pole to steer the craft. This whole operation took two days, and at the end of it Taypi was exhausted. He crawled into the fork of a tree, made himself a bed of moss and leaves, and fell into a dreamless sleep, punctuated by the din of cicadas and tree frogs.

The next day he gathered bunches of aguavas, nuts and other fruits and made neat bundles out of the wide flat leaves of the plantain tree. He lashed these to the raft along with the journals and letters, which the Explorer had wrapped in oilcloth, and stood back critically to view his handiwork. The raft was ready. It was just big enough for him to stand or lie on, and floated low in the water with the ballast of supplies he had loaded on it. He made an offering of papayas to the river spirits and poled himself away from the bank.

As it turned out, making the raft had been much easier than controlling it. Constant vigilance was necessary to avoid sandbanks and whirlpools, and the logs and other detritus that swirled in the brown water so that you could hardly see it until you were right on top of it.

The raft took many knocks, so that Taypi was sometimes forced to lay himself flat and grasp the bindings whilst it bucked and shuddered. He was constantly soaked by the water splashing over the side, and by the sudden rainstorms that came down so hard that the surface of the river turned into a boiling cloud of mist and made breathing difficult. Earth temporarily became a place of water, filling his eyes and lungs so that he was chilled to the bone and thought he would grow gills like a fish. After these showers the river became swollen and angry, and his raft was rushed pell-mell with the current, but he made steady progress downriver. The showers rarely lasted for long, and provided him with fresh water to drink, which he collected in cannonball gourds. The sun soon returned with fiery heat and dried both himself and the surface of the raft as if the rain, and the thunder and lightning had never been.

Just as he had begun to feel confident in his control of the raft

Taypi nearly came to grief. The river had widened, with red mud cliffs along one side where the land had fallen away in the floods. The current here was very rapid, and Taypi kept the raft as close to the bank as he dared, to avoid being swept away. But as he turned a bend the raft was suddenly and swiftly taken by the current and flung into the centre of the river. Taypi nearly lost his balance, but clung to the fibres that held the raft together and managed to stay on. The pole fell into the water and was swept out of sight.

Taypi was carried along pell-mell until the raft hit a large obstruction. A temporary island had been created twenty feet or so from the bank by an earlier landslide, where a large chunk of riverbank, including a tree that had happened to be growing there, had detached itself during the rains. The island had grown in size as brush collected on the upstream shore, and formed a dense floating mat. It was this that had snagged the raft.

Taypi shifted his position slightly, but the raft held solid. He rocked back and forth as much as he dared, but there was no movement. It seemed to be fairly firmly wedged, and he cursed the moment of inattention that had led to the loss of the pole. Not only was he now stuck on this island, unable to push the raft away, but he wouldn't be able to navigate towards the bank with any safety. He sat up and considered his options. He could try and swim to the nearest bank. It was mid-morning, and not a particularly dangerous time for swimming (the piranhas and other carnivorous fish tended to swarm at dawn and dusk) but the river here was strange to him, and the unpredictable currents made it risky. He would have to try and cut a new pole from the brush and flotsam that had built up to form the island.

Taypi unrolled a coil of palm rope from around his waist and lashed the raft to a sturdy trunk as best he could. Then with infinite care, and keeping his centre of balance as low as possible, he crept off the raft and onto the floating mass of junk that the river had deposited there. In amongst the tree branches, vines and other vegetable matter were the skeletons of animals that had been swept along the river and drowned. Small plants had taken root and begun to carpet the temporary island so that footing was treacherous, and Taypi had to take great care not to cut his bare feet, toughened though they were by a lifetime without shoes.

All of a sudden he heard a shrill song of alarm, coming from somewhere by his feet. When he looked down he saw a tiny monkey, no larger than his hand, curled in a crevice between two branches. It looked shrunken, as though it were dead, and certainly not capable of making the shrill noise that appeared to be coming from it. As Taypi looked closer he realized that an even tinier monkey clung to its neck, frantically trying to rouse its dead mother. Taypi reached down and felt the warm body. The creature was shrieking in terror, and he felt its heartbeat thudding against his fingers. He'd seen these monkeys in the jungle – his people called them the 'little lion sagui' – but they were so small and so shy that he'd only ever caught the most fleeting glimpse of one before. Taypi drew his hand back slowly. He didn't want to frighten the little creature to death.

"You and I are both trapped here, Sagui. Perhaps if I find a pole for the raft I'll take you with me, eh? You certainly won't survive here on your own. There's not much for a little monkey like you to eat. And not much for me either."

Taypi stood up and continued looking through the brush, Eventually he found a branch that would do and dragged it back to the raft, where he set to work cutting it down to size. The sun was blazing overhead by now, and he was hot and thirsty. He cut open a stick of raw cane and took a long slug of the sweet and refreshing juice inside. Then he remembered the tiny monkey. He scrambled back over the brush to where he had left it, guided by the shrill song that started up again as the monkey heard him approaching. Taypi reached down and carefully plucked the little creature from its dead mother's neck. He cupped it between his hands and made his way back to the raft, feeling it gradually calming in the warm dark space, although it still trembled uncontrollably.

When he had got back to the raft again he tried to put the sagui down, but it squealed and clung to his fingers so that he couldn't bring himself to do it. Then he had an idea. He lifted the little monkey up to the long queue of hair that grew at his crown. It seemed to get the idea immediately and transferred its grip from his fingers to the hair, hanging on quite happily and settling itself in with a birdlike chirrup. It was so light that Taypi had to put his hand up to check it was still there, and it seemed to fall asleep immediately.

Taypi stood up and, grasping the makeshift pole, positioned it against the brush and pushed with all his might. The raft moved fractionally and then settled back in, but he was heartened. He pushed again, throwing the full weight of his body behind the pole. The raft bucked but stayed solid. He realised that the rope still bound it to the brush and felt very foolish. He quickly untied the knots he'd made, coiled the rope up again, tied it down and shoved the raft off into the current. He steered around the island using the pole, and did his best to direct the raft towards the bank. After a while he found himself in a slower current and was able to relax a bit. He steered the raft along the bank until he found a tree growing low over the water that he could moor the raft to, and set about making himself a meal of fruit and fish that he tickled out of the water. The little monkey woke up and scampered down his arm at the smell of the fruit. Taypi gave him some and smiled at how enormous the morsel of papaya looked in its tiny paws.

Now that he had a travelling companion Taypi felt less lonely. He found himself talking to the little creature more and more, and spilling out his concerns about the enormous task he'd been given. The Explorer had told him that it would take less time for him to find the settlement on the river than it had taken the Explorer to travel to the lands of the Caposcripti, as the river coming down from the mountains would take him there. All Taypi had to do was follow the river downstream for twenty days, and he would find Iquitos: a settlement of some three hundred and fifty people, along with a bustling port where ocean-going steamships called to pick up sarsaparilla, tobacco and salt fish, before returning down the Amazon to Brazil, and the sea – an unimaginable distance away, at the other side of the continent.

At night he saw the red eyes of caiman glinting on the banks in the light of the moon and the stars, and heard the splashes as they slid into the water around him. The surface of the water was like glass, broken only by the rings made by fish as they leapt for flies. One dusk a dozen small silver fish leapt onto the raft, and he moored so that he could cook them over hot stones. He shared them with the little monkey, along with giant grubs that he dug out of the rotten boles of fallen palm trees.

In some places trees formed a canopy over the water, where quiet anacondas waited to snag unwary prey. His pole did double duty, both for steering and for repelling the attacks of the giant reptiles, and after a while he learnt to sleep in snatches, with one eye always watching for danger. In this semi-awake state he felt as though he were travelling through a dream world, where anything were possible. It seemed as though he were living constantly in the spirit world, which he had previously visited only briefly with the aid of the Speaker's drugs and concoctions. He began to experiment with the possibilities of this, discovering that he could communicate with the Speaker, who was able to send his spirit out in the form of a toucan. He listened for the cough of the jaguar at sunset, and for the sound of the great tree trunks, which his people beat with sticks to send, coded messages to each other.

But just as he was beginning to get the hang of distant communication, his raft moved out of range of the sound – and knew that he had left the tribal lands for good, and that henceforth the jungle would get stranger and stranger to him. It was soon after this that he began to see the first signs of settlements along the riverbank. Temporary jetties had been built at the water's edge for women to wash clothes, and dugout canoes were moored to sticks that had been sunk into the riverbed. Taypi was wary of these settlements, and kept the raft as far as possible to the other side of the river. The river was very wide now, so he felt himself fairly unobserved as he was swept past the settlements on his raft. Small children playing around the canoes moored to the banks looked up as he passed, but he was gone almost as soon as they spotted him.

In this way Taypi travelled on for several more days and nights, mooring each evening as the sun fell, to find a place to sleep, with the tiny monkey clinging to his hair.

42. Exploring the Apartment

Nina came around slowly. It took her a moment to work out where she was, and then she remembered bringing the chair crashing down on the Photographer's head. She wondered how long she had been out. Her face felt stiff and crusted, and putting her hand to her head, she felt the ridges from the tattoos, the blood on them long since dried.

She looked across at the Photographer. He lay still, his body unnaturally twisted, in the same position as he had fallen. He did not appear to be breathing. Around his head was a pool of blood, which had spread out and soaked into his clothes. It clung to the polished wooden floor and shone dully in the dim light. She forced herself to reach and touch him, to confirm what she already knew. His hand was cold, the fingers beginning to stiffen. She had never killed anyone before, but she knew that if he had woken while she was unconscious she would now be dead. It was the purest luck that the blow from the chair had been sufficient to kill him.

She pulled herself together, raising herself to her hands and knees. She'd never killed anyone before. He was dead and now she was a murderer. She had never killed anyone before. Now how did that feel?

"Jesus, that's not going to go down to well at the next confessional, is it Nina? 'Bless me father for I have sinned; it's been seventeen years since my last confession. I killed a man, Father. And I'm not sorry – it was me or him.' Survival. If it hadn't been him... She stepped over his body, through the door and found herself in a corridor. She felt a burning need to wash the blood away, the remnants of his touch. Not the bathroom though. She flinched at the prospect of seeing her reflection. No mirrors yet. The kitchen would do.

On the counter, evidence: a sachet of powder, a few scattered grains, a tiny measuring spoon. Nina headed for the sink and turned both of the taps on full. She put the plug in and stared dully at the water as the sink filled. She held her hands just below the surface, watching as the ripples distorted them, and blood began to separate from the skin in little eddies. She reached up a hand to turn the taps off and looked around for a towel. A pristine pile of them lay folded in a recess near the sink.

Dull background of pain. Flakes of dried blood fell from her face as she winced, and floated on the surface of the water. Nina dipped one end of the tea towel in the sink, wrung it out and slowly began the work of removing the clotted blood. All around her was the dead silence of an empty house, save for the ticking of a clock, the background roar of London – or was it blood rushing in her ears? She felt curiously divorced from her own body, even as she watched the blood colour the water in the sink, forcing her to empty and refill it several times. Finally she judged she had removed all of the dried blood, while more oozed from the fresh tattoos. She grabbed another tea towel from the neat pile and wrapped it around her head before emptying the sink a final time. Suddenly she wanted nothing so desperately as a nice cup of tea.

All around her in the tiny kitchen was a profusion of cupboards and drawers. Where to start? On one of the surfaces was a shining kettle. It seemed logical that tea-making ingredients would be close to hand. Once Nina had filled it with fresh water and switched it on she started opening the cupboards and drawers, looking for anything that might resemble tea bags. By the time the kettle had boiled she had found some, and a cup, and made herself some tea.

She sat down on the kitchen floor, arms wrapped around her knees and tea cupped between her hands. She noticed they were shaking.

She must be in shock. A part of her mind knew this, but the various tasks had kept that part occupied whilst the rest went on automatic. Now she felt herself shuddering with reaction, and the shock kicked in. She put the tea down and went through into the sitting room to find something stronger, stepping over the body of the Photographer as she did so. She would have to find somewhere else to put him.

The drinks cabinet was open as the Photographer had left it, and stocked with bottles of whiskey and other spirits that looked as though they had never been opened. Nina grabbed one and took it back into the kitchen. Pouring a large slug of whiskey in her cup of tea, she sat down again to think. Then picking herself up, she began the search.

～

It had taken Nina nearly thirty-six hours to piece together the hidden, secret self that had not been apparent from the outside. Her search was not systematic. She wandered through the rooms in a daze, opening doors, drawers and closets at random; his legacy to her. The flat was soon littered with things she had found – shrunken heads, notes, photographs, bunches of unidentifiable herbs, vials of prescription drugs obtained under a number of different names (or taken from his victims?) A collection of carefully labelled DAT tapes. Finding the hidden room, blacked out with its padded walls and microphones, she decided to keep him in there for the moment, whilst she worked out her next move.

She found dozens of shrunken heads. Blackened and polished they seemed hardly human – no repository for the soul. And how did they fit in? What was he going to do with them? What was he trying to discover? Was this the 'work' he had been talking about?

In another drawer she came across a series of photographs, eerie documentaries of the transformation of each subject. And notebooks, mountains of notebooks it seemed, filled with tiny handwriting. She began to get an inkling of the scale of the Photographer's activities.

She listened to the tapes, those voices coming from the darkness and silence – pleading, cajoling – by turns angry and desperate; the gradual slide into incoherence, the voices tailing off to whispers, weak entreaties. How many of them? How often had he succumbed to that need, stalked the streets for the victims that he knew no one would miss?

Each fresh proof of his actions shocked her gradually back into a sense of herself, but also intrigued her. She sat for hours in his austere study, immersing herself in the notes and tapes that she had discovered, with the tools of his work laid out around her, as if by osmosis she could discover what he was seeking.

The Photographer had stored all the heads away in sealed boxes, hidden in the dark mahogany cabinets in the living room – each one carefully labelled and cross-referenced with their notes. Nina removed them all and arranged them around the room, strangely uniform and dark with their scrolls of bluish black tattoos and the neat threads, but in close-up each one was as individual as a snowflake or a fingerprint. The sight of the heads before her was eerie: there was no denying that each had once been a human being with thoughts and feelings like her – their cries still resounded in her ears, the gradual loss of words. But as she looked at them she remembered a quote she had read once at art school, made by Paul Thek on visiting the Capuchin catacombs: "it delighted me that bodies could be used to decorate a room like flowers."

Nina wondered if the Photographer had ever taken them out and arranged them like this, if he had looked for meaning in their juxtapositions. He reminded her of Doctor Dee, and his endless search for the philosopher's stone, experiments with homunculi and alchemical marriages. But what if it was not a thing but an idea that he was looking for? Were all these shrunken heads the end in themselves, or just a by-product of something much more important?

As she stared at them she began to see different ways in which they could be arranged, groupings and structures, similarities and differences that suggested new combinations in their layout. But there was still something missing. She thought back to the beginning of her relationship with the Photographer; the days when she had watched him in the library and tried to piece together a personality and a history for him based on the books that he chose for his research. Nothing had prepared her for this though: what was the connection? Why the shrunken heads? She had never heard of a serial killer treating his victims like this before. There must be something more, something that her haphazard searching through his apartment had failed to turn up so far.

Some time later she pushed aside the last of the notes and turned off the tape recorder. She sat motionless for a long time with her mind reeling, her thoughts grappling to comprehend the mentality of a serial killer, the mind of the Photographer. She too had killed – but knew somehow that this would be the only time, and that the killing had completed something in her and launched her into the next stage in her existence. She returned to the hidden room, where his body lay just as she had left him, and dragged the stiff corpse through into the kitchen.

꿈

Nina spent a long time thinking about what to do with the Photographer's body; it had kept quite well in the small room where she had been storing it, but she knew it would become a problem soon. To begin with she didn't have the slightest idea how to dispose of a body. Well, this wasn't strictly true. Like everyone else she'd watched the cop dramas, read the stories in the papers and books by Ruth Rendell. But TV shows and detective novels are woefully short on details. For example, where do you get hold of quicklime if you don't happen to have any lying about? She ran through options in her mind. Bury him? That would involve leaving the flat, and she'd have to pick somewhere remote enough that his body wouldn't be discovered by accident. And she didn't have a car. Acid bath? Where would she get that much acid? And wouldn't it mark the bath?

Nina had a suspicion that the answer lay somewhere in the flat. The Photographer must have had some way of disposing of the bodies of his own victims: maybe she could discover it. One thing was for sure. She needed to make the Photographer disappear so thoroughly that people would assume that he had fled to another country to avoid retribution for his actions. There was only one thing for it: she would have to try and burn him.

Cutting up the Photographer was a messy job, despite the plastic she had laid out over the tiles. Both Nina and the kitchen were bloodied when she finally sat back on her haunches to look at the dismembered torso, limbs and head before her. She would have to saw some of the larger pieces, but luckily the coal box on the oven was big enough to fit the pieces into without too much more work. She suspected it wasn't the first time it had been used for incinerating bodies.

It took several hours to burn all of the pieces and clean both herself and the kitchen from top to bottom. It would be mildly suspicious that there were no fingerprints anywhere on the taps or surfaces, but the main thing was that no trace was left of her presence. Nina went back through to the sitting room and began to scrub the wooden floor, to remove any traces of blood.

Finally she made a great heap of the heads, the notebooks, tapes, and all of the other grim paraphernalia of the Photographer's experiments in the centre of the dark polished floor. Viewed in totality like this it made a surreal collage. But there was still something missing. The whole was still more than the sum of these parts. Nina sat cross-legged, staring at the strange sculpture she had made. In the Photographer's notes there had been mention of an Explorer, a tribe, a hidden language. She leaned forward and plucked one of the notebooks from the pile, flicking through it to see if she could find the reference again. That damned tiny handwriting. It had been somewhere near the end, accompanied with sketches of strange symbols. There.

"The old man was onto something. The Caposcripti hold the key. Locked in the heads in the jungle. No one will find them now. No one else has seen the journals. Must keep it that way. The lost tongue must be mine alone."

A single reference – but it seemed to hold the whole key. In general the notebooks were not personal – the Photographer had maintained an objective tone whilst describing his atrocities. It was this that had made her notice and remember the aside.

So where were the journals? They must be somewhere in the flat – she couldn't imagine that a man as secretive as him would entrust them to anyone else.

The one room she had not turned over was his bedroom. She went down the corridor and opened the door.

Like the rest of the rooms in the house it was spartan. The same dark polished floor, the same shadows cast by windows heavily draped. There was no furniture in the room except a bed, a nightstand and a straight-backed chair. Built-in cupboards stretched along one wall.

Where to start? Nina opened the first of the doors set into the wall and peered inside. A light had come on as the door opened which threw everything into stark relief. Black suits and coats hung in neat row. A long shelf stretched above them. She started feeling the pockets of each garment, looking for any clue – but there were no books hidden there. Nothing but a few old bus tickets and dry-cleaning receipts. She dragged over the straight-backed chair and climbed up to see if there was anything on the shelf. Shoeboxes stacked neatly concealed nothing but highly polished shoes. She climbed down and moved on to the next cupboard. Shirts. Socks. Underwear. There was something unnerving about rifling through the dead man's things, the trappings of normality. And they were so very normal, after what she had discovered in the other rooms. But still no journals, no clues.

An anglepoise light was positioned on top of the simple nightstand, throwing a well of light onto the single bed when she turned it on. Under the mattress? She reached down and lifted it up. Nothing. And nothing underneath the bed but dust. Damn. She threw herself on the bed and her eye fell onto the nightstand. Surely he wouldn't keep it in such an obvious place?

She tried the drawer. It wasn't locked, but slid open silently on well-oiled runners. The cover of a book slid into view. Fuck.

A bible? Nina stared at the cover, her mind racing. A bible. A Gideon's bible at that, pilfered from some hotel room. The Photographer had not struck her as a particularly religious man. Perhaps he had kept it there for comfort?

As she reached down to pick it up she noticed it felt odd, the weight wasn't quite right. And when she opened it she realised why. The centre had been neatly cut out to leave a hiding place, inside of which was a stack of crisp fifties. Nina took them out – shit, there must be five grand there at least! – and noticed, that underneath was a key with a tag on it. On the tag was written "Paddington: 5606".

"Of course. His get-out clause. He'd never leave the journals where they could be found if someone raided the house."

Her voice sounded loud in the empty room, and Nina started guiltily. She pocketed the wad of notes and the key and went back to the sitting room. It was time for her to leave now.

Donning a pair of rubber gloves, she went around the entire apartment polishing the handles of the doors and anything else she might have come into contact with. She went back through into the sitting room with a bottle of paraffin she had found underneath the kitchen sink and soaked the pile of notebooks, tapes and shrunken heads thoroughly, before lighting it. The whole pile immediately went up with a 'wumph' of blue flames, which died down almost immediately, while yellow tongues began to lick at the corners. Nina picked up the Photographer's wallet and watch, took a last look around the apartment and let herself out through the front door. She failed to hear the click of the hall camera as the door closed behind her.

43. Meeting Sam Clements

On the afternoon of the sixth day since he had seen the first of the Mestizo dwellings Taypi realised from the increasing number of settlements and boats tied up at the river's edge that he was nearing Iquitos. Soon it would be time to abandon the raft and to put into practice what the Explorer had taught him about making words in his language.

He had been poling the raft at the side of the river, where the current was not as strong as in the middle. He guided the craft to the bank and leapt off, driving his pole deep into the mud and testing it with his weight to make sure that it was firm. He made the raft fast to the pole with his palm rope, and then began to pile brush over it to hide it from view.

He felt sad to be leaving the craft that had been the one constant since he had left his home. Travelling by raft had felt effortless and exhiliarating. The journey home was a different matter; upriver in more senses than one.

Taypi hid the raft well. Henceforth he would continue on foot. He quickly made a bundle of his possessions, ensuring that the journal was securely fastened around his waist. The little monkey woke from his doze on Taypi's queue and began to run up and down his arm excitedly. He sensed a change in the tempo of their journey.

Dusk was not too far off, so Taypi decided to find a place to camp. In the morning he would follow the Explorer's advice and walk up to the settlement with his peace flag. Taypi thought of the piece of white silk the Explorer had given him, and took a moment to dig it out. He felt its texture between his fingers, and examined the fabric. Soft and smooth as a flower petal, yet yellowed and stained like all of the Explorer's possessions. He did not doubt it possessed strong magic. He only hoped it would be enough to protect him.

He started walking with his little sagui for company. Its chattering helped fill the gap that had always been completed by the others of his Tribe in the past. This loneliness was different to what he had experienced on the spirit journey. Then it had been an adventure – a journey from boyhood to manhood, which had happened in his own backyard. Now it felt as though he was leaving himself behind completely. He had already witnessed so many strange things that he felt he would never be able to share them completely with the others of his Tribe. The Speaker would have to come up with an entirely new set of symbols to tattoo on his head – and how would future generations interpret what had been written?

But, Taypi reflected, how many Caposcripti would there be to hand down the ancient language to?

What he had seen of the riverside settlements had shown him that these foreigners were hungry for land and ate it up ravenously – like a boa that snatches a week's food in one go and then digests it slowly. They had already requisitioned vast tracts of land, which they stripped of their people and wildlife and which they would soon turn into plantations. As for the peoples that had been displaced, they had melted back into the jungle, or died in their hundreds from epidemics of smallpox, yellow fever, whooping cough and influenzas.

The Iquitos that Taypi would find was a still a sleepy hamlet of three hundred and fifty-two inhabitants and had been a Jesuit mission for the last hundred years. Settling there had been a particularly daunting task, as the missionaries faced the task of converting the fierce Iquito Indians, renowned as marksmen with their long poison-dart blowpipes. By the time Taypi arrived there were only a couple of families of Iquitos left, and they had moved way up the river Nanay.

The river had not yet receded and the hamlet stood at a fortunate juncture of the Mazan and Amazon rivers – which meant that ocean-going ships could dock there and load shipments from the interior. The area which was to become Loreto was the fabled El Dorado, long sought by the Conquistadores- but it was not gold that was to make men rich beyond their wildest dreams, but rubber. And that boom was only just beginning. Within twelve years, Iquitos would have fifteen thousand inhabitants.

Taypi stood on the cusp of an era that would change his homeland forever, and whilst he had an sense of that change, he could have no way of knowing how drastic it would be. The Speaker had seen it; it was those intimations of a diaspora that had so frightened him when he looked into the Explorer's mind.

Almost immediately Taypi began to stumble across paths worn by earlier feet, and other indications of habitation. He also smelled smoke and began to walk more carefully, skirting the edges of clearings so that he could spy them out before crossing. A little further on his caution was rewarded, as he saw a man encamped, with no effort at concealment. He had a hammock strung ready for sleeping, and appeared to be busy gutting some fish that he had caught earlier, reminding Taypi that it was too long since he himself had eaten.

Something about him reminded Taypi of the Explorer. He watched him for a while, concealed in the brush.

"All right. You can stop spying on me now, and come and introduce yerself. I ain't gonna bite ya."

Taypi struggled to make sense of the words, spoken in a strange and unfamiliar accent. There was no mistaking the man's tone though: he sounded friendly, even welcoming. Maybe he could provide the introduction Taypi needed. He remembered the white cloth, and holding his hands out wide, he stepped out of the shadows and into the clearing.

The traveler looked him up and down – from his naked and tattooed head, to the intricate patterns that covered him. Taypi gazed frankly back at him, though he had already had ample time to observe his outfit and equipment.

"Whooey boy. I been all over and I ain't never seen one o' your'ne type before. What tribe are you? Well, where's my manners. I'm Sam Clement, and you're welcome to set here awhile." He looked expectantly as Taypi sorted out the mess of split infinitives and other curiosities of grammar that peppered Sam's speech.

"I am Taypi. I came here on a raft. I am going to Iquitos."

"Well, Taypi, pleased to meet you. Take a load off there. Just set down boy. Have you come far?"

"My people live many days from here. Up the river. I come to bring papers for my friend. To men in Iquitos. They will take it to England for his family."

"I see. Well set down here apiece boy. I'm waiting for a ship meself – but I figure it's better camping out here than paying those mealy-mouthed Jesuits for my board. Are you fixing to go into Iquitos tonight?"

"No, sir. I think it better to find the Padre at morning. It is to him that I must give the papers of my friend. I sleep in the forest tonight."

"Well you're welcome to a share of my dinner, if'n you want

to eat with a crusty old traveller like me that is?"

"Thank you Sam Clements. I am hungry."

Taypi seated himself next to the fire whilst Sam Clements busied himself with roasting the fish and some plantain. Taypi felt nervous: this was only the second person he had ever spoken to who was not Caposcripti. He thought about the words he had spoken, and felt proud that the man had been able to understand him. He didn't wonder at the fact that the first person he met spoke English, rather than the Castiliano that was the *lingua franca* of the Loreto settlers.

As for Sam Clements? He reckoned that all these jungle tribes had their own languages, which he could never hope to learn. Few even spoke Castiliano. So he might just as well use his mother tongue as any. The fact that the boy spoke and understood made him very interesting indeed.

Sam Clements was a remarkable person himself. He was a street boy from San Francisco, and had never known his father. He barely knew his mother; born in a brothel, he was thrown onto the street after her murder by a disgruntled client. He had had to do a lot of things to survive in his time; travelled a lot of roads. He did not consider himself to be a bad person. But he was certainly an opportunist, and known to be unscrupulous. He could smell money.

He had come to Iquitos because instinct told him there was going to be a boom – and he wanted to see for himself what the area held. The significance of the recent free trade agreement was not lost on him. But judging from what he had seen it would be some years yet before the boom hit this sleepy little settlement. Sam Clements was after something a little less long-term. And here was a mystery. A native of a tribe Clements had never heard of, who spoke English of all things – and had a package to deliver.

What was in this package? What kind of native tribe took in a foreigner and went to the trouble of running deliveries for him? Whatever was in the package must be pretty darn important... That's what Sam thought anyway. After all this area had once been known as 'El Dorado' – hundreds had lost their lives searching for the fabled gold, for lost cities and fabulous wealth. Surely all those hopes were based on something?

"Well blame me, Taypi, but I think these critters are about ready to eat now. Help yourself."

Sam used his own knife to spear the roasted fish and plantain and heaped them onto his mess plate. Taypi thought it was a strange and unfriendly way to eat, but picked up one of the discarded plantain leaves and helped himself to what was left. His little monkey was obviously hungry too, for he ran up and down Taypi's arm in anticipation of the feast to come, letting out birdlike shrills and whistles. Taypi found himself a seat across from where Sam was ripping into his food like one half-starved, and sat down to share his dinner with the monkey. They all ate in companionable silence for a little while. Then Sam pointed his knife at Taypi's little monkey and asked, "What about your little friend here? Do your people often keep spider monkeys as pets?"

The word was unfamiliar to Taypi, but he got the gist.

"No. We find each other on the journey. Our Speaker can talk with many animals, but we do not live with them. Monkeys are not our friends, but food. This monkey's mother die... died? And I find him. So he is my friend now."

"Well, it sounds like you've come a long way from home. You need all the friends you can get. How many days were you on the raft?"

"Many, many days. And many rivers. I think it is a long way back to my people."

It was the longest speech Taypi had yet made in English – and told Sam more about him than the seemingly innocuous words conveyed. His expressive face registered every mood, and Sam Clements saw sadness, loneliness and no little fear there. He realised that the boy was afraid of the journey back. Not because the jungle frightened him. Something else was at the heart of it.

"So who was this guy anyway? Anyone I might have heard of? Only a few men crazy enough to go exploring in this jungle. Curious types have a tendency to disappear in these parts. If the natives don't get 'em, jungle fever does, or some other hazard."

"He nearly die. But Speaker bring him back. He better. Then he got sick again and did not get better. He was my friend. I miss him."

"So I guess he asked you to take letters from him to his family. That's pretty brave of you, to make such a long journey. You must have thought a whole heap of him."

"He said papers very important. Otherwise his family would not remember him. He said his… legacy… would be lost."

"Yes I see. But people round here get kinda jumpy when there's unfamiliar natives around. They might figure you're staking the joint out for a raid."

When Taypi looked at him blankly, Sam laughed and translated: "Looking at the town to see how easy it would be to attack it. The locals ain't been able to drive the Jesuits out for a century, but every so often they have a damn good go at it. I guess he gave you letters of introduction, this friend of yours? Maybe I could see my way to helping out apiece. Course there's no such thing as a free lunch in this world; I guess there'd have to be something in it for me…"

He trailed off and pinned Taypi with a cocked eyebrow.

Taypi understood he was offering to help, but wanted something in return. What that something could be he couldn't imagine; and wasn't quite sure if he trusted this stranger. Maybe it was money, which Taypi didn't quite understand yet, although he knew it was valued in this man's society. At least he hadn't asked to see the journals or the letters. The contents of the bundle seemed of no interest to him. He was just offering to act as a go-between.

"But what about your ship? Will it will leave without you?"

"Damn thing will more'n likely be late anyway. Ain't nothing happens on time in this jungle. I'll take you to the Padre in the morning. Do you speak Spanish?"

"Few words," admitted Taypi. "He teach me to speak like him – English only."

"Hmm. Damn lucky you ran into me then – can't be more'n one or two folks round here speak more than a word of English. Spanish is the lingo you want boy, ever since the Conquistadores hit these parts."

Taypi had noticed a travel-stained hammock which had probably once been multi-coloured, but had now faded to earthy hues and blended into the rapidly falling darkness. He felt a wave of tiredness roll over him – his first hot meal in many days sat warm in his stomach and made him feel sleepy.

Sam saw the sudden droop of his shoulders and realised that the boy was exhausted. "Well, I'm going to turn in now. You look about bushed. Feel free to hitch your horse with me till morning."

Taypi looked blank. "Horse?"

"A big animal with four legs. Eats grass. We use them for riding." Taypi's blank look remained, and Sam laughed.

"You got a lot to learn, boy. You got a lot to learn. You can sleep here. We'll get started on your further education once we've had a mite of sleep."

Saying that, Sam started undoing his boots. He carefully removed them to reveal a pair of sweat-stained woolen socks, much darned and in need of further darning. He tied the laces together and hung them from a nearby branch. He grabbed his blanket and swung himself into the hammock, wrapping himself up so well that not even his eyes showed, and was almost immediately asleep.

44. Finding the Journals

Although Nina was dying to know what was in the locker in Paddington she decided to head back to the squat in Elephant first to change her clothes. The bloodstains didn't show up much on the black outfit she was wearing, but the skirt was still damp from where she'd tried to rinse it out. She'd taken a scarf from the Photographer's wardrobe and tied it around her head to hide the shaven scalp and slowly healing tattoos, but it was at best a temporary solution. And she couldn't afford to look too unusual – she didn't want anyone remembering her.

Back in the relative safety of her room, with the door firmly locked against any unwanted intrusion Nina unwrapped the head scarf and took a good long look at herself for the first time since that fateful moment – Was it really only thirty six hours ago? – when she had decided to board the Oxford train at Paddington. The face that looked back at her seemed unfamiliar, altered. She followed the lines of mysterious characters that seemed to mark out different areas of her scalp. That the Photographer had only had time to sketch the vaguest outlines was clear from the heads that Nina had found in his apartment. Some had been almost totally covered with the mysterious tattoos.

Nina ran a hand over the soft and slightly prickly fuzz that covered her scalp. The hair would probably grow back in a few weeks. Until then she'd have to resign herself to wearing hats all the time. Luckily hats were one thing she had plenty of. They'd come in very useful for spying on people at the library. The tattoos also seemed to be healing fine, although the skin around them was still very tender. Nina had never had a tattoo before, but had an idea that you were supposed to put Vaseline on them to keep them supple. She found a pot of it amongst a mess of make-up and empty glasses at the foot of the mirror, and started rubbing it on her scalp. Then she hunted around until she found a velvet cap and a change of clothes, and quickly stripped off the ones she was wearing, throwing the wallet, key, wad of notes and the Photographer's watch onto the old mattress that served her as a bed. Bruises marked her pale skin in a few places, but apart from that she felt in surprisingly good shape.

Nina dressed again quickly, and sat cross-legged on the bed to count the money. It was definitely more cash than she'd ever handled before: one hundred crisp fifties. Five thousand pounds. The wallet yielded a couple of platinum credit cards, and another two hundred quid in cash. A few business cards and his British Library reader's card completed the haul. Nina kept a twenty, slipped the watch on over her wrist, and put the rest carefully underneath the mattress. She took one last look at her reflection in the mirror, squaring her shoulders and adjusting the angle of her hat slightly. Then she left the room, locking the door securely behind her.

Nina took the Bakerloo line to Paddington. On the tube she studied the faces of the other passengers and wondered what their stories were. It was mid afternoon, according to the Photographer's watch, and the carriage was almost empty. The few passengers stared vacantly into space, avoiding one another's eyes, or buried themselves in newspapers. No one seemed to take much notice of her, but then why should they? Baker Street came and went, and the train began to fill up. A woman next to Nina unwrapped a sandwich and Nina realised that it was at least thirty-six hours since she'd last eaten. Well, that could wait.

The train burst out of the tunnel and Paddington arrived. Taking the escalator up to the station concourse, Nina followed the signs to the left luggage at Platform 12. It was tucked around a corner and there seemed to be no one about, but she knew that CCTV would be filming her every move. Still, she was pretty sure that only two people knew the significance of the brown paper parcel, and one of those was dead. She took the key out of her pocket and looked for 5606. There it was, near the end, and the key turned smoothly in the lock. Nina peered into the deep narrow space that was revealed as the door opened. Right at the back was a package wrapped in brown paper. It looked just about the right size to contain a couple of notebooks. Nina felt a sense of elation as she reached inside and slipped it into her jacket. She hurried back down into the tube, and retraced her steps to the Elephant and Castle.

45. At the Mission, Padre De Vero

Sam snored loudly. Taypi had one of the Caposcripti's string hammocks, woven with fibres from the heart of a palm, but didn't string it up yet. He sat and watched the fire's dying embers, and thought about the journey he had just completed, the strange man he had met, and Iquitos, which he would experience tomorrow. He did some meditation and tried spirit-calling as the Speaker had taught him. But amidst Sam's snores, the sounds of tree frogs and birds and cicadas, the rustle of small creatures and the occasional crash of large ones; the distant cough of a jaguar and the muffled screech of a monkey, the Caposcripti voices were silent. There would be no more guidance from that quarter. Only when the fire was quite dark did Taypi string his hammock: working by feel and the glint of starlight. Then he tumbled into it and felt himself gradually drifting towards sleep.

The next morning Taypi woke to the usual chorus. He lay there for a moment and then remembered Sam Clements and their conversation the night before. Realising that he was awake, the little monkey Sagui ran down out of his perch on Taypi's queue and began loudly demanding its breakfast.

"Bossy little critter, ain't he?"

Taypi sprung up and looked across to Sam's hammock. He was sitting up, fully dressed with his boots on. It looked as though he had been up for a while, and had been patiently waiting for Taypi to awake. Taypi absently stroked Sagui's head whilst he sorted out Sam's strange dialect.

"Yes – he wants some *platano* I think. He is big enough to find it himself now, but he likes to stay with me."

"Well, whenever you're ready, the day ain't getting any younger. These official types like to get all their work done in the morning – they can't take the heat, so they spend the afternoons lounging around. If we're going to deliver your documents, then we'd better get going, boy."

Taypi blushed as he realised that the sun was already in the sky; he had slept deeply and long. He quickly rolled up his hammock and fell into step behind Sam, who surprised him by being very much more comfortable in the jungle than the Explorer had been. He held his machete in a business-like manner and used it efficiently, removing barriers to his passage, instead of slashing wildly like the Explorer. His practised movements told Taypi more than words. This man had spent years in jungle, and for all his affable exterior and friendly smile, was more than capable of looking after himself. Taypi had learnt about lying from the Explorer. Although his instinct was to believe in Sam Clements, Taypi knew that he was naïve in the ways of these people. It would not do to be too trusting.

Shortly they came upon a hut, which Sam said was on the outskirts of Iquitos. After that they began to encounter more huts, most of which did not seem any more elaborate than those in the settlements Taypi had passed on his journey. Then they caught sight of a much larger building. The Jesuit mission at Iquitos was not elaborate, but had survived a hundred years of aboriginal incursions. Built of wood, and unusual in being shingled with wood and rubber instead of the usual palm thatching, it boasted a tower atop which was a cross.

"This is where we will find the Padre. He doesn't speak English – only Spanish and a few native dialects – so I'll do the talking. Got the documents ready?"

Taypi nodded, his eyes wide, and patted the oilskin package that he wore strapped to his side at all times. At the front of the mission he could see a long covered porch, with a couple of rude chairs and benches all along under the eves. He could see that one of the chairs was occupied by a man in black, who gazed out from under the eves, but seemed not to see anything that was around him. Taypi wondered if this was the Padre, and as if reading his thought Sam rumbled from behind him.

"Ah; it looks like the old Padre's out taking the air. Well, here we go then. I'm not promising he'll be happy to see me, but at least I'll be able to give you the introduction you need."

Sam strode up to the porch, and made an ironic bow to the man seated in the wicker chair.

"Buenos dias Padre? I trust you're well?"

The Padre blinked and lost his faraway gaze. His eyes narrowed as they took in Sam and widened again as he saw Taypi standing behind him.

"Sam Clements. I see you have returned. Not for long, I hope! Who is this beautiful boy with you, old ruffian?"

"He says his name is Taypi. We met on the way here and got to talking about how he was looking for you. Would you believe it he's got some documents to deliver to you. Said they belonged to an explorer that his people found stumbling around their territory. He's dead now. Taypi tells me his last request was that this package be delivered back to Iquitos so it could be forwarded to his family."

"I remember that explorer. Inglesa? I told him he would not find anything out there. Hmm. Maybe I was wrong. He found you didn't he?"

Ignatius looked Taypi up and down. Taypi shifted uncomfortably, but apart from the odd word he couldn't understand what the old man in black was saying. Sam smoothly continued over the momentarily charged silence.

"He doesn't speak any Spanish. Just English – and I've a suspicion you don't know that lingo?"

"No I don't."

Ignatius examined the tattoos that wound around Taypi's features. He'd never seen such designs before. They seemed abstract, yet more representational than those of the local tribespeople; symbols he almost felt he should recognise, ghosts of Aramaic, ancient Persian.

Taypi was becoming nervous at the scrutiny of the Padre. Although he couldn't understand what they were talking about, he could tell that the reception was a positive one. He looked questioningly at Sam Clements, but the Padre took the initiative and addressed him directly, trusting Sam Clements to translate for him.

"Taypi, I am sorry for staring, it is most rude of me, but I confess that I have never seen anyone quite like you. Of course I will take care of these documents for you. I remember the Explorer coming through here a few months ago; to be honest I am surprised that he lasted that long. I had a feeling I had seen the last of him."

He paused a moment, to let Sam catch up.

"Have you got the documents here?"

He held a hand out, and Taypi handed over the oilcloth parcel that he had carried so carefully. And that was that. He felt a couple of misgivings, but this was after all the person that he had been told to entrust it to, so in fact his task was done, and he could begin the long journey home.

The Padre untied the bindings and found the letter addressed to him that had been placed at the top of the package. The handwriting was so shaky that he had trouble making out the words, and the Spanish was terrible, but he was just able to make out the Explorer's meaning.

> To Padre Ignatius de Vero

> Unfortunately if you are reading this then I am no more, and Taypi has carried out my last request, which was to bring these journals here so that they can be returned to my family. Padre, you were right, the jungle has eaten me up; but I hope that some small part of me will make it back to my homeland, if only so that my family should have news of my passing, and something to remember me by. I enclose letters of introduction, and some small gratuity to ease their passage.

> I ask also that you look after Taypi, and render him all assistance to return speedily to his people.

> I remain your servant and in your debt,

> Yours Sincerely

> W_____ S_____

"Well Taypi, all seems to be in order here. These are indeed the documents of the Explorer, and he has charged me with ensuring that they are sent on to his people. Soon an American naval officer will be arriving in Iquitos, on his way to Rio, and he will be able to take them on to Brazil for us, and ensure that they receive safe passage to England."

"You have made a long and dangerous journey to reach us. It was kind of Sam to bring you here to me."

Here he raised a rather ironic eyebrow, as they both knew Sam Clements would never do anything for free, and Sam grinned rakishly.

"The Explorer has included some funds which should cover Sam's help. The mission is not large, but you are welcome to rest here for a couple of days before you start your journey home."

The Padre had another motive for his apparent kindness. As Taypi was to discover this fascinating and peripatetic man was an amateur daguerreotypist, and had recently received a shipment of the crucial chemicals required to make daguerreotypes. He was itching for a subject to practice on.

Light might be an issue for the dark countries to the north – but Ignatius had created the perfect solution by enlarging the tower above the mission. Now it had become a small room containing a chair, to which he had affixed a head-clamp, and a high shelf, where he could climb up to release the shutter on his carefully crafted camera obscura.

It had taken several years of letters, waiting and disappointments to assemble the kit needed to create the delicate daguerreotypes in a place as remote as Iquitos; but once captured and treated they would never fade. And Ignatius had time aplenty in the jungle. It was the one thing he was not short of.

Only a man of astonishing patience could have prepared the copper plates by hand; each was polished to mirror smoothness, coated with silver and polished again. Iodine and bromide had made the uncertain journey by boat down the river from Leticia, along with the levelling stand, peculiar dish, plate holders and mercury cabinet which were essential tools of the daguerreotypist's trade. Ignatius was not troubled that he was the only practitioner of the art this side of Bolivia, that almost all pictures were flawed, and that to achieve a perfect exposure was the result almost more of magic than science. Apart from the odd raid and the infrequent arrival of boats from downriver, little happened in Iquitos.

Now that all was assembled, however, his patience was no more. As he thought of Taypi he began to get excited about the possibilities. The beauty of the daguerreotype is in the detail, which never fades. Ignatius had never managed to create a perfect blemish-free image, but somehow looking at this young man he knew that he had found the ideal subject.

Hard as it was, he made himself wait just a little longer. He would let the boy rest a couple of days, chat and build up a little rapport with him, and then ask him if he could make an image of him. Sam Clements would have to stay too, to translate. How strange that the boy should only speak English.

46. South London to South America

Nina went back to her room, hunkered down, and didn't
leave for seventy-two hours straight. She read the journals
from cover to cover, and gradually began to find a framework
for the strange reasoning of the Photographer; his obsession
with language, with representation. When she came
across diagrams of the Caposcripti symbols, she began to
understand the significance of the tattoos. But the scene in
the apartment was still too fresh in her mind for her to accept
any connection between these writings and the macabre
activities of the Photographer.

"South America is where it all began. Maybe that's where it's
supposed to finish? There's no doubt I can't stay in London
any longer... my DNA must be all over that apartment, and
the police are going to start asking questions sometime. Yep,
South America seems as good a place as any to disappear to
for a while." With the descriptions of the Explorer still fresh
in her mind, and those occasional lapses into poetry still
ringing in her ears.

Up west to the Trailfinders on Regent Street. Booking a ticket
for Bogota. For Tomorrow. Single, return or tour ticket?
Nina doesn't know; has never done the Traveller routes; she
buys a return ticket to be on the safe side, and because that
five grand is burning a hole in her pocket. Regent Street
also furnishes a couple of travel guidesm and a moleskin
notebook, complete with elastic, a waterproof jacket and a
teeny-tiny mosquito net. The Explorer's descriptions of the
army of small biting creatures, both land and air-borne were
too fresh in her mind. Finally, an unobstrusive bag to carry

them and whatever disposable clothes she picks up as she goes.

She's booked to Bogota, an overnight stay, and then on by smaller plane to Leticia/Tabbatinga – a small river port straddling the border between Brazil, Columbia and Peru. The flight is uneventful; Nina spends much of it sleeping – the rest of the time too occupied by the minutiae of passports and tickets and Customs and the whole mechanics of moving a human being from London to Bogota that she doesn't have time to think. She's going to South America. That's where it all began; and maybe it will somehow make sense when she gets there.

It's only when wandering around the streets of Bogota that it really hits her; the years in London a chapter now closed, and a new one beginning. Bogota is a city of contrasts – *favelas* set back from the street spill flowers onto broken gutters, jostle slums. The city feels like a giant building site and gives the impression it's been like that for decades. All kinds of vehicles are everywhere, and the ringed mountains nestling close around give the city an intense feel; a literal melting pot.

Everyone is very young, or very old. Signs of Catholicism strike her from unexpected quarters; street poets accost her in the *artisanas* district and she finds tiny origami dinosaurs and giant elaborate *graf* pieces decorating unlikely spots. Bogota draws her in, in a way that London hasn't for a long time; and she'd like to stay longer, but the Amazon's pull is stronger, and by the next morning she is on her way to the small domestic airport to catch her connecting flight.

The flight: down through the mountains to the endless vistas of dark green jungle, giant silvery rivers snaking through, with here and there the almost visceral shock of vast chunks literally eaten out of the landscape.

The arrival: passport check through a tiny little airport where the air is thick with cigarette smoke. Wandering around Leticia she is struck by how laid-back it feels; from the *billares* halls to the working girls drinking rum out front of the *Voces de Mis Recuerdos*. Cars are rare but scooters and mopeds are ubiquitous. Everyone on the streets seems young and people stare openly, frankly, invitation in their gazes. It had not been like that in Bogota. There she felt much more like a tourist. Here on the border of three countries, where the only way out was by air or water, she could disappear... if she chose. But something drove Nina on. South London to South America. And here is where it all starts.

47. Tabattinga, Iquitos

Nina sat in a café overlooking the river port at Tabbatinga and watched the sun setting over the Amazon. She was waiting for the boat that would take her on the first leg of her river journey, up through the basin formed by the confusing mass of tributaries that fed into the Amazon proper. The boat was late, and would be even later by the time it arrived, but that was only to be expected: the few short days she had spent in Latin America so far had already taught her that nothing here happened on time; it felt as though her journey to this point had mostly consisted of waiting – for planes that never came, promises that didn't materialise. She didn't mind too much though; it gave her the opportunity to sit and watch the sun going down across the great river, and think about what she was going to find.

Where had the Photographer gone wrong? Nina had read and reread the Explorer's journals on the plane to Bogotá, again on the subsequent flight to Letitia and even now could not help flicking through them. It was the journals that had acted as her guide so far – the Explorer had obviously been intentionally vague about the location of the Caposcripti – but she had one essential clue: the journals had been in the care of Willam Louis Herndon at Rio de Janeiro, who mentioned he had got them from an Indian boy, and who had given them to the captain of an ocean-going ship bound for Portsmouth, and eventually London.

These details survived in letters which each had written as they discharged their commissions, and which Nina had found folded in the flyleaf of the second journal, the stiff characters fading on yellowed paper, and signed floridly. The handwriting contrasted with that of the Explorer, which was curiously similar to that of the Photographer. Nina had been so struck by the similarity that she had wondered if the Photographer was related to the Explorer; and as she pieced the puzzle together she realised that there was indeed a blood connection – through the Explorer's stay-at-home accountant brother. Another document in a slightly different style of crabbed handwriting included the journals in a family bequest.

A man approached her and tried to chat her up. She was still trying to get used to this. Her fair skin, tending to burn too easily; the freckles that appeared at the slightest touch of sun; the redhead colouring; all of these had tended to make her insecure in London, where people made a career out of being beautiful. Yet they seemed to have the opposite effect here. She lied and told him that she didn't speak any Spanish, and finally simply ignored him until he went away, her concentration all for the river and the port and the lights of the boats sparkling now against the darkening sky.

The journey was like this: small epiphanies interspersed by long periods of emptiness, with the whole hectic Latin-American life swirling around her, and she the one still spot, still marvelling at this new Nina, a woman who travels the continents of the world; speaks in other languages, is on a quest.

At last there was a general flurry, and the other passengers who had, like her, elected to wait in the cafe began to surge forward. She didn't move just yet – just watched for the rush to fade, and when she could bear the waiting no longer grabbed her small bag, paid the bill and joined the crush on the muddy gangplank and the chaos of everyone trying to board and cargo being unloaded. The boat would not be leaving for a couple of hours yet, but she had been told to make sure she camped out at the front to avoid the noise and heat of the engines, and the stink of the toilets and kitchen at the stern.

Nina made her way up to the middle deck, and looked about for a place to hang her hammock. She found a small gap towards the front of the boat and tied the ropes as best she could to the metal rails running the length of the deck. The boat was pandemonium, with children running here and there and adults organising their luggage on the floor in preparation for the three-day journey upriver to Iquitos. Nina decided that the best thing to do for the moment was to get into her hammock and stay there until the boat left the harbour. In any case, the long days of waiting and the knowledge that she would be on the boat for several days made her feel exhausted. She lay down and was soon on the edge of sleep, hearing as if from miles away the sounds of people boarding and the cries of hawkers selling food, hammocks, cigarettes, sweets and other travel essentials. Finally, as though from a great distance, she heard the siren that signalled that the boat was about to leave, and drifted off into a deep sleep, feeling that her journey was now truly started.

She had strange dreams – elements of realism contradicted by the way that they segued into each other, keeping her off-balance. Just when she thought she had the situation in hand she would suddenly find herself in a different location talking to different people. She was searching for something, but what it was never became quite clear in the dream, and try as she might she could not remember, only that it was very important that she find it.

Nina woke properly at 4am to find that the lights on the deck had not been switched off, even though it seemed as though almost everyone was asleep. She wasn't sure what had woken her, except a vague memory of being thirsty in her dream. She untied her water bottle from the end of the hammock and took a deep pull, swilling the water around her mouth to wash away the dust. She felt wide awake and not at all sleepy, so she made her way to the roof of the boat where she could watch the stars and their slow progress upriver.

Nina sat there in the cool night breeze for an hour or so, looking at the stars and the dark outline of the river shores along each side, and thinking on all that had brought her here. The surface of the water was pitch black and it was very quiet, save for the dull rumble of the engines and the splash of the boat's wake. The river was wide here, and the far bank felt very distant: it was hard to imagine what was behind the murky line of trees – thousands of species not yet categorised and named. Nina knew she was going to have to penetrate those dark shores to find what she sought.

The last entries in the journal still echoed in her mind. There was something so terrifyingly sad about them; the desperation of a man who knew there was no escape from imminent death.

Nina closed her eyes for a minute, felt the breeze rushing past her, through the hair, starting to grow back to cover the tattoos left by the Photographer, swirling around the crown of her head. When she opened them again the scene was still there, the endless ribbon of black shores against the dark bowl of the heavens, the limitless and tangled jungle streamed past the boat on both sides.

Suddenly she felt strangely vulnerable, perched there on the roof of the boat, the metal surface cool and slightly rusted beneath her. She edged carefully towards the metal ladder that led to the next level of the boat and carefully made her way back to her hammock.

As she worked her way into it, wrapping a fold over her face to keep off insects and the glow of the ever-present deck lights she thought she would never sleep, that the days remaining would drag.

But she soon got into the rhythm of boat life; the days spent steaming past impenetrable banks, with odd stops at small towns and villages. Finally, on the third day, they reached Iquitos.

48. Making the Daguerreotype

Once Taypi agreed that the Padre could make an image of him, the priest became like a man possessed. Nothing would do but that he should start the process immediately. He took Taypi up to the mission tower and showed him the portrait studio that he had created. He had Taypi sit on the chair and checked angles and exposures whilst Taypi shifted around uneasily, uncomfortable with the straps that held even his head immobile. Finally the Padre indicated that he was ready, and after another interminable wait there was a mechanical clicking, and the Padre rushed off to start the chemical process that would fix the image he had captured on the plate forever. Taypi felt no different, but still wondered if he should have let the Padre make the image; it seemed that something of himself must have been sacrificed to create such a representation, and he couldn't help feeling uneasy about it.

De Vero closeted himself away for a couple of days, whilst noxious smells of various chemicals drifted from his quarters. Taypi and Sam whiled away the time by playing cards. Sam taught Taypi pontoon, but felt unusually guilty about taking the Explorer's money off the boy, so they played for twigs.

At last De Vero emerged from his darkroom. His jubilant expression told Taypi that whatever magic he had wrought had been successful. In his hands he held a small object; belying his years he almost ran towards them, brandishing the daguerreotype he had created.

"I've done it! It's perfect! beautiful!"

He reached them, somewhat breathless, and handed the daguerreotype to Taypi with a flourish.

As Taypi looked at the flawless and detailed representation that De Vero had created – small enough to hold in the palm of his hand, and surprisingly weighty – he realised that the picture was inaccurate. The boy who stood there was no longer him. From the moment he had met the Explorer, and started to imbibe his curious philosophies, he had been changing. The daguerreotype was like a skin that he had cast off, perfect in every detail, but too small now. His new skin was soft, the colours and hues still shifting, and he felt newly vulnerable to all the hazards of the world. But in time it would harden to impenetrable armour.

49. Iquitos; Reading the Journal; Jim

Amazonas, 1851

April 18th

I have reached Iquitos, completing the first leg on my journey & the place where I hope to find information about the peoples that live in this area of the Amazonas. I have heard that there are many Tribes, some savage & some enlightened, with very many curious customs & I hope to discover more from the merchants that make their living here from trading in sarsaparilla & other goods brought back from the jungle. My plan is to go first to the mission house & introduce myself & see if I can discover from the Padre who the best people are to talk to & how best to equip myself for a journey in these lands.

April 20th

I have little to report in my quest today. I managed to gain an interview with the Padre, but he either could not or would not tell me very much except that the lands upriver west of Iquitos are very dangerous & I should not go there. On my further questioning him he became quite angry & said that since it seemed I was determined to bring about my own ruin, then I should seek out a certain Chaman who had travelled much in the area & who knows more than any other living about the people that inhabit the area, their customs & languages. I will go & seek this man tomorrow.

April 24ᵗʰ

I have not managed to locate the Chaman yet, despite having made enquiries throughout the whole of Iquitos. It is a small hamlet of only 300 souls & seems completely at the mercy of the Jungle & the river which press in at all sides – it is all the inhabitants can do to keep their houses from being engulfed by the vegetation. I have found many that seem to know of the Chaman that the Padre told me of, but none can swear to have seen him in the last couple of weeks. It seems that he has gone on a journey into the Jungle. I can only hope that he returns soon. In the meantime I have been questioning many about the people that live upriver from here. Most have been taciturn & unwilling to speak about the area, but I have managed to convince them that I am not after trade, or rare species of plants, but simply interested in discovering new Tribes. Their distrust is most frustrating, but perhaps they have some reason for it after all. All I have managed to discover so far is that the lands are populated by a least one violent & warlike Tribe that shrinks the heads of their enemies. These are called the Jivaro & are feared by all the other people in the area. There are rumours of other tribes, but all tell me to talk to the Chaman, who they assure me, knows of everything in the area. I await his return with increasing anticipation.

April 29ᵗʰ

Finally I have been able to speak the Chaman! News travels fast in Iquitos it seems – he presented himself at my lodgings this morning, telling me that he had heard I was looking for him. He was certainly a shifty-looking character – a native of one of the tribes from the look of him, his lowly stature & dark brow & shifty eyes do not invite trust. But for a small amount of silver he claims he is willing to tell me of the tribes which I am seeking & even guide me a part of the way, arranging our passage on the river – although after that I shall be on my own. I have some misgivings about this man but as all my other enquiries have so far turned up precisely nothing, it seems as though I have little choice but to take him at his word.

What he has been able to tell me so far certainly seems to suggest that he knows more about the people of this area than the rest of the inhabitants of Iquitos, but it is hard to tell what of his stories is truth & what exaggeration. He has confirmed the stories of the Jivaros, but says that they are but one of many tribes in the area, most undiscovered by the white man. Others include people he calls the Machiguenga, who pierce large holes in their tongues & earlobes & thread wood & bones through them.

This Chaman likes to drink & his tongue was much loosened by rum. In his cups he told me of a Tribe which no one has seen, but of whom many stories are told. They live in an extremely remote part of the Jungle, some weeks journey upriver & are rumoured to have a complex language & a long written history, but he did not know their name, nor did he know anyone that had seen them, although he said that they could be distinguished by the tattoos which covered their heads & which were preserved after their deaths – although no one knew how.

I have an intimation that it is important that I find this Tribe, but when the Chaman sobered up he refused to say anything more about them & became quite angry when pressed, denying that he had told me anything & claiming that I had imagined all. The Chaman has agreed to be my guide on the journey & we go tomorrow to outfit ourselves in the market.

March 2nd

I write this in the evening, by the light from my candle on the final night before setting off into the unknown. Today I have outfitted myself as best I can for the journey ahead. I should be sleeping, for we have fixed to depart early in the morning, but find myself wide awake, my brain in a fever of imagining at what is to be discovered.

I have made arrangements with the Consul to leave a box at his establishment with some belongings & letters should I not return & my family send to find some news of me. Still I am full of optimism that I will discover & befriend tribes that will make my memoirs as celebrated as those of Darwin, I must sleep now & dream of what tomorrow will bring.

Nina looked up from the journal at the colourful houses and promenade looking out over a flat plain, what had once been river and was now a wasteland, trying to picture the Iquitos that the Explorer had described, as it had been a century and a half before. On all sides the jungle stretched so densely that there were no roads out of it – the only access was by water or air. That much had not changed, but the town itself had grown out of all recognition in the intervening time. She realised that she was looking at a town that had survived an eighty-year slump. In 1928 rubber seeds were smuggled out of Loreto, and overnight the boom ended. Just like that. Rubber was still farmed, but with competition the price had fallen. The rubber barons were no more, and the palaces constructed during those heady decades were gradually crumbling.

Even the rivers that had once surrounded the settlement had changed slightly in their course, so that the route first the Explorer and then Taypi had travelled to reach Iquitos probably no longer existed. It was the only starting point she had in finding the Caposcripti, so Nina knew that she had to go there. The journal wasn't giving much away. Nina had found some clues in her reading and re-reading, but it seemed that the Explorer had been careful not to reveal the location of the tribe he'd discovered and named the Caposcripti - or he didn't exactly know. Only the general direction of their lands emerged from his entries. Nina realised that she was going to have to try and find a guide, as he had done all those years before.

Nina got up from her table and paid for her drink. She walked through the town until she came to the Iron House, constructed by Eiffel at the height of the rubber boom, some years after the Explorer had passed through. Upstairs was the British Consulate – an outpost in the Peruvian town, where the expats hung out. The bar was made of well-shined brass and mahogany, with notes and coins from all over the world as well as cards from well-wishers and football pennants glued to the wood. A huge Union Jack was hung over the worn billiard table, and some overstuffed chairs and coffee tables took up the rest of the interior. Through long windows she could see the balcony that gave out onto the main square. A sign advertised food and afternoon tea, which seemed somewhat incongruous here in the middle of the jungle.

She ordered a beer off the surly barman, who made a point of finishing the paragraph he was reading in the paper before getting up to pour her drink. If she had hoped to get any information from him she was disappointed – he refused to speak and pointedly went back to reading his paper when she tried to question him. Another man was at the bar and looked up with interest when he heard her voice. As she sat down in one of the chairs with her beer and pondered her next move, he came over to her and introduced himself.

"Hello – I'm James Curtis – most people call me Jim. I couldn't help overhearing you. I run the shop next door. From Yorkshire originally. Been living in this godforsaken place for the last fifteen years. Still – worth it if you're into fishing. Do you mind if I join you?"

Nina was suspicious of his motives, but there was little else she could do – any information was better than the void she had at the moment.

"Sure. My name's Nina – can I get you a drink?"

"A gin and tonic would be brilliant – purely for medicinal purposes you understand."

From his reddened nose, the slight slurring in his words and his presence in the bar in the mid afternoon, Nina doubted that this was strictly true, but it was hardly her place to comment. She nodded her head and Jim shouted at the truculent barman "G&T please John. The lady's buying."

John mixed the drink and brought it over, whilst Jim settled himself into one of the easy chairs.

"What brings you here then? Seems like you said you're looking for one of the jungle tribes?"

"Oh, I'm just generally interested in the people from this region. I was wondering if it would be possible to hire a guide to take me upriver?"

"Sure, there's lots of guides for hire in Iquitos. But you won't get far unless you've got permission from the commissioner. The tribes are very protective of their lands. Especially if they think you're a journalist, or connected with TV?"

Nina could tell Jim was probing to try and find out more about her.

"No, I'm not a journalist, just a writer. I'm working on a novel, and wanted to get some location specific research."

This was the cover story she had developed for herself, realising that it was probably best to keep her true motives secret. She would have to come clean about the object of her search at some point, but not yet.

"Ah – have you been here before?"

"No, this is my first trip. I just got in from Tabbatinga

yesterday. I'd certainly be interested to meet the Commissioner though. Do you know how I can get an appointment with him?"

"Sure. He's a very busy man. He's in Omaguas at the moment, but he's due back in a couple of weeks. I can probably get you an introduction if you like?"

"That would be brilliant, if you're sure it's not too much trouble?"

"No trouble at all for such a lovely young lady. Have you any other plans whilst you're in Iquitos?"

"Nothing specific – just research in the library. That's quite near here isn't it?"

"Yes, just around the corner, but it's only open from 8am to 2pm – you'll have to wait till tomorrow to go now. You'll find more of interest at the Amazonian museum, in Malecon Tarapaca. There might be someone there now. If you come downstairs to my shop I can tell you about the area and show you some maps if you like? I'd better be getting back soon anyway."

"Sure. I'd like that."

Jim finished up his drink whilst Nina paid at the bar, and then she followed him down the iron stairs to the street. His shop was a tiny passageway of a place tucked into the ground floor of the Iron House, and opening straight onto the street. Wellington boots, hammocks, sunhats and other equipment festooned the doorway, and Nina had to duck to follow Jim inside.

A strikingly beautiful Peruvian woman was sitting at a table at the back of the shop, and began haranguing Jim in Spanish as soon as she saw him.

"Where have you been? Do you think I've got nothing better to do than sit in this stinking shop all afternoon?" She abruptly left off when she saw Nina behind him, and stared at her with suspicious eyes, whilst Nina coolly returned her gaze, and Jim placated her.

"Sorry love, the time ran away with me. Got a customer here if you don't mind now."

"Well anyway I'm off. You've made me late. I'll see you at home."

So saying she got up and flounced out of the shop, leaving Jim and Nina alone.

"My girlfriend" Jim explained ruefully. "She's a little highly strung." Seeing that Nina made no comment, he hurried on.

"So, here're some detailed maps of the area to the west of here. Do you have an idea of where you want to go?"

He spread the one of the maps out on the table, on top of precariously balanced piles of papers, whilst Nina stared at the map. It was white apart from the winding lines that represented rivers, and the odd dot to indicate a town or settlement. These settlements were, without exception, located on the banks of the main rivers, leaving an awful lot of white space in between. Nina followed the line of the river up to Omaguas with her finger, on the banks of the river Pongo. The river that the Explorer had mentioned in his journals. But Nina wasn't telling Jim that.

"Ah yes – Omaguas. That's where the Commissioner's gone – about a day from here by speedboat – half a day back again, of course, as it's downriver. There's nothing much past Omaguas until you get to Ecuador. You'll need a pass to visit the tribes around there."

"Are they violent?"

"Oh no, not nowadays – although there's plenty of rumours that suggest that we haven't contacted more than about half of them. You'll find the headshrinkers there, although nowadays they mostly shrink monkeys heads. The Peruvian government takes a dim view of tribal warfare."

"Headshrinkers? What are they called?"

Nina kept her voice casual.

"The Jivaro – you must have heard of them if you're studying this area."

"Yes – I've read about them. It would be interesting to meet some."

"That you can, for a price. They certainly know the value of the dollar, anyway."

"Have you met them?"

"Aye, them and others. I've been up and down that river for the last two decades running fishing trips. Got a big American party coming up the week after next on a private charter as it happens. The Jivaro live on the shores of Lake Titicata – largest body of water in Peru. Best fishing too."

"That's fascinating. What other tribes have you seen then?"

"Well there's the Machichuenga, the Shuar – they're just the general names, and each one's split into maybe a dozen sub-tribes. They used to fight a lot, before the Peruvian government started bribing them with satellite TV. Of course that's just the ones we know about. There's rumours of tribes further into the interior that have never been contacted by the white man. The other tribes will tell you about them if you ask the right questions. But not much. I think they're scared."

"Scared? Of what?"

"Powerful magic, allegedly – but that could mean anything. How's your Quechua?"

"That's the *lingua franca* of the basin? Unfortunately it's pretty nonexistent– I've read about it, but never spoken it. I get by in Spanish okay though."

"Well, that's better than nothing. I can probably find you a guide that speaks the lingo – you won't get far without it once you're past Omaguas. And of course you'll need equipment."

Nina looked around the shop at the sad merchandise on display. Of course kindness probably hadn't been Jim's only motive in approaching her in the consulate – still, he'd given her some good information, and could continue to be useful. She smiled winningly at him.

"Sure – I'll bet you have everything I need right here."

Nina made a show of looking round the tiny shop, realising she would need to equip herself for her journey. The small bag she'd carted from London had done her up to now, but was hardly appropriate for a trip into the jungle. Jim told her she would need Wellington boots, heavy trousers, waterproofs, a hammock, and a good waterproof bag to protect them from the heavy afternoon showers. Nina suspected he was charging over the odds for them, but she had plenty of money left from the five thousand she'd found in the Gideons Bible, so she didn't complain. Peru still seemed almost ridiculously cheap to her, with four sols to the pound. She left the shop laden with purchases, and with assurances from Jim that he would look out a reliable guide for her and would tell her when the Commissioner returned from his trip to Omaguas. She dumped the stuff in the small and somewhat stuffy room she'd found a couple of blocks from the Iron House and decided to go straight to the museum.

50. At the Museum; an Old Friend

The guide that Jim had given Nina informed her that the Museo de Amazonas was a 'reconditioned building home to 80 bronze sculptures depicting the different aboriginal communities of the Peruvian jungle including Brazil and Venezuela. The building also holds 40 photographs of early 20th century Iquitos.'

Nina was excited to read this, wondering if one of the tribes would be the Caposcripti. And the statues were incredible – life-sized and with a literally photographic level of detail, the sculptor (a Scandinavian-born naturalized Peruvian called Felipe Lettersten) had created them as casts of living indigenous peoples, which were then executed as bronzes. The casts caught every detail of grain and expression: but of course showed only details of texture and relief; not tattoos. Nina examined them closely, but not even a leap of the imagination could transform any of them into a member of the Caposcripti.

Then, almost hidden in an ill-lit alcove towards the back of the museum, she found a dark metal plate: a single daguerreotype; the work, its caption claimed, of one Padre Ignatius de Vero and simply entitled 'Amazon native, 1851'. The daguerreotype was small enough to fit into the palm of her hand and badly illuminated – but, peering more closely, Nina was struck by the perfect detail that had been captured, the sense of a three-dimensional moment in time, frozen for over a century and a half. Then something else arrested her attention. The boy/man in the picture was Taypi. It could not be anyone else.

Nina felt a cold rush of adrenaline and foreboding wash through her; so strong that she felt momentarily dizzy. She could intellectualise her realisation: the date fitted; the subject's age, gender and appearance fitted. But in fact, the recognition came at a more visceral level than that. She simply knew it was Taypi. It was the first tangible evidence that the Explorer's story was real, and it shifted everything.

Nina had spent a couple of hours at an Internet café *en route* researching what she would find when she reached the Amazon; but the Internet was frustratingly vague about the Amazon region, and all she had turned up were amateur travelogues and excerpts from obscure academic papers, invariably in Spanish, which she still couldn't read well. Books about indigenous people in Loreto seemed to exist only in Castilliano, and were hard to get hold of. They listed dozens of tribes in the Amazon area but admitted that there were still some tribes that hadn't been contacted. Nothing that she had been able to get hold of gave any proof that there was any such tribe as the one described by the Explorer, and named by him 'the Caposcripti'; yet here, she truly believed, was a picture of the boy to whom he had entrusted his journal; those final notes.

Nina dug out her disposable camera to try to take a shot of the daguerreotype, but let it drop back, unused into her bag. In this dark corner there was no chance of getting a clear shot of the marvellous miniature – and who knew what damage a flash could do to its delicate composition. Instead Nina lost herself in contemplation of the image, trying to commit every detail to memory. The boy sat, in a wooden studio of some kind, held curiously stiff and erect by the head clamp that was common practice at that time. A single exposure could take several minutes – and a single movement during the time could turn the whole image into a blur of confusion. Even the process of fixing the image onto the plate was notoriously tricky; a perfect daguerreotype was as rare as a hen's tooth. Nina could not know that she was looking at the only flawless example of a daguerreotype to have been produced by Ignation de Vera despite years of subsequent efforts.

Taypi stood in the foreground, staring into the lens with an unreadable expression in his eyes. He was not tall, but gave the impression of height due to his slenderness. He was naked but wore strings of ceremonial beads, and his skin was dark with many tattoos that would, Nina was sure, have been possible to read with a magnifying glass. A slightly blurred mass on his shoulder revealed itself to be a tiny monkey-like creature when Nina looked more closely. One other thing struck Nina as she traced the contours of his face with her eyes. Taypi didn't look at all like the statues of Lettersten. His face was narrower, his cheekbones higher and sharper; through the mask of tattoos his eyes were hawklike. It did not surprise her that the Explorer had thought the Caposcripti unique amongst the peoples of the Amazon basin.

Judging from the sculptures of Lettersten and the lists of contacted tribes that she had consulted, the Caposcripti themselves had either died out or hidden themselves away from the censuses, satellite dishes and concrete schoolhouses of the Mestizo government. Yet this seemed to be a clue, undeniable, that the hidden tribe had existed. How many hundreds of people had looked at that daguerreotype – and how had it never been asked which tribe the 'native, 1851' belonged to?

The museum curator was flattered by Nina's fulsome praise of the exhibits on show – but unable to furnish any more detail about the daguerreotype except to say that it had been sold as part of the effects of a bankrupt rubber baron who had killed himself in the 20s. Postcards of the statues were available, and Nina bought a couple to cover her interest – but none had been made of the daguerreotype. Few visitors had ever asked about it.

Emerging into the bright afternoon sunlight, in the full glare of the bare city street, Nina realised that only by going further towards the source could she hope to find out any more about the tribe. Jim had said that the Commissioner would be in Omaguas for several more days at least. Nina did not want to wait around Iquitos that long – she sensed that she had already found all that was relevant to her quest. She decided to journey to Omaguas, and find the Commissioner herself.

51. Herndon Arrives

On the same day in November that the daguerreotype was completed, William Herndon arrived, *en route* to Brazil. He had been commissioned to do a survey for the American Navy, and travelled from Chile, over the Andes and down through the foothills to the valley of the Amazon.

His party was small – just him, a mestizo called Antonio and whichever local guides and carriers they had been able to contract. At Iquitos they were looking to buy a large boat and crew it for the journey down the Amazon proper to Brazil. He had come downriver with some Shuar guides, but they would travel no further, and had already set off to return to their people.

Herndon had traveled a thousand miles, by mule, by canoe, by portage, by foot, to reach Iquitos – and his journey would not end there – not until he reached the mouth of the Amazon would his commission be discharged – for it was not less than to travel the length of the mighty river, mapping and measuring and evaluating as he went.

He too kept a journal, detailed and precise (it would be published to great acclaim on his return to America) in which he missed never an opportunity to record local resources, possible trade goods and avenues; whether the people were sick or well, how easy it was to get provender, the feeling of the natives about commerce, and whether they could be made to work, or indeed made good workmen.

Herndon was a contradictory character. He was a refined man with a well-developed aesthetic sense, and an almost poetic turn of expression when describing the beauties of the landscape. At the same time his sharp eyes had missed not a single commercial opportunity during his trip downriver. In his report he described the Indians as indolent and lazy; content to live without work, and not exploiting the riches to be got around them. And if they would not exploit them, he recommended, they should be enslaved or removed to make way for those that would. He noted that most of this aim had already been achieved by the sickness that had decimated the native peoples, and reckoned that it would not take much to get rid of them completely.

At the same time as he calmly recommended genocide, he was still capable of writing, on witnessing an Indian ceremony:

"The tones were so low, so faint, so guttural, and at the same time so sweet and clear that I could scarcely believe that they came from human throats; and they seemed fitting sounds in which to address spirits of another world." He was not insensible to the beauty of the Indian rites; he merely saw them as the expression of a degraded society in which there was nothing worth preserving.

A young man, strong and in his prime, Herndon suffered none of those debilitating symptoms that had broken the Explorer. He had charm and looks fit for the drawing rooms of Boston or Paris, his clothes were remarkably fresh and crisp for a man who had spent months travelling, and his clean-shaven features were urbane and sharply cut. He immediately won Padre de Vero over with his immaculate Spanish.

"Padre de Vero; I have heard much of you – and am little surprised to discover that you exceed the tales of your worth."

"Thank you Senor Herndon, you are too kind. I hope you will accept the hospitality of the mission whilst you are here? I look forward to discussing your travels with you over dinner."

"That is most kind, and it will indeed be luxury to us to sleep again between walls."

Herndon and his man were quartered in a guest room; the rest of his party melted into Iquitos, with strict instructions to return on the morrow.

After dark fell, Herndon and Antonio made their way downstairs to the single room that served as sitting and dining room at the mission. The rude table had been set with a cloth and silver normally wrapped against the jungle's humidity, and hurriedly polished by a maid.

Ignatius was proud of his protégé, and had invited Taypi to have dinner with himself and Herndon – introducing him to Herndon as "a beautiful native boy who has been kind enough to be my sitter. He has travelled all the way down the Pongo, and comes from one of the tribes which have not been contacted yet." Against his better judgement he also invited Sam Clements. The man knew the river and its people as well as anyone not born there could – and he might have useful information for Herndon.

"And this is one of your countrymen, Sam Clements. I cannot vouch for his character, but he knows these parts as well as anyone."

Herndon declared that he was delighted to meet both of them, and the four of them sat down for dinner.

Taypi had never seen such things. The Explorer had eaten as the Caposcripti did, and Sam's table manners were suited to his travelling lifestyle – he speared his food either with a knife, or scooped it with a spoon, depending on what the meal was. But here were silver knives and forks and spoons, and plates of china. Herndon commented on a particularly fine carved silver spoon with an inlaid handle that the Padre had inherited from his family. Sam translated de Vero's account of its provenance to Taypi – "He says it was part of the dowry of a Spanish queen when she married the King – very old." De Vero flushed at Herndon's praise and insisted on making a gift of the spoon. At that point Herndon left the table and returned with a case of Moroccan tooled leather. Opening it he presented the case and contents to "My dear Ignatius" with his compliments. De Vero pulled the case towards him and removed one of the six Venetian glasses it contained. Holding it up to the light he exclaimed with pleasure as the rays caught its intricate facets.

For his part, Taypi was stunned. The glass seemed to him the quintessence of the Explorer's civilisation. Something so fashioned, so engineered, that he could imagine no parallel in nature. That Herndon should have brought this from his home made Taypi want to visit the place where such beautiful things were made.

Herndon told many tales of his travels as the plates were cleared away. Coffee came, and the men enjoyed it with fine Spanish brandy. Taypi had been silent throughout the meal, listening wide-eyed to Sam's whispered translations of the conversation, but now Herndon applied the full force of his attention to him.

He asked him in English to tell his story, and Taypi repeated what he had told Sam; his delivery sharpened by the retelling so that it seemed far more fluent than the first time Sam had heard it. Herndon was amazed and impressed by Taypi, who seemed to be utterly unlike the other Indians that he had met.

He pressed Taypi for details about where he came from, but Taypi, mindful of the effects of colonisation that he had seen on this way downriver, said he did not know the names of the waterways he had used. Herndon did not have time to take a side-trip back up yet another tributary of the river, so he did not press him further. He had stopped in Iquitos to re-equip his party and hire another few natives to row his boat downriver and translate for him.

Padre de Vero said that there were over a hundred souls in Iquitos and native settlements nearby – but he was not sure whether a reliable party could be got together on short notice for Herndon – and promised to make enquiries on the morrow.

By this time Taypi could barely keep his eyes open – not helped by the unfamiliar alcohol which made his head fuzzy and his vision blurred. Moreover he was so starstruck by Herndon's sheer presence that the Explorer seemed hardly real to him now.

Herndon represented all that the Explorer was in flight from; and the very reason that he had hacked his way unaided through the jungle thickets instead of joining a larger party.

But for Taypi, the combination of charm and intelligence had proven a dangerous combination. He was too naïve to understand the essential disdain that a man like Herndon would always feel for him – and thus saw him as a hero and a mentor.

52. Iquitos to Omaguas; Meeting the Commissioner

At some nameless staging post Nina swapped the big boat from Iquitos for a crowded river taxi, which would take her along a tributary to Omaguas. Although it was a small outpost, it was in fact the administrative hub for an area the size of Wales. The small boat was crowded, and had no roof – just a palm awning to keep off sun and rain, and plastic shields on the sides to protect the occupants of the boat from the splashing water and its inhabitants. Nina could see little of the landscape as they passed, and sat cramped on one of the plank seats clutching her bag, ready to hop off at any one of the numerous stops, until she heard the singsong 'Omaguas … aca… todos para Omaguas' announcing that they had arrived.

Like many of these riverside settlements, Omaguas was built atop a high bank with a tortuous mud-slide of a path down to the river proper, where a battered-looking wooden jetty allowed boat passengers to gain the shore. Nina quickly gathered up her possessions and fought her way past other passengers with many apologies and hopped off the river-taxi, just about getting onto the jetty before the driver blew his horn and it was off. She slung her bag securely around her, and slithered up the steep path.

At the top, she found a row of shacks built precariously on stilts, suggesting that in rainy season the river came above the high bank. Facing these wooden buildings was a rather incongruous town square, brick-new and neat with its regular design of flagstones, fountain (dry) and ornamental pillars. There was even a bronze statue of some military dignitary. Plates affixed to the statue, the fountain and the pillars extolled the generosity of Fujimori and the Peruvian government in creating this, the titular head of the vast Loreto district. One block back from the main square, the jungle visibly strained to encroach; the houses a strange hybrid of traditional palm dwellings and breezeblock structures. Another plate, larger than the rest and hand-painted on wood with large letters 'Comisaria de Omaguas Alta Amazonas' distinguished the Commissioner's office. The door was open, and inside Nina found the man himself. He was huge, and sat beneath a ceiling fan sweating in his tight green uniform. He had a round and guileless face and seemed genuinely excited and interested by Nina's visit.

"Charmed to meet you. You would be Nina? I hope your journey was pleasant?"

"Well, it was certainly interesting." replied Nina in careful Spanish. "And I'm pleased to meet you too. It was kind of Jim to arrange this meeting."

"Jim said you are working on a novel. About the Loreto people. You wish to travel upriver to observe the tribes there?"

"Yes. I'd really like to get in touch with some of them. But unfortunately I don't speak Quechua. Just bad Spanish! So I need a guide as well. Jim said you might know someone?"

"I may do. A very reliable man called Fernando. But you must know that an American TV company was in that area a few months back. They gave the tribal people money to parade in their native dress, and pretend that they have never had any contact with civilisation. These people started to think that they are not really Peruvians, subject to the Peruvian government. This has made things difficult. The Rimachi control entry to the area and they will demand a big bribe, even though I have given you permission to enter their lands. They should not do this – it is illegal – but we cannot stop them. In the past it was enough to bring trade goods. Now they want hard cash."

Nina wondered what he was trying to say; whether there was a hidden meaning in the words. Did he want her to bribe him?

"Obviously I'm not rich," she replied carefully "but I have been given a small advance by my publisher for my research…"

"I have a boat you can borrow. But you'll need to buy petrol, and provisions. And gifts for the Rimachi and other tribal people. Fernando will guide you and take you to the market. He's not here now, but he'll be back any day now. He knows the local people and settlements very well – he's taken people to the lake of the Rimachi before. Have you got somewhere to stay?"

Nina didn't, and shook her head sheepishly. This far off the tourist route the usual backpacker hostels were absent, and Nina hadn't though beyond arriving in Omaguas – hadn't even known what she would find there; what kind of reception.

The Commissioner smiled.

"Well you can stay in the government visitor hostel – that's no problem. I'll have someone take you there after this. But Nina, please, take care when you travel upriver. The *selva* can be very dangerous. You must listen to Fernando and do what he says."

"Thank you so much. You've been so kind. I really appreciate this. My novel wouldn't get written without you."

"Well, be sure to put me in it. In a nice light of course! Now, sadly I must get back to official business. I'm sure we'll meet again before you leave. I'm always here in the mornings."

Nina wondered what it must be like to be stuck in that tiny outpost of civilisation. This man was ruler of a region the size of Wales, but seemed to have no pretensions at all. However she recognised dismissal, polite though it was. She thanked the Governor once again, and then followed the uniformed officer that he assigned to take her to the hostel.

They emerged into the bright light of late morning; the plinths and statues cast short sharp shadows on the dusty ground and the streets were silent and almost deserted. After a couple of minutes they arrived at another breezeblock building and the officer handed her over to another government official, who gave her a register to sign. As she went through the familiar ritual of name, passport number, arriving from, leaving for, Nina reflected that she really wouldn't be that hard to track down if anyone had thought to look in the remote Amazon for her.

Her room was a bunker-like space with no windows and no bed – just a selection of hooks set into the walls, the space just wide enough to sling a hammock. There were a couple of lockers built into one wall and Nina quickly chucked her bag into one before turning to thank the hostel manager. A non-committal grunt was her only reply, as she watched his retreating back.

For lack of anything better to do, Nina strung up her hammock, removed the Explorer's journal from its waterproof coverings, and settled down for a read, and a think. She sensed that she was getting closer to the source, but the more she saw of jungle life, the less hope she had that anything had survived a hundred and fifty years since the death of the Explorer. After all, even the homes of the rubber barons were crumbling, and they had been built more recently than that. The idea that any native artefacts had survived in this environment seemed nonsensical. She lay in her hammock and turned one theory after another over in her brain.

Could the heads be kept in a wooden case – like one of the drums she'd seen in the museum in Iquitos? But the Explorer hadn't said anything about drums. The Caposcripti used the exposed roots of trees to send their messages through the jungle. Drums played no part in their ceremonial. She didn't even have a name to go on. The Explorer knew them as the Caposcripti – but he said this was just a made-up name. How could she find a tribe with no name?

At least their appearance was unique enough that she could make up a description.

She thought back to the daguerreotype she had seen at the museum. She was sure it was Taypi. The date fitted, and the description that the Explorer had given of him in the journal. The tangibility of the clue excited her – but the fact that it created a trail that anyone could follow was also terrifying. Except that she had the only copy of the journal, and she had ensured everything else was burnt… hadn't she?

Which she was going to need for this Fernando guy that the Governor had said would guide her up the river. How much could she tell him? She'd stick with the story of the novel – say that it was historically based on the life and travels of a 19th Century explorer and the tribes that he'd found. Hmm.

She felt frustrated. Surrounded by clues but more clueless than ever, she was reduced to coming up with wild theories. The indigenous museum in Iquitos had been interesting, but there was no mention of head-shrinking, let alone the Caposcripti, and books with any detail were frustratingly hard to come by – only the tantalising daguerreotype suggested that she might be on the right path. The maps that she had been able to track down told her nothing: they were almost all characterised by a lack of detail; vast tracts of white space that had still not been catalogued. Nina had a suspicion that she was chasing wild geese. Perhaps the Caposcripti had moved, or died out.

So? How could she find them? What hope does she have of being able to locate the tribe, much less the head of the Explorer? The tribe will be different now. The young may no longer accept tattoos. Maybe only the elders of the tribe are still marked with the ideograms of the Caposcripti as the Explorer would have known them, if any survive. Would they still retain their network of Speakers?

After a couple of hours of musing, scrutinising the Explorer's journal and turning theories over in her head, Nina realised that she was ravenous. Breakfast had been a couple of stale *empañadas*, when the dawn was still pink on the horizon, and by now it was mid-afternoon. Not great timing for a snack, in a tiny place like this where most of the business would be done in the morning, but he was too starved to wait till evening. Nina pulled her few spare clothes out of her bag, stashed them in one of the lockers, and shouldering her bag once again, headed out of the room. She didn't bother to lock the door. The only things she had of value were cash, her passport and the Explorer's journal – and those were staying on her person at all times.

Outside, Omaguas had the hot, dry glare of ghost-silent deserted streets. She made her way back to the waterfront where she had seen the stilted shacks. As she had already guessed, a couple of them were cafés – radios blaring Latin music and bags of water hung around to ward off the ever-present flies. There were no other patrons at this time of day, but a guy was lounging asleep in a chair next to the radio, and a glass case with a few *papas rellenos* and *empañadas* – and what looked suspiciously like a plate of grubs sitting next to them.

"*Una cervecita Señora?*

"*Si, y algun para comeer, tengo mucho hambré, Señor!*" Nina replied.

He pulled a sweating bottle of beer out of a bucket of cold water, and put a couple of stuffed potatoes and *empañadas* on Nina's plate, whilst she sat down at a table overlooking the river.

"*Veinte Sol.*" Nina handed over the twenty and he pocketed it before returning to his seat. Within a few seconds he gave every appearance of having gone back to sleep.

Well, thought Nina wryly as she sipped the beer and nibbled on a corner of *empañada* – this will have to keep me going for a little while.

For the first time since she could remember, she suddenly felt lonely. What was she doing in this remote jungle outpost in Peru? It had seemed important, and exciting, in London, to come all the way out here and track down the Caposcripti. But in reality she was running from the enormity of her actions. Of course the murder of the Photographer had been self-defence; the stake her very life. But when she had decided to dispose of the Photographer's body instead of doing the sensible thing and calling the police, she had crossed a line and there was no turning back.

And she had been so very naive. On the one hand she was pretty sure no trace of the Photographer's skin and muscle and bone remained. On the other, there had been blood;

plenty of it. Modern policing methods could create a full and detailed reconstruction of events from a strand of hair, a few drops of blood; a fleck of skin could speak volumes....

For that matter, how thorough had the Photographer been with his own victims? Nina had picked up a copy of 'The Shrine of Jeffrey Dahmer" from the airport shop and read it in snatches over the long journey that had followed. One phrase in particular had stuck in her head, when the murderer Dennis Nilsen likened the clean-up operation after a murder to 'the dirty platter after the feast'. The grisly pyramid of heads and notes that she had immolated suggested that the Photographer had feasted many, many times. Once the police put him on the missing list and checked his flat, Nina was sure a whole lot of questions were going to be asked. Belatedly she cursed the impulse that had led her to create a flaming pyramid of the heads. Stupid buying into his mythos.

As the one person who knew the answers (for she was almost certain the Photographer had let no one else into his secrets) she was going to make sure she was very far away. There was no going back.

For someone still in their twenties, that was a heady and terrifying prospect.

Don't worry about that now. Lose yourself in the experience. The Amazon is a fascinating place. Even though she had barely scratched the surface (Tabbatinga, the boat journey, the river taxis) she was already fully immersed. Could this place ever be home? Nina had always thought of herself as rootless and independent. Now that she was truly isolated she understood that she had been fooling herself, in her squat in Elephant. She was still part of a tribe, then. Even though they nominally travelled under the same passports, that Nina was an entirely different person. Exhilarating, terrifying. She knew now that the Photographer had succeeded in his final experiment. He had indeed reinvented her, and she was still discovering the extent of the changes he had wrought.

Nina noticed that the sun was setting, and a few more people had started to make their way to the café where she had whiled away several hours watching the river, lost in thought. It was cooler now and the bar was filling up. She became aware that she was a covert object of attention. Strangers were not that common in a place like this; especially tall, apparently single and obviously foreign women. With her redhead colouring, Nina stood out like a sore thumb and the locals were not slow to pick up on it. But no one spoke to her. She began to feel a little self-conscious, and wondered if the Commissioner would pop in for an evening beer. Judging from the number of people out now, Omaguas was bigger than it first appeared. Obviously the Commissioner had better places to be than a waterfront bar. It would probably look bad.

Nevertheless, the coffin-like room was not appealing in this heat. Nina held up her empty beer bottle and tried to catch the barkeeper's eye. Eventually he made his way over with another beer. Nina was still hungry and noticed a couple of the other patrons were tucking into bowls of soup. In a place like this it would just as likely have entrails in it, but Nina had learnt the hard way not to be too fussy about her food during the last several weeks. She gestured towards one of the diners.

"*Quiero sopa por favor?*"

There was no reply from the waiter, but Nina assumed he must have heard her request because he filled up a bowl from a huge pot which had appeared near the glass case, now refilled with fresh *empañadas*, *patarashca* and other snacks.

Nina tried not to look too closely at what was going into the bowl; as he brought it to the table saliva was literally squirting into her mouth. *"Beinte cinquo Sol"*. She handed over more of the Peruvian coins and set about the soup. Actually it was delicious, though she did discard some tube-like things that she thought might be bits of heart, and a few other unclassifiables that she discovered once she reached the bottom of the bowl. The heat of the soup suffused her body, radiated out from her stomach, and she realised it was the first hot thing she'd eaten in several days. As her digestion got to work on the unfamiliar proteins, she felt suddenly exhausted, and staggered back to the hostel to sleep.

53. Invitation to a Journey

Ignatius's enquiries in Iquitos had borne fruit, and he was able to offer Herndon a full complement of men with which to continue his journey. A team of Yagua men had agreed to row him as far as Tabbatinga, where he would be able to charter a steamer.

Herndon asked Sam if he would be willing to join their party to Brazil. They spoke in English, and Taypi could just about follow their conversation. Sam's knowledge of the Amazon past Iquitos would be invaluable to Herndon and Sam had seen all he needed to of South America for a little while; Herndon's invitation couldn't have come at a better time for him.

As they made plans and negotiated terms, Taypi examined Herndon shyly, fascinated by this man that who traveled from the other side of the Andes, all the way from Chile. He was far younger, and more vigorous than the Explorer, and lacked the fanatical eye; his gaze was quantitative, sizing up everything. Taypi did not yet understand that his attention to detail was driven partly by a view to profiteering.

Though he felt himself a man, Taypi was still very young. He had youth's blindness to mortality. He had a vague notion that money was useful in this 'mestizo' world – but that he had in sufficiency, having inherited the Explorer's gold.

Taypi resolved to ask Herndon if he could accompany him on his journey to Brazil, and finally to the sea. He struggled with his conscience for a while, balancing his promise to the Speaker, but knew that in his heart the decision was already made.

In returning to his people he would be returning to an earlier version of himself, which felt long-outgrown now. He discovered a curiosity that was driving him on – so much easier to follow the current all the way to Brazil; through that unimaginably vast last to the sea. Taypi thought of the maps that the Explorer had given him; how he had struggled to explain the lure of places that had never been explored by his kind, full of secrets and wonders. Just a taste of the settler's lifestyle had made him curious. What other wonders did the world contain?

He asked Herndon, in his broken English, if he could come with him. Herndon looked at the boy before him, the innocent light shining in his eyes; the excitement of youth. It filled him with sadness. He had seen too many youths leave their villages and their people to join his party, over the year he had been travelling the Amazon region. And he knew, with a certain feeling of guilt, that some of them never returned to their homes, even though he had sent back several such parties during his journey. How could he explain the sadness that this caused him to this boy, with dreams of travel and adventure shining in his eyes? He didn't want to take him with him, but it was certainly preferable to Taypi journeying on by himself. Although it was clear he was intelligent and able he wouldn't last long without protection. Herndon took Taypi's hand.

"Taypi, we need another in our party, so you may come with us if you wish. Although I must have your promise that you will return to your people when we reach the mouth of the Amazon?"

Taypi had learnt much since leaving the Caposcripti… including how to lie. He looked Herndon straight in the eye.

"Of course I will return."

Herndon allowed himself to be satisfied with that, although he would have had many more misgivings if he'd heard Taypi's silent completion of the sentence. One day.

~≈~

In the pueblo the Speaker felt Taypi's wordless question and his subsequent resolve. It was the beginning of the diaspora he had forseen. The Speaker sat and stared at the head of the Explorer. He tried to see there if there was any way that the man had not betrayed them; but the loss of Taypi was too painful for him; and he could not find any compassion or forgiveness for the man.

He took the shrunken head and sealed it into a waterproof bark case. Then he went walking to conceal it in a cave upriver, off into the jungle, and safe from the diurnal rains. It did not belong with the Caposcripti heads, but neither could he leave it to rot in the jungle. If it should be found it would be far from Caposcripti lands; and not for many lifetimes.

54. Meeting Fernando; Journey to the Pueblo

The next morning, Nina awoke thirsty, and with a rumbling belly, and went straight back to the café, only to find it deserted. She wandered along the riverfront and stumbled upon a huge shed that contained the market. Hordes of flies lit upon the produce, little deterred by the plastic bags filled with water that had been hung up to ward them off. It was here that Fernando found her.

"Hello. I can only assume you must be Nina?"

He came onto her straight away: tone flirtatious; the palm pressed for just a little too long with plenty of eye-contact. He was tall for a local; floppy dark hair and deep brown eyes. In his thirties she thought. Quite handsome, but knew it.

Nina gave him back a long, level look and said "Let's be clear. I'm not interested in romance. I'm on a serious assignment."

Fernando surprised her with an easy laugh.

"Ah – I see you know your own mind. I think we will get on well. Henceforth, Señora, your honour is safe with me."

Looking at his honest, warm brown eyes, Nina believed him. Something about him inspired her trust; this in itself surprised her. She was used to trusting no one. Yet how much could she tell him about her 'assignment'? She decided, for now, to stick to the story that she had told the Governor. The journal, the Explorer, and her search for the Caposcripti could wait for now. She would decide how much more to tell him when there was a need. There was certainly no question of talking about the Photographer; even though that memory felt like a time bomb, waiting to explode sometime in the future if she didn't unburden herself of the pain to someone.

Fernando suggested that they might as well pick up provisions there and then for the trip upriver. He quickly roped in the services of a carrier and started haggling for 'hot' cigarettes – fat *porros* made of rolled coarse tobacco, bags of rice, flour, pasta, fishhooks, twine, torches, machetes, and a turtle which Nina was not to see again for some time. Within an hour they had everything they needed.

They left early the next morning – Fernando dressed simply in jeans, with bare feet and a faded t-shirt with '*Promotor de Salud*' written on the back. The small aluminium boat lent by the Governor had been fitted with an outboard engine and was packed with their supplies, so Nina had to balance precariously on bundles and sacks. The bottom of the boat was filled with brackish water. They travelled all day along the gradually narrowing river, stopping for lunch on a small beach formed at a bend. Towards dusk they arrived at a pueblo, and Fernando told Nina that was where they would be spending the night.

⌒

Satellite dish and football at dusk. Long logs at the end of each dwelling, gradually burning into the centre. These fires were kept burning at all times, so that there was always a flame at hand for boiling water or smoking.

A clearing where all the men and boys have a game of football, which Fernando joins in with – all seeming incongruous in this rainforest, dressed in mismatched football strips of teams she had heard of (Man U, Chelsea) and those she hadn't; and shorts – with even the odd set of studded boots. Once dark fell (suddenly, shockingly, as always) everyone retreated to the largest hut to eat communally from great dishes of food that had been gathered and prepared that day. Nina watched carefully what order people ate in, and which hand they used, and tried to follow suit. Fernando translated odd swatches of conversation, but mostly she felt like a big clumsy alien observing these people from the outside, and being watched, covertly by all those around her. Once the evening meal was finished, Fernando told Nina it was time to give their hosts some gifts. The women and children vanished, and torches, batteries, fishing hooks and line, and sacks of rice, flour and sugar were duly handed over. Nina smiled and Fernando translated as gifts were presented in turn: a bag woven of *chonta* fibre; a necklace incorporating coloured seeds, catfish spines, and a toucan's beak. Then one last bowl of *chuchuhuasi* went round the circle and everyone retired to their beds.

The next morning Fernando woke Nina just before dawn and they packed up quickly, fired up the boat's engine and continued on their way. The river was gradually getting narrower and they moved from the main course to a tributary, and traveled through a series of 'black lagoons' where the water was the colour of a pint of Guinness and the blackened stumps of mangrove trees thrust from the river like writhing arms. Fernando caught a number of giant black *piraña* for lunch and they moved to a sandy beach to build a fire and ate the *piraña* straight off the bone with a sprinkling of salt. Then they were off, navigating a series of jewel-like clearings, until they reached a giant freshwater lake. It was much larger than Nina had imagined – so large she couldn't see the distant shore.

Crossing the lake was terrifying in the boat which suddenly felt tiny and precarious. They rolled and dipped into giant waves, dwarfed by the islands of floating debris which suddenly swung into sight as they navigated great peaks and troughs. Fernando aimed the prow into the giant waves and laughed with each loud thump as they crashed back down. After one particularly hair-raising leap into the air Nina found her feet sharing the bottom of the boat with an angry-looking turtle which had been tightly bound. Fernando quickly shoved the turtle back under the seat and shouted "a gift for the Shuar" over the roar of the engine.

At least an hour of punishing travel followed, and the far shore gradually came into view as the water became more placid. Nina could make out a two-storey block structure that seemed very incongruous in the setting and she shouted over the roar of the engine to ask Fernando about it. Fernando immediately cut the boat's engine and they idled in the water.

"Fujimori built it for them – he built many schools in the jungle. But now there is no more money, and no more teachers, and the building is too dangerous to use as a school – but no one came to take it down. The pueblo is behind it."

"Nina, it is very important that you do exactly what I say when we are here. We are very far away from the city, and the police – and anything can happen to you in the jungle. Your very bones could vanish and none but the jungle to tell what happened to you. It is very important that we do not make these people angry, because there is no telling what they might do. Not directly; they will not scream and shout. A couple of quiet darts, tipped with curare, and we would be very easy to dispose of, with none the wiser."

Nina gazed back at him unfazed. Of course he couldn't know that she was already a murderer. Had killed a man. Was on the run. Fernando looked earnestly at her and continued.

"So please follow my lead. We may need to give them money. The Governor told you this. How much can you afford? One hundred dollars?"

It seemed little enough, compared to what it had cost her to get that far. And it looked as though she had no choice. Nina nodded. "You're the guide, Fernando."

"Good. We'll be there in another ten minutes or so. I'll do the talking and you just smile a lot and have the money ready, okay? They may demand more but we won't give it to them."

"Are you sure? I could afford a bit more. I really need to get to Yanamono, Fernando."

"I'm sure. We'll be in even more trouble back home if the Governor finds out we let the price be driven up. He might be forced to send the police in. This region likes to think it's autonomous, and it's definitely a long way from Lima – but the government needs to show it's in charge too. It's a fine line we walk, Nina."

So saying, he revved up the boat's engine again and set the prow towards the pueblo. As they approached, Nina could make out more details about the old concrete school, built right on the water's edge, with crumbling pilings – the teachers long-departed, but the community still living there.

As with their arrival at Yanamono, the noise of the boat's engine had the whole population on the bank, waiting to see who these rare petrol-powered visitors were. Their own dugout canoes were tethered to posts all along the shoreline, with a single outboard motor between them.

Fernando guided the boat to a jetty, as it had a deeper draught than the native canoes, and they waded the last few feet to shore.

Two long, tense nights of negotiation and exchange of presents followed before Fernando and Nina were allowed to continue down the tributary that these people controlled. On the second day, Nina stayed in the pueblo, whilst Fernando disappeared on a hunting trip with the men. Before he left, he told her not to be tempted to go for a walk in the jungle by herself. She could be lost in minutes and might not be found for days. She would not know what hazards to avoid, and it would be extremely embarrassing to return to Omaguas without her. Nina promised to stay put, and when he had gone she got out the Explorer's journal.

The day in between. Chickens roosting in great clay pots amid the ruins of the government school; They have moved into the downstairs classrooms, leaving those upstairs empty, filled with overturned and rusting school desks; peeling blackboards; windows missing and open to the elements. Children playing like eels in the shallow water, constantly in motion and seemingly self-reliant. Women grinding seeds and chattering to each other – occasionally casting glances in her direction, but no one speaking to her directly.

55. Quentin Gets a Call from the Police

At three-thirty Quentin got a call from the police...there's been a fire in a south London apartment – belonging to a Mr James Crichton? They wouldn't bother Quentin normally, but Mr Crichton appeared to be... un-contactable. Perhaps Quentin knew of his whereabouts or might be able to help the police with their enquiries? There were certain... irregularities that they would like to clear up.

What kind of irregularities? Quentin was curious, being long used to unusual behaviour on the part of his clients.

"I'm not at liberty to reveal that over the phone, sir, but we'll be happy to tell you everything down at the station."

Quentin wrapped up what he had been doing and headed down to Lambeth North Police Station.

⚓

A series of mysteries awaited him, which he mentally listed under the following categories:

A rubber-padded room with an elaborate airlock.

A charred pile of what appeared to be shrunken human heads.

Deliberate arson – and no sign of the flat's occupant.

Quentin had not seen or spoken to the Photographer since their last business meeting, several weeks before. Mr Crichton was a very private person and didn't like to be disturbed unnecessarily. No, Quentin didn't think it was odd. Mr Crichton was a celebrated photographer, and many celebrities are known to be jealous of their privacy. His client was no exception. And did Quentin have any idea of the present whereabouts of Mr Crichton? No, Quentin did not. Mr Crichton rarely made it his business to appraise Quentin of his movements. It was possible that he had decided to go on a trip. He had travelled widely.

The policeman laid something on the table that Quentin did not immediately recognise. As he got nearer to the blackened object he realised that it was a charred human head, reduced to the size of his fist. As the sight of the thing his gorge rose. He raised his eyes to those of the police officer across the table from him.

"You realise that this is potentially deadly serious sir? This is just one of the remains we found on the premises. There is a possibility that these were old specimens, bought for the Photographer's collection."

Quentin was said nothing. Implacably, the policeman continued.

"Our forensics department is already trying to identify their origin. But it's equally possible that Mr Crichton has been responsible for an awful lot of murders. We'll need to consider that possibility too. We appreciate any help you can give us with our enquiries, sir."

Quentin was silent. He thought back to his final interview with the Photographer; the man's insistence that the world wasn't ready to see what he had been working on. His refusal to divulge one detail of it even to Quentin. And the oddly out-of-character humour in his statement: "If I told, I'd have to kill you." He couldn't help wondering how serious the man had been.

56. Terminal

They arrived at the tiny settlement of Yanamono in the late afternoon. Fernando cut the engine of the boat and leapt out to tie the painter to a small wooden jetty. Nina stood up and looked around her. After several hours crouching in the small boat her legs were stiff, and she welcomed the chance to stretch them.

A narrow path was cut into the high mud bank. Nina scrambled up as best she could, and suddenly found herself at the top. The houses of the villagers surrounded her in a semi-circle, all built from palms and open-sided so that she could see the occupants resting in hammocks away from the afternoon sun.

A man stood waiting for them by a sun shelter, in the centre of the clearing. He was simply dressed in cutoff jeans and a t-shirt, and wore no shoes. Red ochre lines ran across each cheekbone, and his hair was cropped short. Nina looked questioningly at Fernando.

"It is the Shaman, who knows the use of Ayahuaska." Fernando informed her in Spanish.

"He is the one that we are looking for here."

This, then, was the spirit guide who would show her how to find the Caposcripti. Nina walked towards him and stopped a couple of paces short. She cleared her throat and addressed him in her broken Spanish.

"I am very honoured to be in your village. I have brought gifts for you and your people." She held out the hot cigarettes, fishhooks, matches and fishing line that Fernando had advised her to buy in Omaguas. The Shaman made no move to take them from her. He sent a quick blast of quechua at Fernando, whilst keeping his eyes steadily on her. Then he turned on his heel and walked towards one of the huts. He mounted the shoulder-high platform with a bound, and seated himself cross-legged on the wooden floor.

Nina wondered whether she should follow him. Fernando cut across her thoughts. "He says the first ceremony will be tonight. It's important that you don't take any food, only water. He thanks you for your gifts, and says that you must pay him two hundred sols for conducting the ceremony. It will last three days, and we will stay in this hut. Go and sit with him while I go and get our baggage."

Nina rapidly translated the Spanish and arrived at Fernando's meaning. "What is his name, this Shaman?"

"That is not a question to ask of a Shaman. But you may call him 'Rimani', which means 'Speaker' in quechua, more or less.

Fernando ran back to the riverbank, and Nina walked over to the hut where the shaman was sitting, first laying her gifts carefully on the edge of the platform, and then scrambling up there herself. The shaman inclined his head to indicate that she should sit with him. In all this time he had not spoken a word. Nina looked around her, and wondered what would happen next.

A woman approached carrying several clay bowls, and a jug. She placed the bowls in the space between Nina and the shaman, and poured a thin white liquid into them, straining it with a woven net. The shaman leant forward and picked up one of the bowls, balancing it carefully. He tilted it back and took a long drink, before replacing the now half-emptied bowl before him. Nina immediately followed suit, and took a long drink of the bitter liquid, grimacing at the unexpected taste. Fernando came back with their bags and laughed at her expression. "It's *masato*, pressed from the juice of the yucca plant. It's supposed to be refreshing." A huge smile suddenly suffused the shaman's face – the first glimmer of emotion that he had revealed, and Nina felt more relaxed. It seemed that she had passed some kind of test.

Fernando was tying his hammock and nets up to one of the beams of the hut, and Nina jumped up to do the same. Her mind was buzzing with questions about the ceremony, but she kept them to herself. She would find out everything tonight. Not least, she hoped, what had become of the Caposcripti.

❦

Nina had read the accounts of Ayahuaska ceremonies both in the Photographer's and the Explorer's notes. The Photographer had taken it once, in Brighton and recorded, in his precise way, the stages and effects of the ceremony. But it seemed he had derived little enlightenment from the experience. The Explorer had described repeatedly fasting, purging and taking the drug – and being taken to a dark plain where he had learnt the language of the Caposcripti. She had some idea of what to expect from conversations with Fernando in the boat during their journey from Omaguas. But she still felt some trepidation as the night drew on, and the shaman began to make preparations for the Ayahuaska ceremony. She could feel hunger pangs in her belly from fasting all day, but she knew that if she ate anything, it would make the purgative effect of the Ayahuaska worse, so she ignored them.

The Shaman lit a candle and placed it next to a metal pot full of dark liquid and an empty bowl. He placed a bundle of hot cigarettes nearby, and a bottle of Vicks. Fernando told Nina to make herself comfortable, and Rimani handed her a cup of the dark liquid to drink. She drained it all, and then sat back wondering what would happen next.

Rimani extinguished the candle and they were all plunged into darkness. He began to shake a bundle of leaves and circle Nina, singing in an unearthly high voice in a language she didn't recognise. Gradually he speeded up the song, accompanying it with violent rustling from the leaves, until Nina heard a loud buzzing in her right ear. She closed her eyes, feeling very disoriented, and suddenly felt a huge wave of nausea hit her. Someone – was it Fernando? – handed her a bowl, and she grabbed it as she retched convulsively, bile dribbling down her chin. She would rest for a moment, and then it would start again, until it felt like she was trying to vomit out her entire stomach – surely it couldn't continue any longer? She felt floaty, disconnected from her body. She couldn't place herself, or remember what it felt like to have sensation. She seemed to be everywhere, as if her essence had thinned and spread, like gas. The song of the Shaman continued, but she seemed to hear the calls of animals intermingled with it; the melody had become more gentle, and interspersed with whistling, like birds singing.

Gradually Nina came back to a sense of herself. She was lying in a foetal position on the bare boards of the platform. The faintest glimmers of dawn were lighting up the sky. Fernando was fast asleep in his hammock, and the Shaman pointed her towards her own. Then he gathered up his belongings and disappeared, presumably to sleep somewhere else.

Nina was pretty wired, and lay awake in her hammock, feeling curiously divorced from her body, and turning the whole experience over in her head.

This is where the Photographer went wrong – he had been right about the power of the Caposcripti. The language gave it to them. A language that could describe the future or the past with equal accuracy, that gave them knowledge undreamt of in the West, with its linear modes of thought. The clue was the tattoos; layering experience like a palimpsest on the skin: not that different to the parchment used by the Gnostics, the monks, all those other ancient writers.

The Photographer had missed the truth after all – for him, finally and fatally, it had been an intellectual exercise. The language of the Caposcripti was like their souls, entwined in the tangled jungle like the bindweed, which wraps itself around the papaya and the *taberiba* tree and grows into the *marihuana*, which fights for space and light with the *ciguelan* and the *ciguelan* with the *aguaje* and the *aguaje* with the *liana*, until it is no longer possible to be sure where each plant begins and ends. And growing in amongst these is language, which holds all together. And what if you pluck this vine from its natural habitat? It dies and fossilizes, or evolves, becoming something completely different. The Photographer had recreated the language of the Caposcripti in south London, but it was an incomplete lexicon, composed only in terms of pain, loss and fear. There was so much that he had missed.

⇌

The following night the ceremony was repeated again. During the day Nina hadn't eaten anything, only drinking pints and pints of water, so she was beginning to feel very light-headed. The second time the retching didn't last as long – once she had thrown up all the water that was in her stomach, the acids began to come up, but they didn't seem as dark and bitter as the previous day. The disconnected feeling kicked in almost immediately, and this time she found she had left her body entirely, and was observing her slumped form, with Rimani circling it and Fernando sitting off to the side. Something seemed to be connecting it to her, and she could hear a babble like a thousand people talking at once underneath the monotone of the shaman's voice. She was suspended like this for an incalculable time, and then all of a sudden everything went dark and she found herself back in her body. She felt stiff and cold. Fernando looked at her with concern in his eyes, and she returned a weak grin to show she was ok.

The third night was different. This time when she left her body she realised that she'd left the world behind as well, although the Shaman's singing was still there, somewhere in the background. Nina discovered that in the darkness it didn't matter – or she couldn't tell – whether her eyes were open or closed; all she was aware of was his voice – alternatively buzzing like a swarm of hornets in her ear and chirruping like birds or monkeys. She heard jaguar coughs and the cries of children.

Suddenly she found herself on a plain. All around her was… nothing – yet more than nothing, for she didn't seem to be standing on grass, or rock, or bare earth. Her feet made contact with… nothing. It was as though something forced her eyes away. A short? Distance away (perspective was difficult with no reference points) she seemed to see a river – although she couldn't say she actually saw it, it was more as though her mind knew that a river should be there, so it had created one for her. She wasn't aware when the Shaman's voice had segued into a general background of many talking together, or at what point from this babble she noticed that one of the voices was addressed to her.

"What are you doing here?"

The question was not so much heard as felt, as though the

words swam into focus somewhere in her cerebellum. She felt connections being made, and meaning suddenly became apparent, like an insight.

"Where are we?" Nina had only to think her question as the answer arrived.

"It is not important; you would not understand the answer."

"I am looking for the Caposcripti."

"You will not find them."

"And their language? Is that lost too?"

"That will never disappear. It is engraved on nature; it travels with the wind; it is everywhere; we speak it now."

"But the journals speak of heads? Surely they have been preserved?"

"The past is another continent. Do you imagine you could find that place again?"

Nina cast around for more questions – but nothing more would come. Her thoughts flew around like leaves on a windy day. She tried to cling to something, feeling herself lost in this maelstrom. Nina. I am Nina. I am.

When she came to she found herself lying in a clearing. No trace was left of the Shaman's ceremony on the hard-packed earth but the butts of hot cigarettes. A ray of sunlight broke through the canopy and touched her face with its warmth. Nina communed silently with this messenger from another place.

About this book

This book was researched on location in Peru, Columbia and Brazil, as well as London. In 1999 I set off with an intrepid friend, Christian Shields, to find the Jivaro – perhaps the last known tribe in the Amazon to keep the ancient ritual of headshrinking alive.

We travelled down the Amazon, and then the Janamono rivers to the Loreto district of Peru, with a local boatman for a guide (thanks Lorenzo!). After much negotiation with other tribes who controlled territory along the route, we finally reached one of the Jivaro villages. They were very welcoming, and invited us to stay and learn about their way of life.

The Jivaro are not the Caposcripti – and there are few parallels to be drawn in the modes of thought of the two tribes. Nevertheless I am indebted to the Jivaro for their hospitality, and for giving me unique and valuable insights into their world.

Thanks

Thanks are due to many people, as this book has been a long time coming, and had a lot of help along the way. Thanks to Scott Pack for patient re-reading and brilliant editorial suggestions, to James Wallis, for proofing it, and to Emma Pickard, for being encouraging. Thanks also to the Commissioner of the Loreto district for the loan of a guide and a boat, and letters of introduction to different tribes, and to Lorenzo for being unflappable, a great guide, a great fisherman and loads of fun.

Thanks to my patient and loving husband, Stuart Taylor, for keeping me going.

---

* The Jivaro don't take the heads of enemies killed in battle any more: this is of course now illegal in Peru. However, they were willing to show me some monkeys' heads that they'd shrunk, just to keep the old methods alive.